GOLD, GREED, AND A HIDDEN HOARD

A RETIRED SLEUTH AND HIS DOG HISTORICAL COZY MYSTERY

ONE MAN AND HIS DOG COZY MYSTERIES
BOOK 5

P. C. JAMES

Copyright © 2024 by P. C. James

All rights reserved.

No part of this book may be reproduced in any form or by any electronic or mechanical means, including information storage and retrieval systems, without written permission from the author, except for the use of brief quotations in a book review.

Important Notes:

1. While the **places** named in this book are **REAL**, the **people and events** are **NOT**.

2. This is a work of **fiction** and any **resemblance to real people** then or now is **entirely coincidental.**

Created with Vellum

1

AWAKENED TO LIFE... AGAIN
ROSEBERRY TOPPING, NORTH RIDING OF YORKSHIRE, ENGLAND. OCTOBER 1966

Ex-Detective Tom Ramsay stood on the summit of the mountain, pulling his hat down over his ears and squinting at the view through the sharp wind that threatened to sweep him and Bracken, his border collie, off the peak and over the nearby cliff. To the north, the smoke and steam of Teesside's chemical plants reminded him of his years in Newcastle and its industries, to his east he could see whitecaps on the North Sea, westward lay the Pennine hills and south, Yorkshires moors and dales. On a better day, the sight would have made his heart soar, as it had so often before. And not just on Roseberry Topping. The two explorers had hiked to the summit of many peaks since Eliza had left them for the bright lights of London and he'd been able to be more selective in what 'mysteries' he chose to investigate. To be precise, he hadn't chosen any of the many requests for assistance that had poured into the *Mysteries De-Mystified Agency* since their success at solving a drug-trafficking ring and the death of the well-known author, Carole Tolworth.

Instead, he'd climbed the Three Peaks, Ingleborough, Pen-y-Ghent, and Whernside, as he'd promised Bracken, in a glorious week of summery weather during late September. The view and the air had washed away all the doubts he'd felt throughout the unhappy case they'd investigated most of the summer. His decision to keep the sleuthing agency going began to look more and more foolish that wonderful week. The pile of letters waiting on his return almost convinced him to chuck it all in and hike the heights forever. Reading the letters, however, reminded him there were a lot of people who needed the help of someone they trusted. Only, he'd thought that couldn't be him. Now, standing on yet another peak, staring out over the countryside below, he thought, *if not me, who?*

"Let's go home, Bracken," Ramsay said at last. Bracken was shivering in the cold but manfully sitting by his friend without complaint.

Bracken didn't need to be told twice. He leapt to his feet and began trotting down the path they'd climbed up.

Ramsay laughed. "Hey, wait for me."

He caught up with Bracken while his companion had waited in a sheltered spot. "This will be our last climb of the year," Ramsay told Bracken. "My ears are numb."

Making their way steadily down to ground level, Ramsay found the air warmer and his ears aching as they recovered. "I hate to say this," Ramsay continued, "but I think we need a mystery to solve, Bracken. Something mind-taxing but not dangerous would be perfect. And something close to home. I don't want to travel all over the country in the bad weather."

Bracken's glance suggested he agreed with that.

"Not even for the mystery Eliza wrote about, asking for our assistance," Ramsay continued, remembering the letter he'd received that morning from his now departed youthful assistant. "It's best she and Steve do their own sleuthing down there in London. You and I are better suited to the countryside than dodging gangsters in that great sprawling city. Or any city, if it comes to that."

Bracken didn't know what his friend was saying but he nodded his agreement. Generally, he did agree with his friend and this time seemed to be no exception.

"There was one letter," Ramsay continued, as they reached the ground and headed to where his car was parked, "I thought might interest us. It sounds like it might be a treasure hunt, and you enjoy searching out things, don't you?"

Bracken ignored this, he'd caught the scent of a rabbit nearby and was already off the track and into the long grass.

"Exactly my point," Ramsay continued, grinning as he saw Bracken's tail waving to-and-fro above the grass. "I'll read it again when I get home. It's a week old but I'm sure nothing will have changed since she wrote it."

Bracken rejoined him on the track, happy at the chase and disappointed that once again the rabbit had dived into a burrow and beyond his reach.

They reached the car and both jumped inside, glad to be out of the wind. "And the beauty of this case, if it is a case, Bracken, is it's right on our doorstep at Demerlay Hall, not fifteen minutes drive."

2

THE DISCOVERY

TEN DAYS EARLIER, DEMERLAY HALL, GRASSMOUNT, NORTH RIDING OF YORKSHIRE, ENGLAND.

ANNE WATSON LET her eyes scan the cluttered cellar, stacked full of the detritus of centuries of life in Demerlay Hall above. Everything the Demerlay families down the centuries had wished to remove from the rooms above, but couldn't quite bring themselves to throw out, was here. As the owner, and principal worker, of the *Watson House and Estate-Clearing Service*, it should have filled her with delight. The cellar, however, was cold, damp, and smelled of decay and so it depressed her. All those lordly people, all those important lives have come down to this. An empty house, in abandoned grounds, and the whole ruin being picked over by her and her part-time assistant, local historian, amateur antique appraiser and gift shop owner, Judith Palmer.

"Anne," she heard Judith call from the dim recesses of the cellar, "come and see this."

Anne wended her way among the old furniture and tea chests that prevented all but the slenderest people moving around, until she found Judith, who was running her fingertips across a peeling surface on the cellar wall. "What is it?"

Judith turned to Anne. "When I moved that old

screen, worthless, by the way, though it would have been valuable if it hadn't been left down here since I don't know when..."

"Never mind that," Anne interjected, grinning. Her friend and colleague tended to wander off the point if anything old swam into view. "What is it you see?" In the gloom, the wall where Judith's fingers were probing looked like all the rest.

"The wall here is covered and painted," Judith replied, "but you can see there's something behind it here. Something square."

Anne stood beside Judith and now she could see the faint outline of the square, where the covering had sunk leaving a shallow depression. "The damp has damaged the covering, I expect," she said, feeling the edge with her fingertips. "Have you a knife or anything to remove the covering?"

Judith shook her head and looked around until she spotted a broken splinter of chair leg. "This might do." She ran the sharp end of the broken leg along the straight edge of the depression. It parted, leaving a gaping slit she could get her hand in. Tugging firmly, she pulled the soggy fabric from the wall.

"A safe," Anne exclaimed, as the hidden object came into view.

"This might make up for the disappointing haul of bric-a-brac we've found in the Hall so far," Judith replied. "We'll need Arnold to help us open it." Arnold was the locksmith in the nearby town of Whitby.

Anne wasn't pleased at having the Hall's contents described as bric-a-brac. A lot was, of course, but she'd hoped Judith would find some gems among them. "It would have to be something spectacular in such a small safe to outweigh that awful Georgian bedroom set upstairs," she replied.

Judith laughed. "The family jewels are what I'm thinking. Forgotten when the only person who knew where they were, died suddenly, like in a novel."

"My contract says, 'house and contents' so I share your hopes on that," Anne replied, though the idea gave her some misgiving. If there were valuable jewels, there could be a legal challenge to tie up her small company in court for years. There was always some descendent somewhere wanting a share.

"Should I drive into Whitby and get Arnold?" Judith asked. "Or will you?"

Anne peered at her watch. If Arnold wasn't busy, he could open the safe today. Otherwise, it would be an anxious night guarding the cellar or worrying about it in bed.

"You go, Judith," Anne said. "He'll do anything for you." It was true. Arnold had a soft spot for Judith, which he didn't have for Anne.

Judith laughed. "You're matchmaking and I'm no longer interested in being matched." Judith's husband had decamped ten years before with his secretary and now lived in Leeds with a family of four. Judith had stayed on at her shop and remained steadfastly single.

"We need Arnold to open it today," Anne said. "You're our best hope of that happening."

"I'll go," Judith replied, "but you behave when he gets here."

Anne agreed she would, but spoiled it all by calling, as Judith was leaving the cellar, "Don't forget me for bridesmaid." She grinned when the cellar door slammed shut.

* * *

ARNOLD, a middle-aged morose man who, like Anne, had kept on his father's business, soon had the safe door open. "It was my father that sold them this safe," he said.

Anne was too busy grabbing the contents to reply but Judith asked, "When was that?"

"Sometime in the fifties," Arnold told her. "I'd have to dig out the old records to be sure. I don't remember Dad mentioning anything about it being built into the cellar wall, mind you."

"Maybe that happened later," Judith replied. "I think originally it would have been in an upstairs room, wouldn't you?"

"Aye, very likely," Arnold told her, watching in fascination as Anne carefully extracted yellowed documents and cotton pouches, placing them into her briefcase. "These safes are often built into walls behind paintings and the like. For jewelry or cash to hand, usually."

Anne held the last pouch she'd extracted from the safe into the beam of Judith's flashlight, saying, "Maybe that's what's in here."

She gently tugged at the drawstring closing the pouch and it came apart. "Oh, well. I'd hoped not to break anything, but this fabric is very old." She tipped the pouch, and a glittering gold and bejeweled necklace slid into her waiting hand.

Arnold whistled. "As I said, jewelry. But why down here? No lady would come down to the cellar to get her necklace for a party, would she."

Anne, who'd been staring at the necklace, realized the pouch still contained more, and tipped it again. Two matching earrings fell into her palm alongside the necklace.

"Are they real?" Arnold asked, awed by the glittering pile of gold and stones cupped in Anne's hand.

"They're real," Judith replied, and then added, "but not old."

Anne nodded. That had been her own appraisal of the set. "This century," she said, "and quite late. Late forties or fifties, I'd say. Judith?"

Judith agreed. "And more likely fifties. There wasn't a lot of jewelry like this being produced in the late forties."

"Maybe the documents will tell us more," Arnold suggested.

Anne was suddenly reluctant to involve Arnold any further in the business. "We can't read them down here in this light."

They made their way up the steps to the ground floor and found a table to lay the documents flat on. They read them silently for a moment.

"This one's about the garden," Arnold said, at last. "Are yours any more help?"

"Mine isn't," Anne said. "It's like it's in code." She turned the paper carefully so the others could see.

"Nor is mine," Judith said, after studying the papers her colleagues had been reading. "It's more like household accounts than anything else."

"What about the journal?" Arnold said, gesturing to the thick notebook with its closed metal clasp.

"I think we'll get an expert to open that," Anne said. "It's likely to fall apart if we mess with it. And you should be getting back to your shop, Arnold. You probably have a line of customers outside the door."

Arnold laughed. "I've never had a line of customers outside the door, though you could be right. The day I'm away from the shop is when they'd come."

"I'll drive you back," Judith told him, "and Anne can lock up here." She led the way outside.

Anne watched them go, before locking the cellar door. Returning to the table, she pulled up a chair and began reviewing in detail the second pouch and documents she'd pushed into her pockets. After the necklace, they were disappointing, a collection of old gold sovereigns and silver shillings, valuable but not excessively so, gold and silver rings, a gold and jeweled brooch, more papers, and another, but very ordinary, diary. The papers had the same cryptic symbols the first had.

She was still reading and puzzling over the trove, when, an hour later, Judith returned.

"Is this the rest of the safe's contents?" Judith asked, when she stood looking over Anne's shoulder.

Anne nodded. "Yes, and it's equally puzzling."

Judith frowned. "You know, this doesn't feel right. I've helped you with a number of these clearances and we've never encountered anything like this. It feels," she paused, struggling for the right word, "dangerous," she decided, at last.

Anne laughed. "It's an interesting puzzle, but hardly dangerous. Like you said earlier, the start of a novel. Only, the Hall has stood empty or been rented to fly-by-nights for ten years or more now and whoever owned these is long gone and probably dead."

Judith shook her head. "You may be right, but I still don't like it."

"Maybe you'll feel better about investigating all this," Anne gestured toward the documents and trinkets, "if we studied them at home with a nice cup of tea."

"I would," Judith replied, looking uneasily around the decaying room with its dirty windows and rubbish-strewn floor. "If we go to my place, I can consult with my books of jewelry and put a better date on these pieces."

"Your place in one hour," Anne told her. "I'll lock up here and go home to feed Rex." Rex was her golden retriever and a very distinguished dog.

"Bring him with you," Judith said. "He can guard us while we work."

THE LIGHT WAS ALREADY FADING when Anne and Judith settled down at Judith's kitchen table to study their find. Judith had several textbooks piled in front of her ready to research the jewelry, which she peered at through lenses, noting hallmarks and makers' symbols. After a moment working on the necklace, she opened a book and flipped through its pages. "I was right," she said, at last, "the necklace and earrings were made in London for the Festival of Britain exhibition in 1951. They were bought by a film star, then sold to a London financier, or whatever those people in the stock exchange are called, for his wife, then bought by someone who remained anonymous. They were reported stolen in 1954."

Anne listened to Judith's recounting of the gems' history with a puzzled expression. When Judith finished speaking, she said, "It would be interesting to know who owned the Hall in 1954."

"And after," Judith replied. "We can't be sure they were immediately locked up in the cellar safe after being stolen."

"We need Arnold to tell us when his dad sold that safe to the occupier of the Hall," Anne agreed.

Judith frowned at Anne's suggestion. "I wish we hadn't involved Arnold. You know what an old gossip he is."

Anne grimaced. It was true. Like many lonely people, Arnold did have the habit of chattering to anyone who would listen. "It can't be helped. I'll phone him right now and ask him to hurry with his research on the safe and tell no one of what we found."

Using Judith's phone and phone book, Anne called Arnold and outlined what she needed from him. He was inclined to take exception to the suggestion he would tell others about the find but agreed to start immediately looking for the details of the safe sale.

When Anne recounted her conversation with Arnold to Judith, Judith said, "Me thinks he protesteth too much, as Shakespeare has it."

"You think he's already told someone?"

Judith nodded. "I fear so. You asking him not to, made him realise what he'd already done."

"We could say that, when we looked closely, the jewelry was just paste and not worth anything at all," Anne countered.

"Arnold is a locksmith," Judith reminded her. "He knows what is put in safes. Still, if we could persuade him to go along with our story, it should be all right." Her tone suggested she didn't think that a likely outcome.

Anne suddenly realized Judith had told her about the owners of the necklace and earring set without saying what it was worth asked, "How much is the set worth today?"

"I'll have to do some research on that to be sure," Judith replied, guardedly, "because there may be fans of the film star willing to pay more just because she owned it. Face value, I'd say a minor king's ransom. More than you and I will ever be worth."

"Oh," Anne said, unable to collect her thoughts coherently as she gazed at the necklace and earrings spread on the table beside Judith's hand. Judith's word 'dangerous' leapt into her mind. Even the gold's luster and the diamonds' sparkle now seemed menacing.

"We need to keep these in a safe," Judith said, her eyes following Anne's gaze to the gems. "I suggest a bank's safe, not ours. If word is out, our safes may become targets for robbery."

"If we put them in a bank," Anne replied, "people will know they're not paste."

"I think it will be soon all over the neighborhood, anyway," Judith told her. "Best we just err on the side of caution."

Rex, who'd been warming himself by the Aga range, lifted his head and growled. Anne and Judith looked at Rex, saw he was staring at the now darkened window, and swiveled in their seats to see what had attracted his attention.

The window was simply black, no face or movement could be seen. Judith rose to her feet, crossed the room, and closed the curtains. "We'll shut the night out," she said, returning to the table.

Anne smiled in reply, but she could hear the concern in Judith's voice. She shared it. Rex did too. He was now on his feet and at the kitchen door.

Anne and Judith exchanged glances. Without a word, Judith raced to the door and locked and bolted it.

"We've only had these things three hours," Anne whispered, "and already I'm afraid. It's nonsense because we don't know anyone except Arnold knows we have these and yet..."

Judith nodded. "I think that knowing they were stolen and never seen since makes it even worse."

"Can I leave them in your safe tonight," Anne asked. "I don't want to walk home in the dark with them."

"You can," Judith replied, "but I can drive you home as well."

"Maybe that would be best," Anne replied. "It isn't fair to ask you to risk having them on your property."

"We're being silly," Judith replied, bracingly. "Jumping at shadows and wild imaginings."

"Rex isn't imagining things," Anne said, gesturing to her dog, still staring and listening at the door.

"It's probably the neighbor's cat," Judith told her. "Now, what did you find among the papers?"

"A mix of lists and information you'd expect from household books and what looks like coded messages, which doesn't make sense," Anne replied. "It could have been children of the household using old books and papers for games on wet days, of course. Only they look to me like they're written in an adult's hand." She pushed over a sheet of paper for Judith's examination, pointing out the strange hieroglyphics at the bottom of the page.

"If these are related to the theft of the jewels," Judith said, "we probably should tell the police."

"I'm sure the perpetrators will be long gone, and the owner of the jewels will have been paid by the insurance," Anne replied. "These belong to me now, so it isn't a police matter. Still, I take your point, and I know somebody who could help. He 'de-mystifies mysteries', or so his advertisement claims. I'll write to him when I get home."

3

SHADY DEALER

After Judith had dropped her off, Anne sat down at her desk with a coffee and began writing her letter to the detective agency. It was harder than she thought it would be because every time she wrote about the find and what little she'd learned; the story grew less and less worth involving a famous detective like Tom Ramsay. She'd seen the advertisement in the paper and read the articles after that big case in the summer but had never considered there'd be a reason for her to ask his help. And now she came to ask, she thought how feeble the whole story sounded. She was ready to stop when she found she'd described her problem well enough to not look foolish. Before she could change her mind, Anne folded the letter, placed it in an envelope, and wrote the agency's post box number and address on it.

The following morning, when she made breakfast, her courage wavered. Before she could change her mind, Anne placed a stamp on the envelope, walked to the nearby postbox and slipped the letter inside.

Back inside her home, Anne pondered her next steps. The necklace was in Judith's safe, but she still had the brooch, rings and notebooks. There was another person in the village who had an interest in these kinds of objects, Nigel Hawtry, the owner of an antique shop and a collector of antiquities as well. Anne had mixed feelings about Nigel. She had many dealings with him over the years and thought him someone who you needed to watch closely. She didn't think him actually crooked, just cunning and sly. However, on this occasion, she needn't mention the necklace, just ask for his thoughts around the remainder of her little treasure trove.

When she was ready to go, she called Rex, and they set out for his morning walk. The walk ended at Hawtry's shop and home where she knocked on the door.

Nigel was taken aback by her early start but welcomed her in when she showed him the brooch and told him of the other minor items.

He studied the brooch carefully with his magnifier, saying, "This is a nice piece. You say there's more?" He stroked Rex who had gone to greet him. Nigel usually had treats for Rex.

Anne pulled two rings from her pockets and handed them over.

"They're nice too. Yes, I think I could find buyers for these," Nigel told her as he examined the hallmarks carefully. "They aren't particularly valuable, the rings are early Twenties and the brooch is Edwardian, still they will fetch a fair price."

"I'm more interested in what you can tell me about them right now," Anne said. "I found them during my clearing out at Demerlay Hall."

Nigel gave her a penetrating stare, as if assessing her truthfulness. "I'm surprised these would have been left behind when the family, or a later tenant, left. They may not be hugely valuable, but they are nice pieces, and they would have meant something to someone."

Anne nodded. "It puzzles me too. Then there's this." She pulled the smaller diary from her bag and gave it to Nigel. "There are more papers with similar messages on them."

Examining the pages slowly, Nigel's round face creased in puzzlement. "It's a code, as I'm sure you know, but what kind of code or what it means, I can't say."

"You've seen nothing like it before?"

He shook his head. "I haven't. I don't think the code is antique at all. I'd say it's quite recent. After the war, anyway. The letters and symbols were written by a biro pen, unlike the words on the page, which are older. They're written using a fountain pen."

Anne took the book from him and looked at the pages again. "I never noticed that."

Nigel's plump body shook as he laughed. "Not your field of expertise, Anne, so no reason why you should."

Anne nodded. "Do you think it might be a wartime code?"

Shaking his head, Nigel replied, "This isn't sophisticated enough for those boys. It's more like schoolboys or regular people inventing something on the fly. The trouble is to decipher it, you need the translation sheet. The one that shows how each symbol aligns with the letter, or even a word."

Anne's spirits rose. "Maybe one of the other sheets I have at home is just that. Thanks. I'll study them closely when Rex and I get home." She turned to go and then realized Nigel hadn't returned the two rings. "The rings?" she asked, holding out her hand.

Sheepishly, almost furtively, Nigel extracted them from

Gold, Greed, and a Hidden Hoard 17

his jacket pocket and handed them over. His gaze followed them as Anne placed them back into her pocket.

"When you're ready to sell those rings," Nigel told her, as she and Rex walked to the door, "and any similar pieces you find up there at the Hall, don't forget your friend and neighbor."

Assuring him she wouldn't, Anne and Rex walked briskly home. "Rex," Anne said, as she opened her door, "did you sense something more than usually creepy when we spoke to Nigel? I did. But what was it?" She'd barely finished speaking when she realized what it was. First, he'd never tried to pocket something like the rings before, not in her presence anyway. And more disturbingly, the expression on his face every time he looked at the rings said more than any words could. Something about those rings fascinated him. Were they more valuable than he'd told her they were worth? Judith would know someone who could give her a more honest appraisal.

* * *

As they'd agreed the night before, Anne drove to Judith's house to talk about the treasure trove before they began their day at the Hall. She told Judith what Nigel had said about the rings and brooch and the code.

Judith frowned. "Are you sure telling him about what we found is wise?"

"I only showed him those few items and I didn't mention the necklace and earring set," Anne explained. "What did you learn from studying your books?" She didn't tell Judith about her misgivings. That could wait.

"As I mentioned, the coins are gold and silver and varying ages. The silver shillings are mid-Victorian and in excellent condition. I think they were kept as heirlooms, rather than currency."

"Given to children at their Christening, that sort of thing?" Anne suggested.

Judith nodded. "The sovereigns are also hardly worn, so taken out of circulation soon after they were minted. Again, I'd say gifts of some sort, which makes it so strange. If they had value beyond their metal content, why were they abandoned?"

"Maybe the owner died before they could tell anyone where these things were?" Anne suggested. "Any thoughts on the codes?"

Judith shook her head. "I've never seen anything like them. I'm guessing children. They look like the sort of thing children invent when they first hear about codes."

"Nigel suggested there should be a translation sheet somewhere," Anne told her. "You look through those and I'll look through these." She handed Judith half the loose sheets of paper and they studied each one in silence until Rex caught their attention with a low growl.

Anne and Judith looked to the window at once. Rex padded to the door and growled again.

The two women rose and made their way to the door. Judith peered through the nearby window. Seeing no one, she opened the door with one hand while holding Rex's collar with the other. When even this showed the garden to be empty of suspicious visitors, she stepped outside and scanned the path to the gate and then across the garden. When Anne reached her side, Judith laughed, saying "I told you it was next door's cat."

Anne followed Judith's gaze to the fence where a tabby cat watched them in quiet content. Smiling sheepishly, Anne nodded. Again, she'd been alarmed for nothing, it seemed. She told Judith about her letter to the *Mysteries De-Mystified Agency* and wasn't altogether surprised when Judith shook her head.

"I know," Anne cried, "but I was alarmed last night, and anyway we need someone who knows how to do these things if we're going to get an answer about that necklace."

"They were in the news, Anne," Judith replied. "They do big cases, spies and murder, things like that. Our mystery is trivial by comparison."

"Back to the codes," Anne said, deciding to get off a subject that she found embarrassing in the cold light of day, "could it be lovers?"

Judith nodded, smiling. "It could. In days gone by, lovers often needed a way of communicating without being noticed by nannies, governesses, chaperones, and other gooseberries. I hope you're right. I'm partial to the intrigues and affairs of others."

"As we're both too old for such nonsense in our own lives," Anne agreed, "it would be a fun find to read their story over the long winter nights ahead." She was only in her mid-thirties but somehow, she felt, the business was going to be her future.

Judith asked, "Will your detective be able to decipher codes? Or know someone who does?"

"He might," Anne replied. "After all, I imagine the cleverer kinds of criminals often use codes."

"I've never heard of them doing so," Judith replied, frowning. "I mean it isn't mentioned in the newspaper articles about trials, or radio and television news, is it?"

Anne nodded. "I know what you mean, still it might happen. And Ramsay has solved crimes with spies and I'm sure *they* use codes."

"Maybe we can break the code," Judith suggested. "Look for patterns among the symbols, for instance."

Nodding, Anne studied the sheet of paper in front of her. After a moment, she said, "I think this circular symbol," she held the sheet so Judith could see where she was pointing, "is likely to be the letter 'e'. It appears more than any of the others."

Judith looked back to the sheet she was holding and said, "It does on mine too. We should start our own translation sheet with that." She drew a sheet of writing paper from her desk and wrote the alphabet down the left-hand side of the sheet and then, in pencil, put the symbol Anne had identified beside 'e'.

"I've a three-letter word here, ending in two of our 'e' symbols," Anne said. "It can only be 'see' don't you think?"

Judith giggled. "Unless the writer was a golfer and was talking about a 'tee'."

Anne smiled, saying, "Don't be silly, Judith. I've just remembered something dad told me years ago. He said the people at the Hall had fallen into bad company."

Judith nodded, smiled and said, "I was right then, golfers."

"This is serious, Judith. Concentrate! What do you remember about that time here in Grassmount?"

Judith sighed dramatically, before saying, "I remember that when I first came to the village there was a lot of gossip about goings-on at the Hall. Was it the Demerlay family then or one of the tenants who took over after they left?" Taking Anne's suggestion of the word 'see', Judith wrote the possible 's' symbol on the sheet beside her.

"We can find that out for ourselves," Anne said, still carefully looking for patterns among the scribbles. "We don't need any detective for that."

"Hey," Judith cried. "If that is 's' and that is 'e' then this word," she pointed to a four-letter word on her sheet, "might be 'safe'."

"Pencil them in on the sheet and see where they take us," Anne agreed. "You know, I don't think the people who created this code were very sophisticated. Our children theory is beginning to look disappointingly likely."

"The children may have seen or heard something and wanted to talk about it without adults knowing," Judith suggested, hopefully. "It may still be good information."

Anne didn't look convinced, but said, "Maybe. We can continue working on it over the coming days and see what we find. Meanwhile, we have a Hall to clear and sitting here isn't going to get that done."

LATER, after they'd finished cataloguing furnishings in two of the many bedrooms of the Hall, Anne dropped Judith off at her home and set off for her own home, only to make a detour to Nigel's antique shop.

The store was empty when Anne entered and the tinkling bell at the door brought the owner out into the room.

"Hello, Anne and Rex. Two visits in one day are a pleasant surprise," he said, smiling. He patted Rex and the two walked to the counter where Nigel took a dog treat from a drawer. He offered it to Rex who snatched it greedily. Rex enjoyed their infrequent visits to Nigel's shop for he rarely left without something nice to eat.

Anne didn't enjoy her visits to Nigel's business and the dog treats were only part of it. "I wish you wouldn't do that, Nigel," Anne protested. "Too many treats will spoil him.

Nigel laughed. "I want a fierce looking fellow like Rex," he bent to pat Rex who was still contentedly crunching the treat, "to think kindly of me. I'm not a brave man, you see."

"You might see us both more often on this house clearance, Nigel," Anne replied. "I've never had something like the Hall to value and empty before and could use some help."

"Have you something new? More of that jewelry, perhaps?"

Anne smiled and shook her head. "There are pictures on the wall I'd like your opinion on. They may not be worth much, but they might be worth something."

"That's a convoluted sentence," Nigel replied. "Still, if you think I should look, I will. Later tonight?"

"I'd rather you see them in daylight," Anne replied. "The electricity has been shut off at the Hall and torchlight won't do them justice."

Nigel considered. "Tomorrow morning then. Mornings aren't my busy time in the shop."

"I'll pick you up at 7:30 am," Anne told him. "I have another question I think you could answer. Do you remember anything about the goings-on at Demerlay Hall in the fifties?"

"What sort of 'goings on'?"

'I don't rightly know," Anne replied. "My father would say something about things 'going on' at the Hall when I was younger, but I took no notice. They had good parties there, I remember that. Only we local people weren't invited."

Nigel laughed. "I wouldn't have been either," he said, "but yes I do remember hearing about them." He paused, then continued, "There was talk about treasure hunters and people going missing. Surely, you remember that?"

Anne shook her head. "I worked in Edinburgh when I left university. I only came back here when Dad fell ill and needed help with the business."

"I'd forgotten," Nigel said. He frowned in concentration. "Let me see. I came to the village in fifty-eight and people were still talking about it, so it was before then. Yes, the Demerlays moved out in the early fifties, and it was a taken by businessman from Huddersfield, or was it Bradford? I'm not really sure. Before my time. Self-made man, war profiteer people said. Wasn't liked. His family, grown children who lived at home, were a nuisance and grew worse as they got older." He lapsed into silence.

"When did they leave?"

"That's what I'm trying to get right," Nigel replied. He spoke slowly, still searching his memory for details. "They'd leased the Hall, I think, and left soon after the Demerlay boy died. End of fifty-four or early fifty-five. The Demerlay boy was staying with them and was involved in a car accident. I'm sure that's right. Whoever managed the business side of the Hall back then could give you the timeframe for the tenant's comings and goings."

Anne too was considering how best to piece together those years at the Hall. "There must be someone in the village who worked at the Hall in those days, gardeners, cooks, maids, for instance. They would know. It's only just over ten years ago, after all. Villagers have long memories."

Nigel laughed. "They do that. You might try Ned Wishart or Terry Brent, they're both interested in the Hall, though for different reasons. And if I remember more, I'll tell you about it tomorrow when I'm inspecting those paintings you mentioned." This last was because a potential customer had entered the shop, and he was eager to catch them before they could walk out again.

"Till tomorrow then," Anne agreed, and made her way back to her car. "Well, Rex, what do you think now?" When Rex ignored her, she continued, "I think I was right. The jewelry is worth a lot more than he let on."

* * *

ALL THE FOLLOWING DAY, Anne, Judith, and Nigel continued their inspection and cataloging of the Hall's furnishings. Nigel left to open his shop at lunch time, taking with him a list of paintings he thought may be worth something, monetarily or socially.

"Judith," Anne said, when Nigel's footsteps could no longer be heard on the drive, "What's your opinion of Nigel?"

"I don't trust him," Judith said. "Like you, I've had dealings with Nigel down the years. Most have been open and above board but one or two have given me reason to be wary. I think, if you want to keep those paintings, you should have the boys move them all before they disappear in the night."

Anne nodded. "I'll have the boys start this afternoon." The 'boys' were the two men who were her company's only workforce beyond herself. Neither were boys, Ben was in his fifties and Isaac in his thirties. "I'll pop out when we've eaten our sandwiches."

By mid-afternoon, the 'boys' and their van were at the Hall, and paintings were being marched out of the Hall and loaded into the company's van. Two vanloads later and the Hall's paintings were safely stored in Anne's company warehouse by evening.

Exhausted by their day climbing stairs and wandering the rooms and corridors of the Hall, Anne and Judith returned to Judith's home for a glass of sherry and a good natter.

"Have you made any progress with the code?" Anne asked.

"I haven't had a moment to try," Judith protested. "You?"

Anne shook her head, as she sipped her drink and stroked Rex's head. "And I'm too tired for trying again tonight."

"You know, I think it'll be embarrassing if that detective you wrote to turns up," Judith murmured. "I think we were just tired and silly that first night after we found the safe."

Anne grimaced. "I fear you're right. I'm hoping he's too busy and turns me down." They'd worked all day and nothing unusual had happened, not even a growl from Rex as he'd chased mice and rats around the old building.

After an hour of rest, Anne pushed herself to get up and go home. "Early start again tomorrow?" She asked Judith.

"I'll join you later," Judith replied. "Like our friend Nigel, I too have a business of my own to run."

Anne smiled. "And I'm grateful for your help. Rex and I will look forward to seeing you when you get there."

* * *

THE FOLLOWING day was much like the previous one, except Anne, Rex, and her 'boys' were now actively moving items out of the Hall that had been cataloged. It was heavy work, even her two experienced men were tiring by the time Judith joined them

"You're just in time," Anne cried, smiling. "We need a fresh pair of hands."

Judith stared at the piles of furniture and fixings in the hallway and grimaced. "You need to hire more help."

"I should but I can't," Anne said. "We'll just take longer to get it all moved."

"Have you enough space in your warehouse?"

Anne shook her head. "The furniture that's worth saving is going straight to the auction rooms. Only the smaller items are going to my place."

"I worked on the code for a time this morning," Judith said. "The man I was meeting was late. I think I have another word identified, 'stream', and new letters, 't', 'r', and 'm'."

"Stream?" Anne said, looking quizzically at Judith. "Are you sure? It doesn't seem to tie in with the jewels or the safe."

"We don't know the code is only about the jewels and the safe, though, do we?"

Anne shrugged. "Maybe not but if the translation really is just children having fun ten years or so ago, the detective will not be amused."

"Maybe another letter to stop him wasting his time?" Judith suggested.

"If I feel up to it tonight," Anne replied. "I'll do that. In the meantime, help me with this wall hanging. I wish I knew more about so much of what we're loading. I can't help thinking some of it could just be left for the developers to take when they knock the whole thing down, or whatever it is they plan to do."

It was after ten that evening before Anne and Rex were both bathed and ready to relax in front of the fire with a hot drink. Though she was too exhausted to write letters, she had grabbed one of the pages of code to see if Judith's new discoveries helped her decipher a word or two on her sheets.

With a notepad and pencil at hand, she began work on

several four and five letter words that included the letters they'd identified. Her tired brain seemed unwilling to make sense of any of them at first until one word came to her, 'mask'. It didn't seem to be a useful word, but it did add the possibility of 'k' being identified. *Really,* she was thinking, *this is so childishly easy it can't be anything serious,* when Rex lifted his head and growled.

Praying she'd locked the doors when she'd come home, Anne crept quietly to the door looking out onto the street. Through the small glass insert of the door, she saw a figure flitting out of sight at the edge of the glow from a nearby streetlamp but otherwise there was no one to be seen. *Were they listening at a window?* She crept back into her living room and squinted through the gap at the edge of the living room's curtain. She glanced at Rex questioningly. Rex remained alert and staring at the door. Taking a chair, Anne returned to the door and wedged the chair back under the door handle.

Feeling better, she returned to her seat and sherry. Before she sat down, however, she'd decided to make the same security arrangement at the back door. It only took a moment and again, she prepared to return to her drink.

"It's no good, Rex," she said, heading for the stairs, "I want to be sure every window and door is locked before I go to sleep and I'm not writing a letter to cancel the detective. You don't ever raise the alarm at this house and tonight you did. Something is up."

4

BEING WATCHED?

THE DAYS that followed were busy ones as Anne's small team hauled away items that seemed likely to provide a profit on the clearance and sent the rest to auction houses in the hope they'd cover most of the cost. Anne's evenings were short because of the long working days, and she had little time for code breaking. Judith now was almost wholly involved with her own business and, except for the all too frequent visits from Nigel, who claimed he was helping her value the Hall's furnishings, but who looked to Anne to be casing the joint, most of her time was spent alone, except for Rex, in the old Hall. Her two employees were constantly on the move ferrying items to storage sites.

It was during these hours alone with only Rex for company that Anne began to feel as if she was being watched. Occasionally, Rex too would seem uneasy and even growl at doors or windows, but Anne never saw or heard anyone at either.

"It's the Hall," Anne said to Rex, after one such incident. "It's big and empty. Even the smallest of sounds travel along the corridors and echo in the rooms." This thought helped a little, but she was always glad when her employees returned.

One evening, after a particularly anxious afternoon, Anne called in at Judith's house for company and a request for Judith to appraise some small items from the Hall.

As they sipped an evening sherry, Judith jumped to her feet, saying, "I thought you should see this. I found this while researching the Hall's tenants, as you asked me to do." She handed over a photocopy of an old newspaper article.

Anne read the article. "A robbery in a house in Leeds?" she asked, when she was done.

"Here's the next article," Judith said, handing over a second sheet.

"Oh. I see," Anne said. "A necklace, earrings, rings, and brooches. We seem to have found the loot."

"Some of it," Judith replied. "There was much more taken. I think this was the man who bought the jewelry set from the financier."

Anne nodded. "And then was robbed of it. Do you think this was the man who rented Demerlay Hall?"

Judith handed over another photocopy and said, "I don't know if he rented the Hall. It doesn't say."

Anne quickly read the article. "Phew, there's a lot more to find if this is the loot we're finding."

Judith nodded. "Have you had any more nighttime alarms?"

"Nothing since the night I told you about, but I still make sure everything is locked up tight for the night before I go to sleep," Anne replied. "I can't help remembering that Arnold will have told someone of our find. I do feel watched at the Hall, though."

"I have the same feeling of being watched in the evenings," Judith said. "Only, when I look out in the morning, there's no evidence of any prowler, but it's been dry these past nights so there wouldn't be. Anyway, it's why I took the necklace and earrings to the bank today when I paid in my weekly takings. If you want to move it to your bank, I'm happy to do that with you."

Anne shook her head. "We should do as little as possible to prevent anyone becoming suspicious," she said, before continuing, "I hope we hear from the detective soon. I'm now truly concerned."

"You didn't write and cancel then?"

"I didn't," Anne told her.

"You said you think you're being watched while you're working at the Hall?" Judith asked.

Anne nodded. "It's just nerves, of course, but the moment the boys leave, I feel it. Today, I was even pleased when Nigel arrived looking for more goodies."

"Has he made an offer on the paintings he talked about?"

"Not yet," Anne replied. "He says he's waiting to hear back from potential buyers."

"And now he's interested in vases?"

"Vases, light fittings, China tea services, glassware, you name it," Anne said. "He has a new shopping list every time he comes."

"Maybe we should bring in someone with more expertise than I have," Judith said. "I don't think much of it is valuable, but it sounds like Nigel does and he knows his stuff in his specialty areas."

"I agree," Anne replied. "I wish that detective would get in touch. Between Nigel hanging around and the feeling of being watched, I can't help wondering if we're sitting on the loot and others know it. They've been waiting all these years for a break, someone to find something that will lead them to the treasure."

"And you think the safe and the codes are the break they've been waiting for?"

Anne nodded; her expression was grim. "The haul from that robbery was worth thousands all those years ago. It will likely be worth even more today."

"I don't want to depress you, Anne," Judith said, "but it's over a week now and you haven't heard anything. I think the detective has bigger fish to fry."

"Then it's up to you and me to find the loot, and 'high tailing it to the hills' as they say in films," Anne replied. "I can see myself on a sunny terrace in Spain, living under a false name and a sombrero."

"Maybe we should tell the police?" Judith said. "If, as you say, the loot legally belongs to you now, they may be willing to have their patrols go past your house and the Hall more often."

"If I don't hear from the detective soon, I will," Anne told her. "Now, I should be going. I've another early start in the morning. We have an auction house coming tomorrow for the kitchen furnishings."

Arriving at her home, Anne checked around the garden and front of the house before stopping the engine and getting out.

"Quickly, Rex," she told her dog when he seemed inclined to continue napping on the passenger seat. She looked about anxiously as they reached the door, unlocked and opened it, stepped inside and locked it quickly behind them. She shot home the two extra bolts she'd had the boys fit to each door. Breathing a sigh of relief, Anne took off her coat. The evenings were growing chilly now autumn was well settled in.

Switching on the light in her living room she was immediately aware someone had been in the house. Things were misplaced and there was a smell of tobacco smoke. She grabbed Rex's collar and called, "Is there anyone here?"

After a minute without an answer, she entered the living room and inspected the window. It was open. She pulled it closed and turned the old, and now she studied it, insecure latch that locked it. *I'll have the boys screw all the windows shut tomorrow.*

After confirming to herself nothing was missing, Anne spent a restless night and was up long before she needed to be, but she couldn't sit listening for surreptitious sounds from outside. There were always sounds outside. She and Rex had long since grown used to them. Living on the edge of the village, as she did, there was constant movement from wildlife and domestic cats tripping the night away in the darkness.

She could go straight to the Hall, but that would likely be worse. Its situation, a mile outside the village and up at the edge of the empty moorland, made it even less attractive to her in these early hours of the day.

"We'll take a walk into the village, Rex," Anne said. "There'll be people about and the street lamps will still be on." She grabbed an old, heavy walking stick of her father's and they set out.

Rex clearly enjoyed this unaccustomed treat. He sniffed at every corner and followed scents into the hedgerows and gave every sign of a dog enjoying life, which irritated Anne.

"It's all right for you, my lad," she told him. "But I'm too frightened now to be at home, or at the Hall, and I can't walk around the village all day."

She was pleased when full daylight came, and she could return home to a hurried breakfast before driving off to

Gold, Greed, and a Hidden Hoard

meet the auctioneer's van and her two employees at the Hall. When the kitchen range and other items were safely loaded and the auctioneer's van left, she sent her two men off with her house keys and enough money to buy screws and hardware to fasten the windows. Her relief at this next step in her security was short-lived. Rex, who'd happily watched proceedings before trotting off to find rats and mice to chase, suddenly barked a warning.

Picking up a heavy candlestick that Nigel had rejected as bric-a-brac, Anne set out to find Rex. He was at one of the side doors, staring out into the overgrown shrubs that were encroaching on the terrace.

"What is it, boy?" Anne whispered. She peered out of the door to be sure no one was hiding nearby and then, seeing the coast clear, stepped outside. "I hope you aren't frightening me over rabbits or something equally silly, Rex." Rex's rigid frame and intense stare out to the trees, suggested he wasn't.

"I should have had one of the boys stay behind," Anne told Rex as she closed and locked the door. "I'm so nervous now, I can't concentrate on anything but noises."

HER TWO EMPLOYEES were back long before lunch time and Anne was able to settle to her work. Before long, they'd brewed their lunchtime tea on a paraffin stove and the three were sitting quietly together eating and drinking. Neither of the men were great talkers so it was a surprise when Ben, the older of the two said, "There used to be some right tales about this place."

Intrigued, Anne asked, "What sort of tales?"

"That there was treasure," Ben told her. "People came to look for it when the Demerlays left."

"One disappeared," Isaac, her other employee interjected.

"Aye, I remember," Ben replied. "What was his name? Saunders! That was it."

"Morris Saunders," Isaac added.

"Right enough, Morris Saunders. Course, he weren't from around here so mebbe just got tired of looking and went home," Ben said, turning his attention to his mug of tea.

Isaac continued, his face set in an expression of deep thought, "There were another of 'em went missing."

Ben too considered this. He nodded. "I remember. A fellow called Geary but I think he just left. I don't think he was murdered or anything."

"Why do you think the two men's leaving were different?" Anne asked.

Ben looked at Isaac, who shrugged and looked blankly in response, before saying, "I don't know. It were just what people said."

"Do you remember anything about a jewel robbery in Leeds?" Anne asked.

"Leeds?" the two men asked together, shaking their heads. "They get up to all sorts of stuff in places like Leeds," Isaac added. "Nought to do with us here."

"I suppose not," Anne agreed. "You talking of 'treasure' made me think of the robbery I remember from that time."

Ben shook his head. "The story was this treasure was from the Civil War, which is daft. The Demerlays would have spent it long afore then, if they'd found it. And they'd had three hundred years to find it."

"Mebbe they did find and spend it," Isaac said. "Only by our time, it had all gone so they went too."

Ben nodded. "Aye, mebbe you're right cos that's why they left in the end, money troubles and the boy killing hisself. It were the war that started it all. Everyone was poorer after that, even gentry like them. Anyhow, there was a number of different folks here for weeks looking for it."

"After the Demerlays left?" Anne asked.

"Oh, aye! When the first tenants had the place. Who were they now?" Ben wondered. "They were sort of treasure hunters too, I reckon. Any road, they had people come and search the house and everywhere. There were a lot of digging in the grounds."

"Maybe they found it," Anne suggested.

"Nay, old Ned Wishart were gardener here then and he said they were just idiots. Great holes they dug, leaving him to fill them in, and never anything to show for it," Isaac told her.

"Well," Ben said, looking at his old waistcoat pocket watch, "back to work. The gaffer won't be pleased if we sit all day gossiping."

Anne grinned. "The 'gaffer' has found your gossip extremely interesting and entertaining, so I think she'll say nothing this time. But you must tell me more tomorrow."

"Right you are," Ben replied. "That gives me time to put my thinking cap on. It were a long time ago and a lot has happened since so I've forgotten much of it."

Anne thought ten years not such a long time and nothing had happened in Grassmount that she could remember. Maybe Ben lived a more interesting life than she did.

She wrapped up her lunch packages and returned to the Hall's old library. The walls were still lined with bookshelves and many mouldy books. She was working through listing them and growing increasingly concerned. Her contract had less than three weeks left before she had to be finished, and every room had so much in them her time was being eaten away. She had always been uncomfortable around Nigel, his manner was so unctuous, and yet his occasional assistance was a relief, both for his advice and his presence. Judith spent as much time at the hall as she could but most of the time it was just Anne and Rex.

She'd only just looked around for her friend when he leapt at the library window barking. For a second, Anne thought she saw someone disappear into the bushes.

"We'll lock all the doors, Rex," Anne said. "It's probably just someone homeless looking for a place to stay but we can't take chances." Locking the doors was one thing, locking the windows another. There were simply too many. The Hall had two larger wings at the north and south of the main building and a protruding central wing with windows on every wall. Anne decided to retreat to one room and barricade herself in there.

She chose the library, and locked and barred everything that provided an entry, before continuing with her notes about the books and their condition. However, her eyes flitted continually to the window and whenever the bushes outside shivered in the wind, her heart sank.

A loud thumping on the door told Anne that the boys had returned or one of her helpers had arrived and she hurried to let them in. It was Nigel, again.

"Have you shut your shop?" Anne asked as she closed and locked the door behind him

"No, my neighbor, who helps me when she can, is looking after it," He replied. "Have you had intruders?" He gestured toward the door.

Anne explained as she returned to the library with him trailing behind, patting Rex who was trotting alongside hoping for a treat from his friend. Rex wasn't disappointed for a large dog treat was surreptitiously handed over.

"There's a sharp wind today. It was probably just moving the bushes," Nigel said. "Winter is on its way."

"Are you still interested in books?" Anne asked. "I could use some help here."

Nigel grimaced. "Yes and no. I'll help but I'm only interested in notable books in good condition. Most of these are ruined." He gestured to the books on the floor.

"Catalog them anyway and when you see one you think you might take," Anne told him, "I'll give it to you for free."

"It's a deal," He replied, chuckling.

They worked quietly for a few minutes before Anne asked, "Do you remember that big jewel robbery in Leeds?"

"Recently?"

"No, back in the early fifties," Anne clarified.

He nodded. "Yes, I remember it was quite the event. Though I haven't thought about it in a long time. What brought that on?"

Anne explained about her 'boys' remembering the treasure hunters at Demerlay Hall.

"I remember that too," Nigel exclaimed, "though I don't think the two were connected, were they? I'm sure the treasure was supposed to be historical. A Civil War hoard, or something."

"Was there much in the Civil War story, do you think?" Anne framed this question as innocently as she could but watched him closely as he considered his answer.

He does seem uneasy. But Nigel was always a strange mix of characters, sometimes too jovial, others not enough. Sometimes as scrupulous as a woman about things and other times coarser than a sailor. By turns too loud, then too quiet. He never seemed entirely at ease.

"It's possible, I suppose," He replied at last. "When the Parliamentary army battered down Scarborough castle and its Royalist garrison, I can imagine a lot of well-to-do families in the locality running from their homes and maybe leaving things too heavy to carry, like the family silver, buried in their gardens."

"But most would come back when the danger was over," Anne suggested. His explanation was sensible enough, but she couldn't help feeling he was holding something back.

Nigel nodded. "Exactly. And the Demerlays were back the moment it was safe to do so. We know that from the records."

"There goes my hope of a fortune," Anne replied, pretending to be sad.

"It would be 'treasure trove' and the government would want a share," Nigel reminded her. "And there are still Demerlays alive who would claim it for their own."

Anne laughed, to show she was joking. "What makes you think I was planning to tell anyone?"

"Well, now you've said that you won't be able to complain if I find a rare first edition in here and keep all the proceeds to myself. After all, you did agree I could take what I wanted for free."

Anne scoffed. "Any rare book you find in here will likely have a mouse's nest inside made of all the pages. Believe me, I've seen more than one already. It's why I have Rex with me, to keep the mice away."

"Then I fear we are both doomed to finish our work with only the usual collection of small profits for our pains."

They worked in silence for some time before Anne again spoke. "I wondered if the two events were connected, you see. The robbery and the treasure hunting, I mean. The hunting, as I understood it from Ben and Isaac, only began after the robbery."

"Leeds isn't so close that the loot would wind up here," Nigel replied, "and I think the treasure hunts began after the Demerlays left, rather than after the robbery. Though it was all in the same time, if I understood the story right. I'm not the best person to ask about this. I came later and only know the story from hearsay."

Anne felt deflated. "You're probably right. People who'd heard the hidden treasure stories dived in when the Hall became available to rent. It was being told about the two incidents together made me jump to the conclusion they were connected." *That and the newspaper article Judith found that listed stolen rings and a necklace that sounded like the items they'd found in the safe. Not to mention silly cipher messages written on pages torn from books, which she could see now were just games being played by children. How utterly, utterly depressing.*

"Local legends often lead to outbreaks of treasure hunting, I believe," Nigel muttered, as he was studying a book in some detail. "This one I may want," he said, showing her the volume.

When Nigel said he must leave so his neighbor could get home, Anne decided she too should finish for the day. She wanted to talk over what Nigel had suggested with Judith.

Anne's timing was perfect, for Judith was just making a pot of tea when she arrived, and they were able to discuss the depressing news as they sipped their hot drinks. Nigel was right about the cold wintry wind.

When they'd exhausted all thoughts on Nigel's information, Judith said, "In a way, I'm not surprised." When she saw Anne's expectant look, Judith continued, "I've been working on those coded messages in the quiet moments, and I have a number of sentences worked out."

"And?" Anne asked gloomily. She didn't like the sound of where this was going.

"They read more like clues in a children's Scavenger Hunt, or maybe ideas being developed for a Scavenger Hunt," Judith replied. "'Where the stream ran', is one and 'under the mask' is another."

"They still could be clues," Anne said.

"They could but in light of what we've heard," Judith said, "I can't help feeling adults wouldn't have written single cryptic lines over a number of re-used pages if these instructions were supposed to be helpful."

"Maybe they weren't trying to be helpful," Anne suggested.

Judith shook her head. Her expression disbelieving. "Have you heard from the detective?"

"No, and once again, I'm glad I haven't," Anne replied. "What could I say now?"

"Quite," Judith agreed. She went to a sideboard, returning with a sheet of paper. "Here, take this newest, latest version of the code alphabet. Maybe there'll be something on one of your sheets to turn our hopes around again."

Anne thanked her and, waking Rex who'd dozed off, left for home.

5

BREAK-IN

WITH HER NEW alphabet in hand, Anne searched her collection of loose pages for words now deciphered and for words that should be more easily deciphered. With a mug of hot cocoa beside her, she wrote feverishly on clean paper each sentence as it appeared. Sadly, they confirmed Judith's opinion, rather than her hoped for suggestion. They were more Scavenger Hunt than Treasure Hunt.

She was puzzling over a long word with half its letters known, when Rex rose to his feet growling. His attention was again fixed on the room's curtained window, which looked out from the front of the house into the garden and street.

Frowning, Anne rose. Grasping the kitchen knife she now had with her whenever she was alone in the house, she crept softly to the front door where she could see out. The idea of pulling back the living room curtain and being face-to-face with an intruder was too frightening. From the door, however, no one was in view, and she couldn't see enough to spy someone at the window where Rex was still growling. Screwing up all her courage, Anne crept back to the window and peered through the gap between the curtain and the window frame. Still nothing to be seen. She crept to the join in the curtains and, taking a deep breath, swept them apart. No one was there.

Drawing the curtains closed, she said to Rex, rather crossly, "What is it you're sensing? You're frightening the life out of me."

Rex turned away and padded back to his place near the electric fire and Anne returned to her chair. It was some minutes before she was calm enough to return to the puzzle but when she did, something jumped into her mind right away. She grabbed the diary and leafed through the pages until she found what she was looking for. A number, which she wrote down, and continued searching. As she'd remembered, the number 364 was repeated many times throughout the book. It could be some kind of grid reference, though she thought that would need more numbers. A safe key, perhaps? Was there another safe to be found?

She was still puzzling over this and what she could remember of the fifties in the village and what her parents had said about the Demerlays, when the clock struck eleven and she hurried to bed. It would be another long day tomorrow.

* * *

BEN AND ISAAC were already waiting for her when she arrived the following morning, and they greeted her cheerily.

"Sorry I'm late," Anne said. "These long days are taking their toll." She opened the old oak doors of the Hall entranceway and the three made their way inside. Anne stopped. "Wait!"

The two men froze as if playing a game, while Anne's gaze swept around the entrance hall and the furnishings, they'd left ready to load this morning.

"Someone's been in here," Anne said, after a moment. "This isn't how it was when I locked up last night."

"Is anything missing?" Ben asked.

"It's hard to say," Anne replied. "You staged those items for shipping," she said, pointing at one of the piles, "see if you can spot anything taken. I'll look at the books and papers on the desk."

For a short period, there was silence broken finally by Ben saying, "Nothing seems missing here."

"Nor here," Anne replied, looking up from the book-and paper-strewn table, "though it's hard to be sure."

"I'll check the doors and windows," Isaac told them, and set off down a corridor.

"Mebbe one of us should allus be here," Ben suggested.

"Maybe we should," Anne said, trying to imagine the overtime bill.

"Not you, lass," Ben replied. "It's not safe for a woman on her own when there's thieves about."

"Or elderly men either," Anne retorted.

"Thieves don't lift furniture every day like Isaac and I do," Ben replied, grinning. "We'll be fine."

Anne thought on balance he was right but was there anything in this place that she couldn't afford to lose? If there was, it hadn't leapt out at any of them yet, other than the safe, of course.

"If we move these last items today, and I finish the library," she said, 'everything else will be too heavy to carry away in the night. They'd need a truck."

"Aye, well, we're here if you want us," Ben said, nodding. He began lifting items to carry out to the van.

"A window has been broken at the back," Isaac said, returning to the hallway. "They got in that way. I'll board it up when we've taken these things to the warehouse."

After her alarm the night before, this new evidence of an intruder or intruders chilled Anne to the core. Not for the first time, she wished she'd never taken on this contract.

The two men worked steadily for twenty minutes or so while Anne began again in the library. Ben stuck his head through the door and said, "We're off now. Lock up after us."

Anne followed him to the front door and turned the heavy iron key in the lock when he was out. The van started up and she soon heard it rumbling down the driveway on its way into Grassmount. When it was gone, the Hall was eerily quiet, and it made her shiver.

Fifteen minutes later, among all the furtive rustling and creaking of the house, she heard more metallic noises. Someone, she guessed, was at the broken window, their arm through the glass opening the latch Isaac had only just closed. She took her trusty kitchen knife from her handbag and padded quietly down the corridor, only to have Rex go bounding past barking like a wolfhound in full chase.

Anne ran as fast as she could but when she could see the window, there was no one there, though it was opened a crack. She looked out and saw the overgrown raspberry plants shaking wildly and then a figure in brown clothes dive from them into the trees at the farther end of the garden.

"Idiot," she said to Rex, who was looking pleased with himself. "Still, I now know it's a man. Fat lot of good that will do me." She imagined telling the police the trespasser was a man in a brown coat and their polite, but mocking, response.

Rex was now at the door, hoping to give chase. Anne re-locked the window before taking Rex's collar and leading him back to the library.

"You can keep the mice and rats at bay," she told him, still cross.

Ben and Isaac arrived back. Isaac boarded up the window while Ben prepared more furnishings to go. Anne continued cataloguing until lunch time, when she told them in more detail about the intruder.

"Skinny or fat?" Isaac asked.

Anne hesitated. "Skinny, I'd say."

"Old or young?" Ben asked.

"Older rather than younger, but still fast on his feet," Anne replied. Amazed to learn how much she had seen in that moment.

"What sorta coat?" Isaac asked.

"A trench coat," Anne replied.

"Ex-army likely, down on his luck," Ben suggested.

"Or someone who shops in the second-hand clothing shops that sell old army stock," Isaac added.

"Hat or cap?" Isaac asked.

"Cap, like you wear," Anne replied, "and it was brown too."

"Boots or shoes?" Ben continued the questioning.

Anne hesitated. She'd only seen the man from the waist up because of the raspberry bushes. "I can't be sure, but I think if we look among the rasps out there, we'd find prints."

The ground between the raspberry canes was damp from the rain during the night and prints of large hob-nailed boots marked a clear path from the window to the trees.

"A working man, then," Ben said, as they returned to the Hall. "Or one who looks like one, anyway. Maybe just someone taking the opportunity to make a few bob before the old place is gone."

"Well, he doesn't need to terrify me to make his few shillings," Anne replied. "He could come and help lift and carry."

There was no repeat of the incursions that afternoon and by the time the three were packing up to go home, Anne was confident enough to say, "Thank you for the offer to stay tonight, Ben, but I think we've removed anything an intruder could carry alone. We'll just lock up and be back again early in the morning."

The men wished her goodnight and drove off, while she locked up and drove herself and Rex to Judith's house, where the inevitable cup of tea was soon offered.

"Busy day?" Judith asked, as they waited for the kettle to boil.

Anne nodded, slumping in an armchair and pushing off her shoes. "My feet are killing me, and I thought I'd been sitting all day."

"You need to move about more," Judith advised. "Get the blood moving. Oh, I deciphered another sentence, and it mentions an icehouse. Did you know there was an icehouse?"

"No," Anne replied. "My contract is for the house and attached buildings only. Where's the icehouse?"

Judith shrugged. "I don't know but I think we should find it. Maybe this really is a treasure hunt, and something is hidden in there."

Anne laughed. "I think those treasure hunters in the nineteen-fifties wouldn't have missed something like an icehouse. It would probably still have been in use at that time. Even rich folk had little in the way of refrigeration then."

"I still think we should..."

"We'll go together, with Ben and Isaac tomorrow afternoon when it's still light," Anne said. "Now, isn't that the kettle whistling?"

Judith ran off to the kitchen while Anne massaged her feet with one hand and Rex's ear with the other.

They'd only just sat down with their teacups when a crashing of glass outside had them hurriedly running to the kitchen window. No one was to be seen so Judith took a large torch from the top of a cupboard, put on her rubber boots and headed out into the garden.

"Come and look, Anne," she called.

Still in her stockinged feet, Anne walked gingerly over the damp flagstones to stand at her friend's side. The flashlight beam lit the greenhouse and the broken pane midway along it.

"I've started having bother with the children from those new houses," Judith said. "I expect this is their reprisal for me speaking to their parents."

Anne murmured agreement. *Is it though? Or has my intruder followed me here?* She gripped Rex's collar tightly in case he decided to give chase.

6

HOME FROM ROSEBERRY TOPPING

RAMSAY AND BRACKEN arrived at the cottage, still chilled from their minutes on top of Roseberry. So much so, Ramsay lit the coal fire he needed to heat water for a warm bath *and* switched on the electric fire he kept for additional heating in the winter.

With a pot of tea made and fresh water for Bracken, Ramsay began sorting through the many letters the *Mysteries De-Mystified Agency* had received since the summer and which he hadn't answered. He'd given up responding after only a week because there were so many. The agency's fame thanks to the well-publicized case of the missing manuscript and its author's death, had a surprising number of people getting in touch.

"It's in here somewhere, Bracken," Ramsay told his companion, who was too busy gnawing on a bone to be interested in sheets of paper. Reaching the end of the pile, Ramsay frowned and began again.

"The thing is, Bracken," he murmured, as he read each letter more carefully, "I was becoming a ghost again. You won't understand that because what I'm talking about was before your time. When Jeanie," he paused, hardly able to continue, "and the boys were killed, I didn't die. I just wasn't alive anymore. I went to work, came home and slept for an hour or so and then went back to the office. Looking back now, I can see it was why they were so eager to push me out when I was shot. Nobody wants a ghost in their lives, not even in their working lives." He stopped speaking and separated the letter he wanted from the others.

"Got it!" He exclaimed, waving the sheet at Bracken, who lifted his head, saw it was just paper, and returned his attention to the bone.

Ramsay read the letter again. He studied the address and date the letter was written and grimaced. He really should have replied to this one. It being so close, the next village over, and a mystery in which everyone involved was likely to be either dead or long gone from the place.

"Listen, Bracken," Ramsay said. "It's in Grassmount, not ten minutes away, and it's from a woman who found jewelry and papers in an old Hall she was clearing. She thinks the jewelry was stolen in the fifties and never recovered. There's also diaries and papers with cryptic clues that may mean there's more to be found. That's exactly what we're looking for. A case where we don't have to go far from home, and no one is likely to want to hurt us."

He glanced at his watch. "She'll still be at work just now. I'll phone later." He paused, staring into the flames, collecting his thoughts. "What I was trying to say, Bracken, before I found the letter, was after Eliza left, I was becoming a ghost again."

Hearing Eliza's name, Bracken sat up. He missed Eliza and couldn't understand why she wasn't still with them. He thought they were friends.

Ramsay stroked Bracken's head and fondled his ears.

"You see, I dealt with the pain of losing my family by never thinking of them and I was doing the same with Eliza. Up there on top of Roseberry, the cold sank deep into me and somehow it brought me back to this life. It's just you and me now, Bracken, and we're going to be alive. However much it hurts."

They sat quietly until it was time to eat the food that Ramsay made while humming *The Keel Row* softly to himself. He still needed a warm bath to thaw him, but he felt more alive than he'd done in weeks. After his evening meal, Ramsay listened to the radio and read the new Agatha Christie, *The Third Girl*. He wasn't usually a fiction reader, but Agatha was a guilty pleasure for him. At seven o'clock, he put down his book and dialed the number he'd been given.

* * *

ANNE WAS in the act of shutting and locking her front door when the phone rang. "Bother, I must have left something at Judith's."

She picked up the phone and said, "Yes?"

A man's voice, low, northern England or Scotland accent, said formally, "Miss Anne Watson?"

"Who is this?" Anne demanded, perspiration prickling her brow. *Had the intruder moved onto threatening phone calls?*

"Tom Ramsay of the *Mysteries, De-Mystified Agency*. You wrote us a letter."

"That was more than a week ago," Anne cried, annoyed to find she'd once again been made afraid of nothing out of the ordinary.

"I see. Well, if you do..." Ramsay began.

"I do!" Anne cried. "Yes. How soon can you get here?"

"Do you mean this evening?" Ramsay asked, startled.

"This evening or tomorrow morning as soon as you can."

There was silence and then he said, "I could be in Grassmount in ten, maybe fifteen minutes. If you'd rather leave it to a more suitable hour, seven tomorrow morning."

"I've just come in from work, Mr. ...er, Ramsay. Can you be here in forty-five minutes?"

"Certainly, Miss Watson. I have your address but maybe a landmark to guide me?"

"Grassmount isn't very big," Anne replied, chuckling. "Which way will you be coming from?"

Ramsay told her and Anne said, "Then stay on the road through the village past the Rail Station and the street is on your left. You really can't miss it."

"Thank you," Ramsay said. "I have a dog. Will it be alright to bring him?"

Anne grimaced and glanced at Rex. "I do too," she said. "Is yours good with other dogs?"

"If they aren't vicious," Ramsay laughed.

"Then they should be fine," Anne said. "I'll see you soon."

"He has a dog, Rex," Anne said, bending to stroke his head. "He must be a good man, if he has a dog." She left the living room and hurried off to wash and change. Suddenly realizing she hadn't had a formal visitor in a long time, Anne returned to the living room and quickly tidied up. *It wasn't perfect, but he had a dog, so he'd understand.* Once again, she ran upstairs to get ready.

Ramsay was punctual to the minute. Anne suspected he'd been waiting outside for some time.

"Come in," Anne said, opening the door, "that wind is icy."

Ramsay laughed, as he stepped inside. "I know. I was on

Roseberry Topping this afternoon and I'm still not thawed out. This is Bracken, my bloodhound. He's a collie but you get my point."

Anne smiled and stroked Bracken, saying, "How do you do, Bracken. Come and meet Rex."

Anne took Ramsay's coat and hung it up, wondering if he was really the man for the job. He was older than she'd expected and not so tall. Certainly not the six-foot, 200-lb, rugby playing bruiser she was hoping for. Recent events had begun to sway her vision of the help she needed.

When they were settled, Anne described the timeline of events ending with the broken greenhouse pane only an hour or so ago. Ramsay listened quietly. *He seemed a quiet man all around.* Bracken and Rex had spent a few minutes checking each other out and had decided they could get along. Now they lay side by side in front of the electric fire.

"Can I see these coded documents?" Ramsay asked, when she finished speaking.

Anne handed the loose sheets over and he studied them for a moment. "I see your point," he said. "They don't look like the work of sophisticated people. Criminals, however, aren't often sophisticated people, except in fiction where the story's hero must pit their wits against criminal masterminds."

Anne nodded. "It's the same with the incidents. It could be someone trying to intimidate us or it could be naughty children or homeless people. I thought you might be able to shed light on the old jewel robbery and the pieces we've found."

"You disregard the possibility of buried treasure then?" Ramsay asked, smiling.

Anne replied, "I do. Nigel, our local antique dealer and Judith, our local historian, say before the treasure hunters arrived there was never any official mention of the Demerlays hiding their family fortune and losing it."

"Public knowledge is often better than official records," Ramsay responded, "but I'm sure the records are right this time, if the family returned to their home soon after the danger was past. What about the Leeds robbery you mentioned?"

"Again, we aren't near Leeds and why would they bring the loot here? People I've asked, don't think there's any sense in it," Anne replied. "The Demerlays, the family that owned the Hall then, are real old-fashioned aristocracy not villains."

Ramsay laughed. "There's some would say that's what aristocracy are. Villains, I mean. But I take your point. It does seem a stretch."

"Will you help me?" Anne asked. "I know this isn't murder, not yet anyway, and it isn't spies or anything glamorous like that, but it is puzzling, and I have to be honest, frightening at times."

"From my point of view, having a case right on my doorstep and with little chance of meeting seriously violent people, is perfect," Ramsay said. "Only let me explain my rates and see if you're still interested."

Anne wasn't sure his emphasis on not meeting violent people was what she wanted to hear but she imagined there were degrees of violence she, as a new amateur in this world, hadn't yet encountered. *However, like Ben and Isaac, he does have that sense of physical strength you don't see in most men of their ages.* "Go ahead. I'm not rich but I might be able to get some of your costs back at tax time."

Ramsay laughed. "I've never been a tax write-off before. Anyhow, here we go." He itemized the hourly rate and his expenses. "Bracken comes free, but he is an asset, believe me."

Bracken raised his head at the mention of his name and caught Anne's eye as she looked at the collie lying contentedly in the glow of the fire bars. She agreed he was an asset, though not obviously so at this moment, and Bracken lay back down, feeling he'd made his presence known.

"May I take the coded pages and copies of the newspaper articles?" Ramsay asked. "I'll return them tomorrow when I bring our contract."

"Very well," Anne said, "but come to the Hall in the afternoon, I'll be busy in the morning."

With this agreed, Ramsay and Bracken left, leaving Anne feeling strangely relieved. *He hasn't done anything yet*, she sternly told herself. *The proof will be in the pudding.*

* * *

THE FOLLOWING MORNING, Anne and Rex were at Demerlay Hall before her two workers, and she waited impatiently in the car for their arrival.

"We're going to find this icehouse, Rex," she said to her friend who panted and grinned in reply. "And I think I know where it is." She'd often noticed a bump in the landscape of the estate when driving on the lane that brought her to the Hall each morning.

When they arrived, Anne told Ben and Isaac to continue moving items without her for a while. She was going to find an old lost icehouse.

"T'ain't lost, Anne," Ben replied. "It's just through the trees over there."

She was pleased he was pointing in the direction where

she thought it was. "You never mentioned it before," she said.

"You never asked," Ben replied. "I thought the contract was for the Hall. That's what you said."

Anne nodded. "It is but I've never actually seen an icehouse and if there is anything there, well we may forget to tell anyone..." she let the sentence die away with a mischievous grin.

Isaac agreed. "What the eye doesn't see, the heart doesn't grieve over."

The icehouse, when she arrived, and that took some time because the shrubs were so entangled and shot through with briars, looked as depressing as she'd thought it would. The doorway was sunk into the earth and the short flight of steps down was also covered in briars.

"We could have come here to pick blackberries last August, Rex," she muttered to her companion as she hacked away at the stalks with her secateurs, brought especially in case she met exactly this kind of obstacle. She wondered how the old gardener, Ned Wishart, felt when he passed the grounds in these later years. *Maybe he didn't, so he didn't know what had become of all his years of toil.*

When she reached the door, it was held fast with a rusty lock that couldn't have been opened since those famous fifties everyone spoke of when talking about Demerlay Hall. She probed the wooden door and felt it give. The lock was still locked but the hook it attached to was in rotten wood. Putting her secateurs in her jacket pocket, she pushed the door with both hands and, when it flew open, almost fell into the empty corridor that opened out into a wider room.

Stepping inside, she shivered. The air was even colder than outside and damp, smelling of mold and decay. Anne switched on her flashlight and moved farther inside. The floor was strewn with rubble from the roof and wooden pieces that might once have been shelves. A thought occurred, and she retraced her step to the door and wedged it open with the detritus from the floor. "That will slow anyone who thinks to lock us in," she told Rex who was watching her work.

The main chamber of the icehouse, where the ice must once have been stacked until it was needed, was even more cluttered than the entrance. Every shelf was down and lay in pieces on the floor. Her torch beam swept the room, and she had a moment of déjà vu. This was like the Hall cellar when they'd found the safe. With that in mind, she began slowly examining the walls hoping for a sign there was another hidden compartment.

Rex growled and turned to look back to the entrance. Anne abandoned her search and almost ran back to the door. The thought of being trapped in this tomb was terrifying. Ben and Isaac were the only ones who knew where she was and they may not notice her absence for hours, if they were as busy as they usually were.

She could see no one at the rectangular patch of light where the door had been, but she was still careful to move slowly, and listen carefully, before peering out. There was no one in sight and again she wondered if Rex was just growling at squirrels or cats.

Now she was outside, Anne found she didn't want to go back in again until she had someone with her. She pulled the broken door back into the frame and wedged it in place as best she could. "It's encouraging that a coded sentence mentioned the icehouse," Anne told Rex as they pushed their way back through the undergrowth to the Hall. "It's the perfect place to hide loot. Maybe, that means the messages are real." *But those old 'treasure hunters' would have searched it thoroughly; you can be sure of that. Maybe that's why all the shelves are broken.*

Ben and Isaac were drinking tea when she arrived, and Anne was mildly irritated. They'd be sat drinking tea waiting for her return for hours if she'd been locked in the icehouse.

"We didn't like to go away leaving the Hall unlocked," Ben explained, sensing the boss wasn't thrilled to find them on their tea break an hour before it was due.

Anne nodded. "You did right. Get that load off to the auctioneers and I'll look after the place. I have lost time I need to make up in that library."

By mid-afternoon, the library was finished to her satisfaction and the last remaining books were packed in the van and sent off to the warehouse. Ramsay hadn't appeared by the time her workers were out of sight and Anne began to think he'd changed his mind.

Anne wanted to go back into the cellar and the icehouse, but contented herself in wandering through the remaining uncleared rooms trying to estimate how long each would take and whether she could be finished by the time her contracted time was up. She thought she might, if the cellar didn't contain anything of real value.

A thumping on the entrance door told her Ramsay had arrived and she, with Rex alongside, made her way down the grand staircase to let him in.

"I was beginning to think you weren't coming," Anne told him, as she closed and bolted the door behind him.

"I've been doing some digging," Ramsay explained vaguely, not mentioning his early start, train to Leeds and the hour spent among the local Leeds newspaper's back copies, "and scouting out the lay of the land." He returned her documents and handed her the contract. "You can read and sign it later, if you wish."

Anne placed the documents and contract on the hall table they used for staging fragile pieces, before saying, "Before we talk about that, I want you to guard the cellar door while I climb down there for another look."

"That's where you found the safe?"

"It is, but there's a mountain of stuff we may or may not want to shift and my workers are busy ferrying what we have salvaged from the Hall to our warehouse. You're my best hope. Rex tends to follow me instead of guarding the door," Anne added with a grin.

"I've been training Bracken to stay and guard things," Ramsay told her. "This may be my chance to see if all my work has been successful."

Anne led the way to the cellar door and opened it. Switching on her flashlight, she began descending the stairs leaving Ramsay and Bracken at the top.

The cellar was huge, containing what would have once been the wine and beer cellars as well as places for hanging game. Other rooms probably were just intended for storage. Anne didn't believe the stories of how they were once dungeons where rebellious villagers were held in medieval times. Now, whatever they were for, they were all filled with items that needed scrutiny before being consigned to auctioneers, restorers, or antique dealers. Getting some profit from this pile of cast-offs may make the difference between a good year for her business or in the worst case, a loss. She was on the hook for quite a sum with this contract.

"What do you think, Rex?" Anne asked her friend who, she noticed, had not stayed with Ramsay and Bracken.

"All right down there?" She heard Ramsay's call echoing off the cellar walls from what sounded miles away but wasn't more than fifty feet. The piles of furniture muffled everything.

"Yes," she called back. "If Bracken stays, come and look at the safe we found."

She was at the safe when Ramsay arrived. Their torch beams lit the hole in the wall and the open safe door.

Ramsay studied the safe and covering, before looking around the wall for similar possible hiding places. "Have you examined all the walls?"

"I haven't been back down here since that day," Anne told him. "I trust Ben and Isaac implicitly but the fewer people who know about this the better."

"We don't want modern treasure hunters traipsing all over the property," Ramsay agreed. "We're here now, why don't we examine the walls at least. The floor and ceiling can wait for another day."

They spent the next twenty minutes circling the room and Ramsay only had to tell Bracken to 'stay' twice. Eventually, even Rex grew so bored he went and joined Bracken on guard at the door.

"Nothing?" Ramsay asked, as they met at the steps.

"Nothing," Anne agreed. "There's an icehouse as well but it may be growing too late for us to explore today." She led the way back up to the light, which was noticeably failing outside.

"If it's dark inside," Ramsay said, "It won't make any difference what the light is like outside."

Anne shook her head. "We'll go another time and then you'll understand. The whole estate is one giant bramble bush. Even Brer Rabbit couldn't get out of it in the dark."

Ramsay laughed. "You know best and, until you hire me, I'm not supposed to be helping you anyway."

"I'll read this tonight," Anne said, waving the contract in her hands, "and you can drop by and pick it up tomorrow."

"I saw a café in the village," Ramsay said. "I'm going to test their tea and pastries. Care to join me and give me more details?"

"Madge loves dogs," Anne said, "and having two to pet will make her day. Yes, I'll join you, but I'll pay. You helped me a lot this afternoon."

Madge's Teashop was still open when they arrived, and Anne was right. Rex always was welcome, and given too many treats, and soon Bracken's reserve about strangers was overcome by treats that, Ramsay told him, 'Were bad for him'. Bracken treated this advice with all the attention it deserved.

Madge took their order and returned with a tray filled with tea pots, jugs, cups and saucers. "I'll just be a minute with your dainties," she told them, and hurried away.

"You say the icehouse is like the cellar inside, ruined," Ramsay asked, as Anne poured tea.

Anne nodded. "Except I think it was probably ruined by treasure hunters. I'm not expecting to find anything there."

"They must have searched the house's cellar too," Ramsay reminded her, "yet they didn't find the safe."

"You might be right," Anne said. "Maybe the covering that hides a safe in the icehouse will also have become sodden and useless over the past ten years."

Before Ramsay could reply, Madge returned with a three-tiered plate of pastries and an envelope, which she handed to Anne.

"What's this?" Anne asked, looking at the unmarked envelope.

"A lad just asked me to give it to you," Madge said. Then

added, with a grin, "It isn't ticking so I thought it should be safe."

When Anne didn't seem eager to open it, and a nearby customer caught her attention, Madge moved away leaving Ramsay and Anne eyeing the envelope with suspicion.

"I'm not so sure it is safe," Ramsay said. "If you want to open it, do it outside where anything inside can be dispersed."

"Are you saying there could be poison in this?" Anne asked, holding the envelope at a distance.

"I know it sounds mad, and I've probably spent too long thinking about spies," Ramsay replied, "but they do sometimes use dangerous substances placed in packages."

"This is the North Riding of Yorkshire," Anne exclaimed. "Not Moscow."

Ramsay grimaced. "I know and I know what I just said is incredulous in the context of this situation, only strange things do happen."

Anne got to her feet. "Outside, you say?"

"I'll do it if you prefer," Ramsay told her.

Anne shook her head. "I haven't signed your contract. It isn't your risk to take." She headed out the door with Ramsay clearing the way.

Feeling extremely foolish, Anne walked away from the teashop door and opened the flap. Nothing terrible happened so she tipped the envelope upside down over a street drain. A single sheet of paper fell out and she had to snatch at it to stop it going down through the grate.

Glaring at Ramsay, who she blamed for this embarrassment, she uncrumpled the page and read aloud, "Clear the house and leave the land to them what values it!"

"Interesting," Ramsay said, thoughtfully. "Who would be more interested in the land than the house?"

"The estate's old gardener, that's who," Anne retorted. "I'll talk to him tomorrow."

"After you've signed my contract," Ramsay said. "This may not be anything serious, just an old man with a bee in his bonnet about his precious garden, but it's the first real evidence you have that someone has a dislike of what you're doing. Everything else, you've been able to explain away."

Anne nodded. "I won't sign your contract without reading it, but I do want your advice. Old Ned may be just a crank, or he may be more than that. He's a strange old man."

"Advice, I give out freely," Ramsay replied, smiling. "For assistance I'll need a contract."

"I must think it over," Anne said. Now she'd read the note and rationalized it in her mind as being Ned Wishart to blame, her fears were subsiding. She looked up and down the street where ordinary people were going about their ordinary business and shivered. Could she sleep easily in her bed until this job was finished or the person or people behind these incidents were arrested?

"Phone me when you've made up your mind," Ramsay said. "Now, let's go back inside, finish our tea and we can both get away home to think."

7

INDECISION

ANNE'S THOUGHTS were still evenly balanced about hiring Ramsay when she dragged herself out of bed next morning after a night so restless it left most of the bedclothes on the floor. Even Rex looked tired and miserable.

"Didn't you sleep either?" Anne asked, as she placed his food and water down for him.

Rex didn't reply and Anne slumped into a chair to begin buttering toast. She'd talk it over again with Judith before finally deciding.

Judith, however, when Anne and Rex arrived at her home, was too excited to talk about detectives.

"I found another newspaper article, it's from about two months after those ones I showed you," Judith said, stumbling over her words, to Anne as she welcomed her guests inside.

"What does it say?" Anne asked, intrigued to know what could cause such excitement in her friend's normal staid manner.

"A treasure hunter went missing," Judith replied, breathlessly. "Never seen again."

"I'm guessing he found it, or are you going to tell me his body was found later?" Anne asked.

"The article suggests he found the treasure and scarpered," Judith said, pushing the photocopy into her hand. "I got this from Lizzie at the Gazette."

"You didn't tell her about the jewels we found?" Anne cried.

"Of course not," Judith replied. "I told her about the coded messages and how mystifying we found them. She's digging through back issues of the paper for me in hopes to find an explanation for the messages."

Anne read the article quickly. Not just a treasure hunter, the missing man was also a private detective from Leeds. *There's that connection again.* The man, Morris Saunders, had gone missing in February 1955 while researching leads concerning a robbery some weeks before, so the newspaper reported.

"This has to be about the Leeds robbery and the necklace set we have," Judith said.

Anne nodded. "Which means the loot was here and he found some of it."

"I imagine he found most of the rest," Judith replied. "He wouldn't have absconded to parts unknown with only a ring or bracelet."

"It's a relief, actually," Anne said. "If everyone thinks the loot is gone, no gang members or their offspring will be searching for it. And we have just been imagining horrors."

"But what if they don't know it's gone?" Judith replied. "What if Mr. Saunders is buried under the bushes of the estate and the gang is still waiting for someone to stumble upon the loot?"

Anne shook her head in dismay. "Whenever I begin to

feel safe, somebody tells me I shouldn't. Look! Should I hire the detective or not? What do you think?"

It was Judith's turn to be confused. In her excitement, she'd clearly missed what Anne had been telling her when she arrived. "How likely is it the loot is still there and the gang or their children are looking for it?"

Anne laughed. "I don't know. It was your idea."

"I was just playing Devil's Advocate," Judith replied. "I don't know any more than you do."

Anne told Judith about the note that she'd been handed the evening before and who she thought wrote it.

Judith nodded. "He's potty enough for that, it's true. When you speak to Ned, you hear the Middle Ages talking. In his mind, the Demerlays are still the local squire, and one day they'll return to put everything right."

Anne laughed. "Like King Harold or Francis Drake, they'll return when their country needs them."

"Exactly," Judith replied. "Barmy, but he believes it."

"Then," Anne said, "summing up, if the broken greenhouse was children, the people we hear outside by night and day are homeless tramps, and this note came from the Demerlays' dotty old gardener, we have nothing to worry about. We don't need a detective."

Judith nodded her agreement.

"You have doubts?" Anne asked, sensing Judith wasn't sure.

"If we're wrong," Judith said, "and Saunders was killed and buried, and we don't trust Nigel, we might need someone experienced on our side."

Anne groaned. "There you go again."

"Well," Judith replied, bristling, "you're no better. Shall I, shan't I? Will I, won't I?"

They lapsed into silence for a moment. "I'll ask him for

advice for now," Anne said, at last. "His rates are very reasonable but if we do poorly out of clearing the Hall, I'll be stretched to pay him."

"I think that's best," Judith said. "Did you visit the icehouse, by the way?"

Anne told her of her visit to that tumbledown tomb of a place, ending with, "If there was anything there, it will be gone now."

"I deciphered another word," Judith continued, "some of these pages are hard to read."

Anne agreed. "The damp was harder on the paper and ink than it was on the jewels."

"I think the word is 'mill'," Judith added. "Was there a mill on the estate?"

"There must be an old map of the estate in the village records," Anne replied. "One from Victorian times should be far enough back. And remember, we had a reference to a 'stream' on one of the sheets so there's a good chance there was a water mill once."

"I'll visit the village records at lunch time," Judith said. "Will you join me?"

"If I can," Anne replied, "but we still have a lot to shift and time's running out."

* * *

ANNE SPENT much of her time while cataloging and carrying, debating how she would tell Ramsay she only wanted his advice. She still hadn't found the perfect words when he knocked on the Hall door, which was locked because her two workers were 'on the road with another load' as Isaac poetically put it.

"Sorry, I was upstairs," Anne said, when she finally

opened the door to Ramsay and Bracken, who pushed his way in to rejoin his new friend, Rex.

"I've asked some old colleagues for more information," Ramsay told her. "With luck we'll hear back from them soon."

"Oh," Anne said, guiltily. "I hope that won't cost anything because I've decided I just want advice for now."

Ramsay laughed. "I don't deal with police officers who ask for money, so, no, it won't cost anything."

"Good," Anne replied, relieved. "We have learned that a private investigator turned treasure hunter disappeared here in 1955."

"Found the loot and took off with it," Ramsay suggested.

Anne nodded. "We thought that too."

"Are we going to reconnoiter the icehouse today?" Ramsay asked.

Anne hesitated. She had a mental image of them finding Morris Saunders' skeleton rather than jewels and it gave her a shock. "Very well," she said, slowly, "but only when Ben and Isaac are back."

"Will they be long?" asked Ramsay. "I might do some research on this place in the local library records."

"They'll be back for lunch," Anne laughed. "They left their lunch boxes here."

"Then I'll return after lunch," Ramsay replied, and called Bracken to follow him back to the car.

"That sounds like 'work' not 'advice'," Anne called after him, and received a wave in reply.

* * *

RAMSAY RETURNED after a warming lunch of soup at Madge's Teashop, where he managed to learn more about the village than he'd done in the library records. The village hadn't had much going for it until the railway arrived, was the impression Ramsay gleaned from the records. He had obtained two copies of an old map, one for Anne and one for himself, showing the principal features of the Demerlay estate as it existed in 1877, which was outside the timeframe he was interested in, but all that was available.

"Ready to go?" Ramsay asked, after he'd done the obligatory small talk with Anne and her two assistants.

"We're exploring the icehouse," Anne told Ben and Isaac, "so, if you hear cries for help, you know where we'll be."

The icehouse door looked undisturbed when they'd finally made their way there. Ramsay and Anne lifted away the rubble and timbers Anne had used to wedge it and, switching on their flashlights, stepped inside.

"Ugh," Anne said, "it's worse than I remembered it. I can hear water dripping."

"It rained overnight," Ramsay reminded her. "There's sure to be leaks in a place like this."

Once again, they went around the walls searching for shapes that might conceal a hiding place. Bracken remained on guard outside. He liked the dark cavern even less that they did.

"If there'd been something," Anne said to Ramsay, "I'm sure it would have been found. Look how the place has been torn apart."

"The walls and floor would have been in better repair ten years ago," Ramsay reminded her. "And if they had found something, there'd be a hole where that something was. I don't see any hole, do you?"

"You think it's still in the wall somewhere?" Anne asked.

Ramsay shook his head. "I don't know. I'm just saying it

wouldn't have been as obvious ten years ago as it might be now, like the safe in the cellar. Only, I don't see anything to suggest there is a hiding place in these walls."

Anne who was examining the opposite wall, said she couldn't either. "Then it's in the floor, if it exists at all. And it would take days to clear the floor, even with Ben and Isaac's help and I don't want to make them suspicious. We're clearing the Hall, and only the Hall."

"The floor wouldn't take as long as you think," Ramsay replied. "We only need to clear rubbish from one area at a time. We don't have to take it outside."

Further conversation was halted by Bracken barking and Ramsay hurrying off to see why. Outside, Bracken was on his feet growling and staring into the nearby bushes. Rex too was watching intently.

Anne arrived at their side and asked, "See anyone?"

Ramsay shook his head. "Bracken and I will see if we can find a scent to follow."

"I'm not staying here alone," Anne said, falling in step with them.

After exiting the screen of bushes that had hidden the intruder, they found boot prints. "It's the man I told you about," Anne said. "Ned Wishart, the old gardener."

"It's someone wearing work boots, that's certain," Ramsay replied. "But we can't assume Ned is the only man in these parts wearing them."

"If we follow the scent," Anne said, "It'll take us to his cottage. I'm sure of it."

"And what would we say?" Ramsay asked. "He may be trespassing on private land but if your contract is for 'only the Hall', then so are we. And there's no law about wondering who's in the old icehouse."

Anne nodded. "You see my dilemma. We've seen

worrying activities and incidents but nothing that would lead to hiring a real detective."

"I do see," Ramsay replied, "but I suspect something will soon happen to change that. I feel you're stirring a hornets' nest, and it will end badly. It usually does, I remember." He added, grinning at the memories of being stung as a child.

"Shall we return to the icehouse?" Anne asked.

"Yes, even if it's only to shut the door again," Ramsay replied. "We can't leave it as it is, or children will get in and may be injured."

Anne nodded. "There are splinters everywhere, though they're so soggy I don't think they'd go through clothes, let alone skin."

At the icehouse, they stopped. "We should at least finish our search of the walls," Ramsay suggested. "Maybe leave the floor for another day."

They agreed on this and, leaving Bracken and Rex to guard the door again, plunged once more into the darkness.

After some time, Anne found herself back where she'd started. "Nothing," she said, in disgust. The slime that coated the walls and ceiling was in her hair and on her hands and clothes. It was disgusting.

"Same here," Ramsay said, reaching the end of his search. He shone his torch beam over the ceiling where water dripped and ran down the walls. There were holes where cement had fallen off but none of them seemed like a hiding place. "If there is anything in this dump, it's in the floor."

Anne agreed as they made their way back to the entrance, where Bracken and Rex seemed to be sleeping in the sunshine.

"A fine two guards you are," Anne said, laughing, only to stop at the sound of a stick breaking somewhere nearby. She glanced at Ramsay who was already scanning the surrounding undergrowth for a sign of movement.

Ramsay shrugged. "Maybe deer or something," he said, though his eyes continued searching the wooded area.

They blocked up the doorway and headed back to the Hall. "There isn't even water on in the Hall," Anne said, "and I'd dearly like to wash this muck off." She waved her hands at him to demonstrate.

"It'll dry," Ramsay told her. "Before we finish for the day, I have something for you. A map of the grounds as they were in the 1870s."

"Does it have an 'X' to mark the spot where the treasure is buried?"

Ramsay laughed. "No. Maybe you already have a map?"

"I didn't know I was going to need one," Anne said.

"Well, don't let me forget."

8

DECISION MADE

As they parted that evening, Ramsay handed Anne the map and other papers he'd taken copies of at the library.

"These cost me a shilling," he told her. "Remember that if you change your mind about my contract."

"A shilling!" Anne cried. "For four sheets of paper? That's outrageous."

"They are copying paper," Ramsay said, "and the nice old lady in the library had no idea what to charge. Nobody had ever asked before you see."

"Still..."

Ramsay shook his head. "I offered a shilling, and she agreed. No backing out of the bargain. I had no idea what copying paper costs either."

"If this is an example of your cost management, you must move in grander circumstances than mine," Anne scolded him.

"I did meet a Sir Christopher on my last case," Ramsay replied, grinning. "Perhaps, that was what led me into extravagance and, I've no doubt, future debauchery. Good night." He waited while Bracken jumped into the car and, waving Anne goodbye, sat down, closed the door and drove off.

* * *

ANNE AND REX settled down and, after clearing the table of her evening meal dishes, she spread out the map Ramsay had given her. The property boundaries then were as they were now, almost a square with the moors along the west edge, the narrow lane to the main road along the east edge and neighboring farm fields to the north and south.

The estate included the Hall and outbuildings, many of which had gone, though not the stables. She made a note to look into those in the morning. A stream ran through the grounds in the 1870's, running from the northwest corner to the southeast, where it ran under the lane. The whole stream was underground now. The watermill, which was mentioned in one of the coded messages, stood just inside the northwest corner where the stream entered the property. Again, it was heartening to find a message that seemed to be genuine even if it was childishly simple to decipher. Anne thought about the estate as it now was and decided the remains of the mill would be among the trees to the north of the Hall and therefore invisible to modern visitors. Those trees were called the 'new plantation' on the map. When was the stream buried? This evidence of lost features that appeared in the messages, sent her hopes soaring and she continued scouring the map in growing excitement.

The Hall showed its Elizabethan beginnings in its outline, the distinctive capital 'E' shape. Today's building was Georgian but clearly stood on a foundation from two hundred years earlier. The three wings forming the 'E' faced east, looking out to fields and the village of Grassmount, which perhaps would have been seen from the Hall in Elizabethan time. Now, trees obscured the view. The short drive ran from the narrow lane to the central wing and entrance lobby of the Hall.

The icehouse was clearly marked to the south, with a short road from the kitchen door of the Hall. She must see if the bushes along that route were fewer than the way she'd been using to get there. Double dotted lines also ran from the kitchen to the icehouse. What was that all about?

Other double dotted lines ran outward to buildings that were gone. What did they mean? One was the old family chapel so could that mean there was a Priest Hole and an escape tunnel? If the Demerlays were Royalists, then they were likely Catholics, so it wasn't an impossible idea.

She picked up the pages that had the cipher on them and looked for words that might mean 'tunnel' but couldn't see any. If there were tunnels in the 1870s, were they blocked before the coded messages were written?

After an hour of speculation, Anne felt the need for air and exercise. "Come on, Rex, let's go for a walk. And we'll walk by Ned Wishart's cottage and see if he's in."

She put on her coat and head scarf, attached a leash to Rex and opened the door. It was growing dark, and she turned to pick up her flashlight from the shelf above the coat hooks when Rex barked and leapt, tugging her sideways, which was enough to save her head from the heavy cudgel she saw race past and hit her shoulder. She yelled in agony as it crunched her shoulder bone. All she could see of her attacker was the balaclava covering his face and then the cudgel did hit her head.

Rex whimpering and licking her face woke Anne. She smiled at him and tried to rise but felt so ill, she lay back down. After a minute recovering, she sat up again and this time stayed sitting. Rex was so pleased to see her awake he almost knocked her over again and she wrapped her arms around his neck for support and comfort.

"We need help, Rex," Anne said, as she struggled to her feet. "This wasn't naughty children or elderly gardeners. This was a man, tall, strong, and willing to hurt me... but for what?"

She was on her feet now and making her way to the phone when she saw the table, with all her papers, was clear. Everything had been taken. "That's what for," she murmured to Rex.

She dialed Ramsay's number and waited. When the phone was answered she said, "I'll sign your contract, even with that debatable shilling."

"You sound as if you aren't well," Ramsay replied. "Are you alright?"

"No. I've been attacked, and all the papers are gone." She was beginning to feel nauseous.

"Are you at home?"

"Yes." Even to Anne her voice now sounded far away.

"Stay there. I'll be with you in minutes," Ramsay replied.

* * *

RAMSAY GRABBED his coat and hat, called Bracken to join him, and they were soon in the car and on the road.

When he arrived at Anne's house, he found the door wide open and all the downstairs lights blazing. He ran inside and found Rex sitting outside the downstair bathroom. Bracken went on ahead to join his friend. Ramsay arrived at the bathroom door a moment later and saw a white-faced Anne staring at the two dogs.

"We need to get you to a doctor," Ramsay said, appalled

at the swollen lump on her forehead, which was already turning purple.

"It's my shoulder," Anne explained. "I think it's broken."

Ramsay saw what she meant. Her right shoulder wasn't how a shoulder should be. "I'll dial '999' and get an ambulance. It will be better than getting in and out of a car."

He helped her to her feet and into the living room, where he assisted her to sit in an armchair. "Don't move," he said, before phoning for help.

The ambulance arrived much quicker than he'd expected, considering how far they were out of town. When she was in the ambulance, Ramsay told Anne he and the two dogs would follow and be there at the hospital.

It was nearly midnight before Anne's shoulder was reset, her head bandaged, and she was out in a ward where Ramsay could speak to her.

"You have two minutes, no more," the night shift nurse told him when he asked if they could talk.

"There's no point in me asking questions now," Ramsay told Anne. "Rest and I'll look after Rex. We'll all be back for visiting time in the morning. Good night."

"It was the map," Anne said, when Ramsay finished speaking. "He must have seen me with it, or you give it to me, and he thought it meant something."

Ramsay nodded. "Tomorrow is the time for talk." Before Anne could say more, he left taking a reluctant Rex with him.

* * *

AFTER PICKING up Rex's bed and bowls at Anne's house, and having a good look around for clues, Ramsay returned to his own home with the two dogs. The most useful clue he'd found was a piece of torn cloth that looked like a pant leg; there was still evidence of a crease between the ragged edges.

"Well done, Rex," Ramsay said, as he examined the fragment. "This looks like your work." He settled the two dogs and returned to his table where his own copy of the map and pages with ciphers on them lay spread out for him to examine.

The torn fragment of cloth took his notice at first. "Not workmen's trousers anyway," he murmured. "No creases in those." His thoughts continued, Anne hadn't mentioned who her attacker was so not a local man, it seemed. He may learn different in the morning. And someone who wasn't afraid to use violence, which meant someone with a lot to gain or lose. And the fabric looks more like a suit, rather than casual clothes. *So much for my nice safe case close to home.*

Returning to the documents, Ramsay considered what the attack told him. The map was readily available in the library so why attack Anne over it? If he wasn't local, he may not have known the map was available. The man had also taken the other sheets. Why? Could he read the code? Did he write the coded messages all those years ago, but they'd been lost to him? Or were the messages for this man and he'd never received them?

His hall grandfather clock struck 'one' and Ramsay murmured, 'the mouse ran down, hickory dickory dock' before gathering up the papers and placing them in his safe. The unknown assailant may well have followed him home and was waiting outside to burgle the place.

"Goodnight, fellas," Ramsay called to the dogs and went to bed.

His sleep wasn't disturbed by burglars, and Ramsay

pottered downstairs in the early light to let the dogs out into his garden while he prepared them breakfast. While they ate, he shaved and dressed, before setting out for his morning walk with Bracken and Rex.

"Visiting hours aren't until ten," Ramsay told the dogs as they meandered through the late autumn countryside. "We have time to visit Mr. Wishart on our way to see how the patient is this morning."

Bracken stopped and gave Ramsay a quizzical look.

"Did Eliza tell you to do this?" Ramsay asked. "I know Anne hasn't signed the Agency contract; I'm just dropping in on a neighbor. I'm not interrogating them."

Bracken didn't seem convinced but set off again.

As it happened, Wishart wasn't at home, so Ramsay wasn't able to drop in or interrogate anyone.

Anne, however, was ready for a ride home and was waiting with her few possessions in hand. "You're late," she said.

"Good morning to you too," Ramsay said, smiling. "Are we going immediately? Don't you want to say goodbye to the doctor, hear last minute instructions or whatever?"

"I've done all that," Anne replied, stroking Rex with her good hand.

As Ramsay drove her home, Anne recounted the events that led to her injuries. "The doctor says I've strong bones. My skull isn't cracked, and it was just my collarbone that was dislocated. Nothing is broken."

"Still, it's enough for me to say no more shilly-shallying. Sign the Agency contract and we can continue this together."

"I will when I get home," Anne replied. "Now, have you searched for evidence around my front door and garden?"

Ramsay told her about the torn trousers.

"Well done, Rex," Anne cried, twisting in her seat and patting Rex.

"Sit still or you'll be back in hospital," Ramsay said. "We can search this morning while it's light. I suggest we also interview this gardener you mentioned."

"I have to get to work," Anne cried. "I'm paying you to do all that."

Ramsay pulled into the driveway behind Anne's car, a blue Austin Mini. "I'll drive you to and from work," Ramsay said. "You'll never drive with your shoulder bandaged and arm in a sling. I don't know how you hope to work like that."

"I can work. I still have one good hand," Anne retorted. "I'll carry light objects. Ben and Isaac do the heavy lifting anyway. Now, I must go. I'm the only one with the keys."

Ramsay backed out of the drive and drove to Demerlay Hall, where Ben and Isaac were leaning against their van chatting. After opening the doors, Anne returned to Ramsay's car, saying, "I'll stay. You investigate."

Bracken and Ramsay returned to Anne's house to search the path and garden area with Bracken being most successful in the hunt. Following his nose, he found where the assailant had stood waiting out of sight, where he'd left footprints in the border as he ran out avoiding the angry Rex, and a button torn from the man's coat as he ran.

"Well done, Bracken," Ramsay said, fondling his friend's head. "Rex may have torn pieces from him, but you found them. Now do you think our old friend, Inspector Baldock, will deign to have them analysed for us?"

Bracken huffed in a tone that suggested Ramsay would be lucky if that request was done. "You may be right," Ramsay sighed. "If we're catching him on a good day, who can say."

Ramsay and Bracken left Anne's house with the clue

they'd found and went in search of Ned Wishart, the Hall's retired gardener.

Ned was easily found because he was carrying his shopping on the main street as Ramsay drove through the village. Ramsay stopped and offered Ned a lift. Ned took some persuading but eventually got in, even after Ramsay explained why he was keen to see him.

"My friend, Anne, has the contract to clear Demerlay Hall," Ramsay began. "I imagine it's painful for you, seeing the old place being emptied like that."

"Aye," Ned replied, sucking on his pipe and blowing a steady cloud of smoke out of the window.

Seeing this was to be a longer process than a short ride home, Ramsay continued, "You were the gardener there when the family owned it, I understand."

"Aye," Ned replied, and then in a sudden burst of chatter, continued, "boy and man. I began when I were still at school, working part-time, like."

"When did you leave?" Ramsay asked.

Ned chuckled. "When they stopped paying me."

"When was that exactly?"

"About two year after the family left," Ned replied. "The money kept arriving and I kept working. Strangers were in the place then. A Leeds man." He grimaced so Ramsay understood his opinion of the new tenants.

"Did the Demerlays have money troubles?" Ramsay asked. "So many did, after the war. Is that why they left?"

Ned considered this question carefully as if deciding how much family business he should divulge to strangers.

"Well," he said, at last. "That were partly it." He stopped, frowning. "Others'll tell you if I don't, I suppose. The Demerlay children were a wild bunch. Two boys and a girl, nice youngsters but when they grew up it was parties and such shocking happenings. Jeremy, the one who was to inherit the Hall, was in trouble with the police more than once." Ned paused as if to catch his breath after all this talk.

"You say was to have inherited?" Ramsay prodded.

"He was killed," Ned replied. "He drove his car into a bridge at night at high speed. Drunk as a lord, he was."

"Neither of the other two wanted the Hall?" Ramsay asked, as he drew up outside Ned's cottage.

"Miss Joan was left an estate over West Yorkshire way, which she liked better than here, and Mister John has the estate up in Northumberland."

Ramsay nodded. "They may not have wanted to be reminded of their brother's death."

"Right enough," Ned replied. "The bridge is the one you can see from the west windows, where the road goes under the train line."

"I imagine you sometimes visit the gardens you used to keep," Ramsay said. He'd parked the car, but Ned showed no sign of leaving. Maybe he also wanted to talk about the old days.

"I do. It's a sad walk now, though," Ned said. "We had those gardens a picture in the seasons. Now it's just weeds and undergrowth."

"Do you remember treasure hunters coming to the Hall?"

Ned laughed. "Aye. Barmy, the lot o' them. I told them, I've dug up the whole blessed plot and never found no treasure."

"Do you remember one disappearing?"

"Oh, aye. There was a lot of talk about that," Ned told him. "Some say he's buried out there in the garden. Others that he's in Spain with the gold."

"What was your opinion?"

Ned's laughter this time was scornful. "He's more likely buried than sunning hisself in Spain. Treasure be blowed."

"Did you talk to the man who disappeared?" Ramsay asked. "When you were working in the garden and he was scouting out possible places to search?"

"Aye," Ned replied. "He were right taken with the icehouse, I remember."

"He wasn't just pretending that, so you'd be put off the scent?"

Ned laughed again. "Nay, he were all over it some days. Though he did try the floor of the old chapel as well."

"Is that still there?" Ramsay asked. He hadn't seen any sign of it.

"The businessman," Ned paused, "Fewster, that were his name, had me smash up the floor and turn it into a rock garden. It's just weeds now." He added, sadly.

"You've never looked for the treasure then?" Ramsay asked, grinning.

"Nay, lad. Lord Demerlay was here visiting when that fuss was going on and he told me the story was nonsense. He said his descendants did leave the Hall during the Civil War when the Parliamentary army came, but they took everything valuable with them. There wasn't much — the Hall, even then, was little more than a shooting lodge. Their home was the one up in Northumberland, as it is now."

"Did you hear of a big jewelry robbery in Leeds about then?" Ramsay asked.

Ned sucked on his pipe and replied, "Oh, aye. It was in the news and everything. You didn't hear of ought else for a week or so."

"You didn't think the talk of treasure might have been the loot from the robbery?" Ramsay pressed him.

Ned shrugged. "Some said it were, some said it weren't. I didn't think so then. Now I do."

"You think the Civil War story was a cover, and it was really about the loot?" Ramsay asked.

Ned nodded his head almost eagerly. "It's the only thing that makes sense, in the end."

"Did the Demerlays sell the Hall to that Leeds businessman, Fewster?" Ramsay asked.

Ned shook his head. "Only leased it. He were going to buy it, I recall. It was in his time the treasure hunters were all over the place. He hired one group after another. Then there was a falling out with Lord Demerlay on account of Jeremy Demerlay's death and they left. Lord Demerlay blamed the man, we all reckoned..."

Ramsay interjected. "Why would Lord Demerlay blame the businessman? Do you know?"

"Because Jeremy Demerlay and the businessman's son had been at school together," Ned said, looking surprised Ramsay didn't know that. "Jeremy came to stay at the Hall more than once, when the Fewsters had it."

"I see," Ramsay said, slowly. And he *was* beginning to see. "Was Fewster the man who was robbed of the jewels, do you know?"

Ned shrugged. "How should I know? I don't remember it being said but I wasn't someone they talked to."

Ramsay nodded. He imagined it was unlikely tenants would talk to the gardener. Realizing Ned was gazing at him enquiringly, Ramsay asked, "What happened then? After the Fewsters left, I mean."

Ned continued, "Another businessman, from Bradford this time, a woollen mill owner, took it a year or so later but they didn't stay either."

"You don't remember the second tenant's name?" Ramsay asked.

Ned's expression suggested he thought that a foolish question, but he replied, "Nay, lad, they were 'here today, gone tomorrow' kind of people. Folk like that leave no mark in the world."

"It must have been difficult for you after you left working at the Hall," Ramsay mused. "Were you able to get more work locally?"

"Aye. Only part time like, but there's plenty of folks don't like to do their own garden," Ned told him, "and I help fetch and carry for Nigel Hawtry's business and steer Terry Brent in the way of items for his collection."

Ramsay laughed. "I'm learning that's how it is in the country; a bit of this and a bit of that makes for a satisfying life, I think."

"Better than stuck in a factory or shop doing the same thing every day," Ned agreed.

"I'd better get back to the Hall," Ramsay said, remembering he should be helping at the Hall. "Anne has dislocated her collarbone, so she'll need some help. Thanks for telling me about the family, Ned. I hope we can talk again."

Ned left the car saying he would like that 'because no one was interested in the old days now'.

"A good morning's work, Bracken, I think," Ramsay said, as they drove off. "What say you to old Ned being one of our mysterious watchers?" When Bracken failed to give his opinion, Ramsay continued, "Next stop Scarborough and our friend Inspector Baldock."

Baldock was sceptical after hearing Ramsay's story and requests. "A robbery ten years or more ago, an assault last night, a scrap of cloth and a button," he said. "And you want me to spend present day police resources on it?"

"The assault was last night," Ramsay reminded him, "and it was serious."

"I'll have those pieces examined," Baldock agreed, "and I'll even find the background to your Leeds robbery. But you must see these don't constitute an emergency for me or the detective force. It's local bobby stuff."

"I understand," Ramsay said, smiling, "and I'm grateful for what you're doing. I'm not claiming anything here is an emergency but as the house clearing continues there's someone in the neighborhood who is willing to use force to take what they want. It may yet end in murder." He left the police station with Bracken.

Back in the car, he thought over what Ned had told him. *The first businessman who came to the Hall, Fewster, was from Leeds and the later one from Bradford.* It seemed to confirm the mental picture he'd built of the Leeds businessman who'd been robbed. In Ramsay's mind, the man had somehow suspected, though Ramsay couldn't yet see the connection, it was the young Demerlay who'd robbed him, so he'd leased the Hall to find and regain his property.

At the Hall, he found Anne and her two employees hard at work loading the van. He joined them and the pile that had been in the hall was soon in the van.

"I didn't bring lunch with me today," Anne said, as they watched the van drive away. "May I buy you lunch at Madge's?"

"Have you signed my contract?" Ramsay asked, grinning.

"Yes, that's why I'm offering to buy lunch," Anne retorted, "so you can't expense it to me."

"Then I accept," Ramsay replied, "because I didn't make lunch either."

They walked to Ramsay's old Ford Popular, let Rex and Bracken hop into the back seat, before driving off.

"I've just come from talking to Ned Wishart," Ramsay told her, as they exited the Hall's drive and out onto the road. "He seems to have a good memory for the events we're investigating."

Anne nodded. "That was the beginning of the end for Ned's gardens, so I'm sure he thinks on it often."

"I know that feeling," Ramsay replied ruefully. He often thought about his last case as a police officer. He and his team surrounding the building where they knew a gang were hiding. He remembered entering the room where the gang were waiting, one of the gang raising his pistol, the sound of the shot and the bullet entering his chest. The weeks after, when he worked with the medical people to get back to his job, and the way his superiors worked to prevent him returning, until he was left with early retirement as his best choice.

"I've been thinking about last night," Anne said, as they entered the village, "and I think the man must have thought what you gave me was the key to the treasure's location, which means he knows more about this than we do."

"I thought that too," Ramsay replied, as he parked outside Madge's Teashop. "But there's another possibility. He's just been waiting for something to break open the puzzle and he thinks this is it. He knows no more than we do."

They entered the teashop and found a table. When Madge had handed them the lunch menu and rushed off to answer a request from a table across the room, Anne said, "You don't think this proves there is a 'treasure' or 'loot' buried at the Hall?"

Ramsay replied, "I don't think it proves anything either way, I'm afraid."

"Now you're on the case, what are you going to do to find

what's behind all this?" Anne asked, before Madge arrived with water for the two dogs.

Ramsay waited until Madge had gone with their orders, "I'm following two lines of enquiry. One, the story of the Leeds robbery, and two, who hit you last night. I think the two will turn out to be one and the same, though I don't see how yet."

"What about the treasure?" Anne cried. "Find that and we have all the rest answered."

Ramsay smiled. "You and your team are clearing the house and are finding the clues to the treasure, if that's what they are. I'm leaving all that in your capable hands."

"But it's the treasure my attacker wants," Anne hissed, seeing people on nearby tables starting to take notice.

"It's possible, he just doesn't want you finding Morris Saunders' body," Ramsay murmured, also noticing the interest being shown.

Madge arrived with lunch, and they turned their attention to that, letting the conversation in the rest of the café return to normal.

Driving back, Anne continued, "I haven't a map or coded messages now. I need you and Judith to give me copies of yours."

"While you work on the Hall, I'll have my friend at the library make me more copies," Ramsay said. "But it will cost you another shilling."

"You drive a hard bargain," Anne grumbled. "But I do need those papers so I can work on them tonight, if you're not going to help with the treasure hunt."

Ramsay grinned. "Those papers are part of my investigation too. Between us all, I expect we'll have the alphabet finished tonight. I'd really like to know if we have all the messages or there are more elsewhere."

"Like the icehouse?" Anne asked.

Ramsay nodded. "Apparently, Saunders set great store by the icehouse as a hiding place or so Ned told me."

"Can we trust Ned?" Anne asked. "Isn't he the most likely author of that nasty note I received?"

Ramsay had to agree with that. "Of course, and he may be diverting our attention there because he knows it was searched and nothing was found, while he searches in more likely spots."

"When you get back from bribing public officials with shillings," Anne said, "we'll search the icehouse floor and if nothing appears to be hidden, we can focus on more likely spots too."

When Ramsay returned an hour later, he had Judith with him.

"I couldn't resist," she told Anne. "Mr. Ramsay came to borrow my collection of the papers to copy them, he told me of your plans so here I am."

"I'm glad you came," Anne told her. "With my arm in a sling and no heavy lifting allowed, we'll need all the help we can get to clear the rubble away."

Carrying brushes and mops from the Hall, the three investigators and two dogs tried following the route outlined on the old map from the Hall kitchen to the icehouse. It was better than the route they'd used before because the undergrowth hadn't been growing as long, but still not easy.

"All this must break Ned Wishart's heart," Judith said, as they cut away branches and young saplings.

"When I spoke to him," Ramsay replied, "he seemed resigned to it all, rather than angry or upset."

"He's had ten years or more to become accustomed, I expect," Anne told them. "You know, there's a Priest Hole and a tunnel to the chapel here somewhere as well. I saw it on the map before the map was stolen."

Judith grimaced. "Oh, good. Another dark, dank hole to search."

They were still chuckling over this when they reached the icehouse, and Ramsay began lifting the rocks and logs that pressed the old door shut. It took Ramsay a moment to free up the entranceway and the three entered, leaving Bracken and Rex on guard outside.

"Bracken has become well trained in his guard dog role," Anne told Ramsay.

Ramsay agreed he had, then added, "Of course, we don't really know what he does when we're out of sight. He could be off chasing rabbits, for all we know." He laughed to show he was only joking.

* * *

Bracken and Rex settled down to wait for their respective friends' return and stayed settled until it began to rain. Rex rose to his feet and padded down the slope to wait inside the icehouse entrance. Bracken fastidiously trotted over to where the trees provided shelter. The icehouse smelled bad, and he didn't like the green slime that its walls left on his coat.

Minutes passed and the rain turned into a steady downpour. The trees no longer stopped it all and Bracken looked about for another shelter, which he saw beside the entrance. It was a small opening, maybe a badger sett or even a foxhole but too old to be still inhabited for there was no scent of any kind of wild animal using it. He ran quickly from the cover of the trees and pushed his way inside through the screen of autumnal dying vegetation.

It was a pleasant enough shelter, too small to invite Rex to share it, but adequate for Bracken's needs. He could watch the rain's steady patter on the leaves and ground in comfort. Or so he thought. Only a few minutes after arriving, water began seeping through the back wall of his little cave and it slowly grew more alarming. This wasn't a badger's den; it was simply a cave created by the action of running water scouring away the soil that covered and insulated the walls and roof of the icehouse.

Bracken backed away from the growing stream and felt a sharp corner sticking into his behind. Twisting around, he found it was the corner of a rusty box of the kind he saw being handed around to visitors in living rooms, and usually filled with various kinds of good things. He took hold of the box with his teeth and pulled. For a moment, it looked too buried to move and then, in a peculiarly slithery motion, it came out from the mud and Bracken had it held tightly in his jaws. Where the box had been, water was now pouring out to join the rivulet flowing from the back of his shelter. Bracken left the shelter and joined Rex in the entranceway.

He and Rex examined the box, attempting to open it but it remained shut. If there were good things inside, they needed their friends to get them. Bracken set off into the darkness to get help.

Finding Ramsay, Bracken tried to make his friend understand about the box. Ramsay just said, "What is it, Bracken?"

Bracken tugged at Ramsay's pant leg, this often worked.

"Is there someone outside?" Ramsay asked, realizing his friend was serious and not just wanting to go home.

"We may have visitors," Ramsay told the two women. "I'll see what's going on. I'll call if you need to leave."

Bracken led him to where the box lay on the ground, but Ramsay was so sure the problem was outside, he walked straight past it and out into the rain. "Ugh," he said, "this is why it's been getting wetter and wetter inside."

Bracken watched Ramsay looking around the entrance and, seeing no one, step back inside. "I don't see anyone, Bracken, are you sure there was someone there?"

Bracken growled and pushed the box with his nose, before putting a paw on it.

"What have you there?" Ramsay asked, peering at the block under Bracken's paw. For a moment, Bracken thought Ramsay was going to move away and he, Bracken, would have to take sterner measures. Then Ramsay looked closer.

"I thought it was a brick," he said, bending down to lift it from the ground. He took it out into the light, and let the rain wash more dirt from it. "A biscuit box," Ramsay told Bracken, and gently shook it. "Empty though." Ramsay tried to open the lid. "It's rusted shut. We'll take it back to the Hall and borrow one of Ben and Isaac's tools."

Ramsay placed the box back on the floor, saying, "You two, guard this with your lives." He grinned at them and returned to continue work on the floor with Anne and Judith.

"Was there someone?" Anne asked. She was leaning against a wall, resting her arm.

"I don't think so," Ramsay replied. "Bracken had found a biscuit tin and just wanted me to know."

Anne laughed. "Rex is like that. He'll find the oddest things and expect me to praise him to the skies for what he's done."

"Maybe we should stop anyway," Judith said to Anne. "Your shoulder must be painful after all this."

"I'm fine," Anne said, leaving the wall and taking hold of the broom she'd been using to push mud and gravel off the floor that Judith and Ramsay had cleared of debris.

"Judith's right," Ramsay said. "We'll inspect the part you're brushing clean now and stop for the day. Who knows, Bracken's box may be the treasure we're searching for."

"Does it seem like there's anything in the box?" Judith asked.

"No," Ramsay said, "certainly no treasure anyway. Maybe some papers."

"The next clue in the Scavenger Hunt," Anne suggested, as she finished sweeping and leaned her broom against the wall.

"Could be," Ramsay replied, scanning the cleared area of floor with his flashlight, hoping for some sign of a door or panel.

"If so," Judith said, also scanning the floor with her torch, "the hunt never happened. No one found the first clues, and no one found these ones."

"There's nothing here," Ramsay said, in disgust. He swept his flashlight over the rest of the floor. "I'd say we were half done, wouldn't you?"

The others agreed. They too seemed dismayed by the remaining work.

"Then we should go," Ramsay said, "and hope Bracken's find saves us having to come back."

They slowly made their way toward the door. "Even if there are clues in the box Bracken found," Anne said. "we have to come back. We can't leave this undone."

"Ben and Isaac will be upset they've done all the work this afternoon," Ramsay told her, as they reached the entrance and Ramsay picked up the old tin box.

"I know," Anne replied, "but our only time to search for clues to the mysterious treasure and the coded messages is the time I have on my contract to clear the house."

Ramsay handed Judith the box and assisted Anne, who

was struggling, to climb over the rubble in the entrance. He wedged the door shut and they set off for the Hall. The rain was still falling steadily, which only increased their gloom.

"We could date this box by its design," Judith told them, as they walked, and the rain washed the box clean of all the mud that had obscured it. "It's a Christmas gift box and companies know which design they used and when."

"If there's anything in it," Anne said, "that will be useful to know."

"Oh, there's something in it," Judith said. "Papers, I imagine. I can feel them bumping the sides as I walk."

"More codes?" Ramsay asked, laughing.

"I hope so," Judith replied. "We have almost every letter of the alphabet now and they will be quick and easy to decipher."

Ramsay was right about the two workers who were in the Hall doorway, arms folded across their chests, and grim expressions on their faces. Anne's apology lightened their mood a little and when she told them to take their load to the warehouse and take the rest of the day off, that seemed to do the trick.

As they prepared to leave, Isaac said, "That Nigel was here wanting to go through the library some more. He was put out that we'd cleared it."

"Did he leave?" Anne asked.

Ben laughed. "We suggested you could use some help clearing the old icehouse and he skedaddled faster than a rat up a drainpipe."

Anne smiled, looking at her own besmirched clothes. "Nigel is a very fastidious fellow."

"He said he'd visit you tonight and ask to see the rest of the books," Isaac called back to her as the two men ran to the van and climbed quickly into the cab.

"I wonder what he's found that makes him so keen to see the rest of the books," Anne said.

"Likely he's got one volume of a set that he's discovered is valuable," Judith replied.

"I hope not," Anne said. "I told him he could have any books he wanted for free, if he helped catalog the library."

"But he didn't help, did he," Ramsay said.

"It's true," Anne replied. "He's been missing for days."

Isaac had already told Ramsay where the toolbox was hidden so they made their way to there. With a screwdriver and hammer, Ramsay tapped away at the lid until it popped off and papers fell out on the table.

"Ugh," Judith said, picking up one curled sheet. "They're as slimy as everything in that wretched place." She gently opened it, and they all studied the writing.

"It's like the others," Anne said. "A printed page from a book that's been used to hand write a single sentence in code at the bottom."

"I have the alphabet in the car," Ramsay said. "I'll get it."

"Oh, no," Anne protested. "I'm too tired. I'll lock up and we'll decipher them over a cup of tea at my place."

Judith placed all the sheets back in the box, while Ramsay praised and petted Bracken. "Well done, Bracken. You've saved our day."

9

RETRACING FOOTSTEPS

After the three had been home and bathed and changed, they met, as agreed, in Anne's home where they placed all the sheets of coded messages they had on Anne's dining table. To drive out the chill that even her bath hadn't dispersed, Anne had a roaring coal fire lit in the hearth and, with the lights on and the curtains drawn, the room looked warm and cozy. Two dogs lying in front of the fire only added to the effect.

Sitting around the dining table, they deciphered the messages as far as they could and placed the finished translations in a pile. When all the sheets were done, the table was cleared of everything but the pages, and they were laid out side by side. Each individual sheet made no sense on their own and they hoped seeing them spread out before them might help make connections.

"I thought the sheets we found in the safe would be linked," Judith said. "Only, if they were, I couldn't see how. Even now, looking at them all, they seem totally random."

Ramsay agreed. "And these Bracken found today don't

tell a consistent story either, with or without the earlier ones."

"That's why I think we might find something this way," Anne replied. After her bath, the hot fire, and a cup of tea, she felt much more alive. "I'd expect the message that said 'stream' to connect in some way with the one that included the word 'mill', for instance."

They all stared quietly at the two messages for a moment until Ramsay said, "Well, they don't."

"My guess is they really are standalone clues," Judith said, "though clues to what it doesn't say."

"They all point to locations," Ramsay said, "but in a way that's too general to help anyone. 'Bank of the stream' for example, is ridiculous. The stream runs right through the estate. It's quarter of a mile long if it's a yard."

"Saying 'The foot of the mill', doesn't help either," Anne said. "Though it wouldn't be anything like as long as the stream, I suppose."

"We could have Bracken and Rex sniff along the side of the stream and around the foundations of the old mill," Judith suggested.

"The stream is underground, and nothing is left of the mill. There's no scent left at either," Ramsay replied, grinning. "I wonder if these are clues that were never fully worked out. These are the ones that weren't used."

"They must mean something," Anne cried, "or why hide them?'

Ramsay continued, "I think Judith's idea might work. I bet Bracken found this box because the earth around it has been washed away over the years. Maybe, whatever is hidden at these locations will also be visible today, when they wouldn't have been when the messages were hidden."

Gold, Greed, and a Hidden Hoard

"We won't find any at the side of the stream," Anne retorted.

"True," Ramsay replied, "so tomorrow, Bracken and I will start over at what's left of the mill."

Judith suggested, "We have a village historian who collects stories of the village down the years."

"Terry Brent?" Anne asked.

Judith nodded. "I know he's a bit eccentric about the village and everything, but he has kept things that will never go in the official records."

Anne laughed. "Eccentric? He's as mad as a hatter, which is why the things he collects will never get into the official records. They'll need a small army of rubbish collectors to clear that place out when he goes."

Ramsay decided to draw the line at helping here. "Bracken and I to the mill, you two to Mr. Brent's place seems a fair division of labor."

"I have to be at the Hall tomorrow," Anne protested. "I'm paying you to investigate."

"He knows you two," Ramsay protested. "He won't want a stranger like me poking around in his rubbish."

"I'll introduce you, Mr. Ramsay," Judith said. "I have to be near my work tomorrow so I can't help out at the Hall. And Anne has given you a false impression of Mr. Brent. He's a perfectly nice old man and his home is filled with perfectly nice relics and papers. None of it is rubbish."

"Ha!" Anne scoffed.

"I'll be at your place by ten o'clock tomorrow morning, Judith," Ramsay said, grinning. "And we'll research together."

"While I do all the heavy lifting at the Hall?" Anne retorted. "Thank you both."

Ramsay laughed. "I judged from your description of Mr.

Brent's archive that I'd get a better response from the man if I arrived with Judith than I would with you."

"Terry has more than once taken offence at Anne's description of his collection," Judith told Ramsay. "Your judgment is sound on this subject." She and Anne exchanged glowering expressions, and both burst out laughing.

* * *

NEXT MORNING, after dropping Anne at the Hall, Ramsay and Bracken arrived at the spot where, on the old map, the mill was marked. It was hard to see any sign of a building among the bushes in the present day.

Ramsay frowned. "We'll scout around, Bracken. There may be something left to guide us."

They found a shallow rectangular depression in the ground that Ramsay decided must have been the wheel pit, which had been filled and subsequently settled. Standing on the edge, he looked about. "The thing is, Bracken," he muttered, "the mill could have been on either side of this. There's nothing to say which one. We don't even know how big the building was so we can't measure out possible walls."

He made a note of where he was standing and set off directly forward, hoping to come across a footing or floor among the weeds. Finding nothing he returned to the pit and walked around it. "Let's try *this* way this time," he told Bracken, and they set off.

Here they were more successful. Odd mounds among the weeds suggested something was underground. Declaring success, Ramsay and Bracken returned to the pit and began walking what Ramsay thought would be the base of the mill's outer wall. Once again, they found hillocks and holes that suggested something had once stood there. As he progressed, Ramsay snapped branches off bushes and pushed them into the ground to mark out a circle.

"The difficulty as I see it, Bracken, is we don't know if 'foot of the mill' means the outer wall or some inner feature. Below the millstone, for example. We don't even know when the notes were written so we don't know if the mill was still a working mill or a ruin."

Bracken was too intrigued by the new scents he was finding to take any notice of Ramsay's muttering.

"Worse," Ramsay suddenly cried. "We don't even know if these notes refer to the physical features of the estate or just a picture or model of it. What if they're about rooms in the Hall that refer to the estate? The Stream Room, for instance, or the Mill Room, rooms named for the principal feature that could be seen from the room's window, perhaps?"

The despair in Ramsay's voice did catch Bracken's attention and he looked at his friend in concern.

"Exactly," Ramsay said, seeing Bracken's expression, "a disastrous waste of time and resources, as any one of my old bosses would have said."

They arrived back at the wheel pit and Ramsay took stock of the building's size based on the sticks he'd planted along the way. "It would take a day with a team of diggers to excavate that, Bracken. And we haven't the time or people to spare."

Bracken understood from this they weren't going further. He was disappointed. Some of those scents were very fresh and might provide a good morning's sport, if he could flush them out.

"Let's hope we have more luck with Judith's old historian," Ramsay said, as they made their way back to his car.

The amateur historian, Terry, a small thin man,

nervously put his cigarette in an ashtray and beamed with pleasure when Judith explained what they were looking for. "I knew someone would want the information my museum can provide. I've tried so many times to get the authorities interested but they only care about how much it would cost to keep. What period of our rich history do you want to learn about?"

Ramsay said, "The early to mid-fifties and in particular events surrounding Demerlay Hall."

Terry's expression darkened. "A bad time for us all, that was. The family leaving and outsiders coming in." He shook his head. "And now we're told it's to be developed into a country hotel. More outsiders."

"It will provide jobs, I expect," Ramsay suggested. Terry's answering expression wasn't encouraging, so Ramsay continued, "We've been told there were treasure hunters at the Hall, after the family left."

Terry laughed, his face brightening. "Some people will believe anything. Yes, we did have treasure hunters. The tenant brought them in." His face darkened again, "though they didn't look like the sort of people I would have expected for treasure hunters." He became thoughtful for a moment and then said, "I have photos. Here, I'll show you." Grabbing his cigarette, Terry turned away and scurried through the house, leaving a cloud of smoke in his wake. Ramsay, Bracken, and Judith trailed behind, out of the back door, across a small yard and into a large shed.

Inside the shed, Terry switched on the light and Ramsay could see rows of shelves some ten feet high, running the length of the building. Judith was right — it didn't look like rubbish, but Anne had been correct in how hard it would be to shift all this when Brent died.

Brent led them between stacks of shelves until he came

to an area labeled 'Photos'. He scanned the many boxes before them and then trotted off to the end of the row, returning with wheeled steps. "The 1950s are near the top," he told them. Climbing the steps, Terry said to Ramsay, "push me slowly to the right."

Ramsay did as he was asked until Terry cried, "Stop!" He drew a box from the shelf and handed it down to Judith. "They'll be in here, I'm sure."

Descending quickly, Terry took the box from Judith and scurried away to stand under a light. He opened the lid and cried, "This is it. See?" He handed Judith a faded black and white photo of a group of men standing at the entrance to the icehouse.

Judith handed it to Ramsay who, like Terry, didn't think these men looked like treasure hunters, though he also had no idea what a treasure hunter looked like.

"These treasure hunters," Ramsay began, "were they the tenant and family or friends?"

Terry shook his head vigorously. As with every one of his gestures it was too emphatic. Terry's skinny frame and nervous mannerisms made Ramsay uneasy.

"Not the tenant, then?" Ramsay asked again.

Terry bit his lip before saying, "No. The tenant had a family of two boys, young men really. One was the younger Demerlay's age, Jeremy, that was, and they'd become friends at school. The other was even younger. I don't have photos of them. They were camera-shy."

As Ramsay was finishing his perusal, Terry cried, "And this fellow disappeared." He handed a photo to Judith who examined it before handing it to Ramsay.

"Was that Morris Saunders?" Judith asked.

Terry, still excited, nodded vehemently, "Yes, that was him." He turned to Ramsay, "the man standing alone at the front of the group. He wasn't really with the others, I asked him to be part of the group to save on film. Film was so expensive those days."

Ramsay stared at Saunders who seemed to stare back. He was a big man, ex-armed forces undoubtedly, and he looked capable of defending himself. If he was murdered and buried in the grounds, Ramsay doubted it had been easily done.

"Here's another group of treasure hunters," Terry cried, handing Judith another photo. "They came after the first lot." He paused. "No, I'm wrong. Not treasure hunters, civil engineers. They said they'd been asked to look over the Hall to check its soundness for development. Even then the Hall was being marked for destruction." He sighed.

Ramsay and Judith examined the photo together. "They do have the look of engineers," Ramsay said.

Terry nodded. "Civil engineers, that's what they called themselves. They had equipment too. You can see some of it behind them."

"None of these people found anything, did they?" Judith asked.

Terry frowned. "People said the one who disappeared did, but I don't believe it. I think he's buried on the moors somewhere around here."

"Why do you think that?" Ramsay asked.

"When I asked them to be in one photo," Terry said, "there was a feeling in the air. You can even see it in the way the others are looking at him."

Ramsay returned to studying the photo of Saunders and he could see what Terry meant, even though the photo was faded, and the men were long gone, Ramsay could practically feel the hate. *If looks alone could kill, Saunders hadn't long to live.*

"May we take these photos away for a day or so?" Ramsay asked.

Terry shook his head, sending ash from the cigarette in his lips flying. Taking his cigarette out, he said, "No. You found them here because I kept them and all the other records you see around you. No one else did. If I let any of them go, I know they'll disappear."

"We understand," Judith interjected, seeing Terry was becoming upset. "Maybe we can spend some time looking through the records you've kept so well. Will you help us?'

Terry frowned. "What is this about? This isn't just about the past of Demerlay Hall. This is about something today."

"We told you," Judith said, "we found these coded messages and we want to know more."

Terry shook his head. "I don't believe two adults with busy lives would spend time over silly messages found in an abandoned house. You found something else, didn't you?"

Ramsay and Judith exchanged glances. Each wondering how much they could share. Eventually, Ramsay said, "Some small items of jewelry were found with some of the messages."

"So, there is treasure," Terry cried, his face lighting up. "I knew there had to be something."

"You mean you've been searching your records for the truth?" Judith asked.

"What?" Terry asked. "No. I don't mean now, I mean then. When it was going on. That's why I took the photos. I did articles for local papers in those days. I knew I'd have the scoop when the treasure was found. I had everything. Names, photos of people and places, everything."

"Then we need you on our side," Ramsay said. "This time, with your help, we will find whatever there is to find."

Terry considered this. "I would like to know if there is

something there," he said, at last. "Let me show you something." He hurried off to another shelf and selected a box. He returned moments later with an old notebook.

"Where was this from?" Judith asked, as he handed it to her.

"The man who disappeared," Terry said, "stayed at the Station Hotel. He never checked out of his room and when he didn't show up for two days, the hotel alerted the police. His room at the hotel remained as it was when he walked out. I got in after the police because I was known as being a freelance reporter. The police examined his belongings but left them in case he was just off somewhere and hadn't told anyone."

"You stole it?" Ramsay asked.

Terry turned white. "I-I meant to return it. I thought it might help me find him. But the next day, the hotel moved his belongings into storage because they needed the room. Then it became a 'missing persons' search, and the police took everything, and I couldn't easily return it."

"It's hard to read," Judith said, handing the book to Ramsay. "The ink has faded with time."

"It was hard to read even then," Terry told them. "I don't know what he was using for ink. And his writing is just a scrawl."

Ramsay had to agree with that. It was as if it was intended to be impossible for anyone but the writer to read it.

"He mentions the icehouse more than once," Ramsay said, flicking through the pages. "It's such an odd word, it jumps out from the scrawl."

Terry nodded. "I noticed that too and I spent time searching around there after everyone was gone but I never found anything."

"He didn't like the other people searching the grounds," Ramsay said, now reading aloud what he thought was written.

"He thought they were criminals," Terry responded. "It says so somewhere."

"Does he say why he was searching the grounds?" Judith asked Terry.

Terry shook his head. "He mentions jewels once but otherwise calls what he's looking for 'treasure'. I think he was trying to use the 'treasure hunt' to find something he knew was there."

"Did you have any idea what that might have been?" Ramsay asked.

"At first, I thought it may have been the proceeds of a big robbery in Leeds only a few weeks or so before," Terry said. "Only,..." He stopped.

"Only what?" Ramsay prompted.

"Only why would the proceeds end up at Demerlay Hall?" Terry replied. "Young Master Demerlay was a tearaway, which made people suspicious, but there was never really any evidence he was a robber. He was too erratic to have planned something like that."

"He could have been a hanger-on to the gang," Ramsay said, "or even the get-away driver."

Terry laughed. "No one would employ him as a driver; he was hopeless. In fact, that's what got him killed."

"Did you know him?" Judith asked.

Terry nodded. "The family were here often through the year, not just the shooting and hunting seasons, so we did know them a little. He was a good-looking boy and then man, and he was charming. Too charming, many local fathers of daughters thought. But when he drank, he was wild."

"Still," Ramsay said, "it sounds to me like he could have been involved with that robbery."

Terry shook his head. "People thought of all this at the time but, to be honest, it was all just wishful thinking. We all wanted to think that we, in our small village, were part of the big events in the wider world. Nothing was ever found, and we all looked, believe me. There were times when you couldn't move for treasure hunters on the estate."

"Maybe Saunders did find it and made his way out of the country before anyone knew he was gone," Judith suggested.

Terry nodded. "That's what people came to believe. I don't. It would have been less dangerous for him to return to the hotel, pack and leave. Much less suspicious."

"Then what you're saying is he was killed, which means there really was something to be found," Judith replied. "If he found it and the killer took it, we're safe. If it hasn't been found, then what we're doing is dangerous."

"I can't believe anyone is still interested or even knows about the events we're talking about," Terry said. "It's ancient history now."

"Yet you're keen to help us get at the truth," Ramsay added, "so you must believe something is at the root of what went on then."

"Oh, there was something to be found," Terry told him. "What I'm saying is I think the treasure story was a cover, but I also think the 'something' was unlikely to have been related to the robbery, which was the rumor at the time, all of which means I don't really know what it was."

"Then it's even more mysterious than we thought," Judith said, looking at Ramsay.

Ramsay nodded. "We should widen our search because whatever it is, seems to have led to Saunders' death, so it isn't insignificant. For instance, I've heard there was a Priest Hole and a tunnel leading to the chapel. Do you know anything about that?"

Terry nodded. "Every treasure hunter looked there, and I did too. We found nothing. Still, you can certainly look again." He told Ramsay where the hiding place was to be found and ended by saying, "The tunnel will likely have been filled in when the chapel was knocked down."

"When was that?" Judith asked.

"I have photos," Terry said, searching his memory, "it was only just before the events, say twelve years ago. Before the treasure hunting craze, anyhow. I'll get them." He hurried off to the 'Photos' section, returning moments later with another shoebox of faded images.

While Terry sifted through the photos, Ramsay asked, "You mentioned searching the Demerlay estate back in the day, but have you looked since?"

Terry's fingers slowed as he considered his answer. "Sometimes I have an idea, or Ned or Nigel do, and we try again, but it isn't often nowadays. It's been so long, you see." He pulled a photo from the box, crying, "Here's the chapel!" He turned over the photo and read the date, "August 1953. I was right, two years before."

Ramsay and Judith thanked him and, as they walked to his car, Ramsay said, quietly, "Like the stream and the mill, there's little chance we'll find anything hidden in the tunnel now it's filled."

"We don't know it is blocked," Judith replied. "Terry said, 'likely' not certainly."

10

ABANDONED JAG

ANNE AND REX finished the last room in the Hall and, after a brief rest, headed out to the old stables, which had been garages in the last years of the Hall's occupancy. With Ben and Isaac gone, the old buildings seemed once again threatening.

"We should have gone in the van with them," Anne said to Rex, as she pulled open the garage door. The hinges were rusty, and it was hard to move. The effort strained her injured shoulder and made her nauseous. She leaned against the door for a moment to catch her breath when she heard movement behind her. Anne swung around in alarm only to find the yard empty.

"I'm imagining things, Rex," she said, relieved. "I should have known that because you would have heard if someone was creeping up on us."

Switching on her flashlight, Anne stepped inside the building. Her heart sank. She'd the thought the basement was stuffed full of junk but it was nothing to this. She felt a surge of anger that the company who'd hired her never mentioned the full extent of what she was seeing. *They wanted me to fail so they could refuse to pay me the full contract*, blazed in her mind.

She walked back and forth surveying the stacked indoor, and ancient, garden furniture while wondering how Ben and Isaac would react to seeing this. They were pleased to be almost finished, when they'd driven off an hour ago.

She tugged at a rolled carpet standing on end, leaning against the other pieces, and it fell to the floor, unfurling as it went. A painted fire screen caught her eye, and she brought it out into the sunlight. It was too badly damaged by heat and smoke to be valuable, so she set it aside. A small side table looked promising, and she pulled it toward her. At first, it wouldn't move but, after she'd wiggled it side-to-side a moment, it did come away from the rest of the pile. Unfortunately, it had been holding other pieces in place and they slid down to the floor, making her skip away to save her feet.

Her eyes, now accustomed to the dim light, spotted a car number plate through the mess. "There's even a car under all this junk," she told Rex who was investigating rat holes among the bric-a-brac.

Rex looked at her and froze. Anne froze too. Somewhere in the building something was stealthily moving. Not a mouse or a rat, something large, human likely.

Anne hissed a 'heel' command to Rex and, when he joined her, she took hold of his collar and led him growling from the garage. She pushed the door closed and locked it with a sigh of relief. Her relief lasted only a second for she realized at once that whatever made the sounds, hadn't entered through this door and would, presumably, leave through the entrance they'd entered by.

Anne hurried Rex across the courtyard and back into the

Hall, where she slammed and bolted the door. She practically ran through the Hall and did the same for the front entrance, all while estimating how much time it would be before her two employees returned. She retreated to a small study off the library and closed and barred the door with a flimsy, decrepit table they'd rejected for potential sale because it was riddled with woodworm.

Picking up a length of wood, presumably once a chair leg, Anne braced herself in a corner and settled down to wait. "It's up to you now, Rex," she told him as he watched her in puzzlement. "This rotten stick and that rotten table won't stop a determined attack."

Fortunately for Anne and the still puzzled Rex, no attack came before her workers returned. They were as puzzled as Rex when they found her exiting the study holding her stick.

"Somebody was in the garage," Anne told them. "And they weren't introducing themselves."

"We'll go and look," Isaac said, turning away.

"Not without me," Anne replied. "I'm not staying on my own here anymore."

The garage, when they stepped inside, was as quiet as the Hall had been when they walked through it.

"They're gone now," Ben said. "A tramp as likely as not."

"How did they get in?" Anne retorted.

All three and Rex came out of the building and walked along its walls until they found on the back wall of the garage, a small window high up, but with a pile of lumber laid below it.

Isaac climbed the lumber and examined the window. "It's not locked," he called down, and proceeded to climb inside.

Anne, Rex and Ben waited until Isaac reappeared.

"There's quite the den in there," he said, as he climbed down the lumber stack. "It's a shame to disturb him."

"I'd be more sympathetic," Anne retorted, "if he'd spoken. He scared me half to death."

"I'm sure he was more scared of you than you of him," Ben said, laughing.

"I don't see how he could be," Anne cried. "I barricaded myself in a room until you returned. What did he do?"

"He scarpered as fast as he could," Ben replied, still enjoying the joke.

"How do you know it's a man?" Anne asked Isaac, suddenly changing the subject.

"The den doesn't have anything to suggest a woman," Isaac replied, "but I suppose it could be. Not often we see homeless women though."

"Shall we board up the window?" Ben asked.

Anne shook her head. "He can live there a few more days but when we're done, he's homeless again. The developers won't let him stay. The good news, for me, is, now I know who has been spying on me every time you two leave the premises. It's a relief. I've been imagining all kinds of villains out in the grounds."

They returned to the garage and surveyed the mountain of work ahead of them.

"Do you think all these outbuildings are like this?" Ben asked.

"Let's see," Anne replied, and they opened each outbuilding door, growing more despondent at each one.

"It can't be done," Isaac said, as they began closing and locking the doors again. "We must be selective."

"I agree," Anne said. "We pick out only the best pieces. Everything else is carted away to the dump."

"I'd like to see that car," Ben mused. "It should be worth

something. The Demerlays wouldn't have had just an everyday Austin or a Morris."

"Until we shift the junk on top of it, none of us can see it," Anne replied.

"Are we going to make anything out of this place, missus?" Isaac asked, doubtfully. He and Ben were not only paid by the hour but also had a small share in the final sale of goods.

Anne nodded. "I think so. Enough to buy Christmas presents for our family and friends, I imagine."

"That good, eh," Ben replied. He didn't sound pleased.

"Maybe the car will make all the difference," Anne said, smiling at them both. "Now, if you bring around the van, we can start making a dent in all this. And remember, only things that will sell."

* * *

Ramsay and Bracken drove to the Hall after dropping Judith off at her shop. Ramsay's mind was churning with everything they'd learned. How much was useful, it would take him most of the night to decide.

He parked at the Hall entrance only to hear, when he switched off the engine, that all the activity was now at the back of the Hall. He re-started his car and drove around to find the three house clearers moving junk from the garage into the van, except for a growing pile of discarded pieces stacked outside the door. Ramsay joined in the clearing while Bracken went off to assist Rex in hunting rats.

As they worked, Ramsay told Anne what they'd learned from Terry and his archives. "You were wrong there," he said, "they're properly cataloged, filed and kept. He has better records then the British Museum, I'll be bound."

"Huh," Anne responded, unimpressed. "Have they solved our mystery?"

"No but there's nothing we can't find in them when we want to," Ramsay retorted, nettled by her scorn.

"Such as who wrote the coded messages and why?" Anne asked.

"Not that, no."

"Or what happened to Saunders?"

"It wasn't just Saunders," Ramsay said, ignoring her question. "Another person went missing some weeks later."

"Ben told me," Anne said as she placed a cracked vase on the pile of discards. "It isn't just a murderer we need to watch out for, it's a serial killer. You do realize the killer may still be alive and living nearby? And but for Rex, I could have been victim number three?"

"I do," Ramsay replied, grinning. "Which means you and Judith shouldn't spend any more time alone here until the job is finished. If Ben and Isaac can't be here, and I'm not here, you go with them."

"I'm hiring you, remember?" Anne retorted.

"For my expertise and experience," Ramsay replied, unconcerned at her outrage. "We'll use both from now to the end."

"You really are worried, aren't you?" Anne asked.

"I am," Ramsay told her. "I thought it was a local with a bee in his bonnet about the treasure. Now, I'm convinced there's much more than that going on. It still may be the loot from the jewel theft and the city thugs who stole it, but whoever they are, they're serious."

Anne nodded. She told him of her fright before the discovery of the tramp's lair among the junk they were removing, ending with, "Every scare now feels worse than the last. Being attacked and injured does that to one, I find."

Ramsay nodded. "Part of what worries me is that Saunders was a professional and even he seems to have been done away with. Anyway, now we're both awake to the danger, we should plan our next steps accordingly," Ramsay said. "And we need to be sure Judith knows she may be in danger too. The person doing all this may think Judith knows enough to be a threat, and we can't have that."

"You don't think the man living in the Hall's garage is the one who attacked me, do you?" Anne asked.

"Do you?" Ramsay replied.

Anne shook her head. "The one who hit me was bulkier, not someone living on handouts."

By late afternoon, everyone was tired, even Ramsay who'd only been working for a few hours.

"It isn't going to be as bad as it looked," Anne told the men, as they gathered around the back of the van. "Like the basement, most of this is just junk we can leave behind."

Ben and Isaac wished them goodnight and drove off to the warehouse with the van load of saved items, leaving Ramsay and Anne to lock up.

"I want to inspect the Priest Hole," Ramsay told Anne, when she'd pocketed the garage door key.

"It's getting late," Anne said. Her shoulder ached. She should have stopped hours ago, she knew.

"I'll step inside, see if the tunnel is still there and step right out again," Ramsay told her, grinning. "Exploring can be for tomorrow, if it is."

In the library, Ramsay examined the shelves where Terry had told him he'd find the door mechanism. It took some time. The handle was part of the bookshelf support and so long unused, it appeared to be all one piece. Dusting off the debris, Ramsay carefully pulled on the lever, hoping it wouldn't simply break in his hand. Years had passed since anyone had done this and at first nothing happened. He waggled the lever and pulled gently again and this time a soft sigh seemed to come from the bookshelf and Ramsay felt it move.

He and Anne exchanged anxious glances as Ramsay drew the lever further toward him and a section of the bookshelf swung away from the wall. A man-sized entrance was before them, dark and forbidding.

Ramsay switched on his flashlight and examined the small room that lay before them. It was a measure of the desperation of the time that anyone would want to hide for hours or days in such a space.

"Terry said the tunnel runs out from the back panel," Ramsay said, stepping inside and rapping his knuckles of the wood. "It sounds hollow. Maybe we're in luck."

"I thought Terry also said everyone had searched the tunnel back in the fifties," Anne replied. Even the excitement of the Priest Hole couldn't overcome the dull ache from her shoulder.

Ramsay was pressing the wood and the edges, searching for the mechanism to open this next door, as he replied, "He did. Only, remember, they all searched the icehouse and yet Bracken found the box because time and wear has exposed things that were more deeply buried back then."

He turned his attention to the other walls and found what he needed. Pressing on a small button that was part of the decorative trim unlocked the back panel and he was able to push it open. Unsound-looking wooden steps led down into the darkness with an equally wood wormy railing along the wall to his right. "Wish me luck," Ramsay told Anne, and gingerly placed one foot on the first step. It groaned under his weight, and he stepped back quickly.

"You said we'd leave exploration until tomorrow," Anne

reminded him. "And I think we should. I can't carry you out of there if the steps collapse and you break a leg."

Ramsay nodded. "It would be useful to have Ben and Isaac here when we go down those steps. If only to rescue me if they do collapse and I can't get back out." He pulled the panel closed, stepped out into the library and wiggled the Priest Hole door shut.

"I need to rest," Anne said. "It's been another long day."

Noting her almost gray face, Ramsay agreed. After locking the Hall, Ramsay drove Anne home and helped her make a meal and feed Rex.

It was late when Ramsay arrived back at his own home. He was in the act of removing his jacket when the phone rang.

Grumbling, he picked up the handset.

"Are you ever at home?" Baldock demanded, when Ramsay said his name.

"It's long days in the private sector," Ramsay told him. "What do you have for me?"

"First the easy bit," Baldock replied. "The cloth and button are from a man's suit, not new but expensive when it was. The man you're looking for is either wearing his old suit to go out murdering people, or it's someone who picked up an old suit at a used clothes shop. Maybe a jumble sale or something like that."

"Not too much help," Ramsay mused, "what about the rest?"

"The Leeds robbery is interesting," Baldock told him. "The goods were stolen from a high-end jeweller, not your run-of-the-mill high street store. The owner, a wealthy man himself, had just bought a famous necklace and earring set sold by one of those fifties' starlets, you know the sort, masses of blonde hair and cleavage. Mini-Marilyn Monroes.

She had one big success, became quickly rich, bought the jewels, or had them bought for her, and quickly became poor again, which is when she sold them. Rags-to-riches-to-rags in under five years. Quite the life, the entertainment field."

Ramsay laughed. "It's why I never went in for it," he said. "The police pension is a lot safer."

"I hope so," Baldock growled. "I can't wait to get there. Where was I? The jeweler brought the set to his shop in Leeds, showed it to a select crowd of potential buyers, there wasn't any publicity, all word of mouth, and within a week, the necklace set and lots of other expensive pieces were stolen."

"So the tip-off came from the upper-crust of our honest society," Ramsay mused.

"Exactly. The investigation didn't get far, from what I can see," Baldock said. "It wasn't a smash-and-grab, it was a professional job. The robbery was Saturday night, and nothing was noticed until Monday morning. The jewels and the thieves were probably out of the country by then."

"How much was the haul worth?" Ramsay asked.

"You know what it's like," Baldock told him. "The newspapers use the value of the finished pieces as they were for sale. But the thieves will have to break up the pieces to make them unrecognizable and so get only ten percent of their retail value."

"The newspapers suggested two hundred thousand pounds," Ramsay remembered. "Twenty thousand if what you say holds true. A nice sum, if split only one or two ways, but not worth fleeing the country for."

"There are people in Amsterdam who'd fence them for a fair sum," Baldock reminded him. "Ferry to Amsterdam on Saturday night or Sunday, sold by Monday, and back home by Monday night. No one would hardly know you'd been gone."

"All this was checked?" Ramsay asked.

"It was, but nothing came of it," Baldock said.

"It sounds to me the loot never left the country," Ramsay told him.

"No one admitted to seeing any of it for sale in the weeks that followed," Baldock replied.

"Probably made into new pieces and now in jewelry boxes all over the country," Ramsay suggested. "I have two names for you to research, if that's all right?"

"It must have been your persistence that made you mildly successful as an inspector," Baldock growled.

"I like to think it's my best feature," Ramsay agreed. "Morris Saunders, a private investigator, and another man, Oscar Geary. Both went missing while hunting for treasure here at Demerlay Hall in 1955."

Baldock's silence suggested he was wrestling with this new request. "You do remember you retired a year or so ago, don't you?"

"What I'm investigating will lead to criminal charges," Ramsay told him. "I'm sure of it. You will be the officer laying those charges and getting all the glory. Wouldn't some promotion be welcome? Add a little more to your pension?"

"This is close to bribing a police officer, and a criminal offense too," Baldock reminded him. "You're sure about this?"

"As sure as I can be in such circumstances," Ramsay said, fighting a childish urge to cross his fingers to cancel out the untruth.

Baldock growled. "All right, I'll put someone on it. Now, I'm going home for my dinner. Unlike you fellows in the private sector, we public servants are at work all hours of the day and night."

Ramsay thanked him and hung up. He grinned. *We know where some of the loot is and, if no one found it, the rest can't be far away.*

11

A VAGRANT

Next day, as arranged, Ramsay drove Anne to the Hall. Driving was still out of the question for her.

"The tunnel first?" Anne asked.

Ramsay nodded. "Then the church, I think. Parish records often have interesting information, and I think two disappearances in the parish might lead to something being mentioned. The records may also contain the Hall's chapel records. The most likely place for them to go, don't you think?"

Anne said, "It might be best if I do the Parish Records search. I know the vicar and I still ache everywhere. I probably shouldn't be doing what I'm doing; it's slowing my recovery."

"Will the vicar be at the church?" Ramsay asked. He didn't like the idea of Anne sitting out of sight of others.

"He'll be at the vicarage, and we can ask."

Ramsay nodded. He parked the car, and they got out to start the day. Bracken and Rex trotted off to investigate the area for interesting smells, while Anne opened the garage doors.

Ben and Isaac arrived as she did so, and they entered the garage. The sound of the squatter clearing out of his den at the back of the building had Ramsay, Ben and Isaac racing off to see who emerged from the window. They were in time to see a shabbily dressed figure disappear into the shrubs that pressed upon the old buildings.

"Did you recognize him?" Ramsay asked, seeing Ben's expression.

Ben nodded. "We see him around the village sometimes. I wondered where he called home."

"Not someone we should worry about then?"

Ben shook his head, as they walked back. "I'd say he's a harmless old man. I doubt he's even aware there's a story of treasure here."

"Someone hit Anne so hard it dislocated her shoulder," Ramsay reminded him. "It may just be because she's turning what he thinks of as his home upside down."

Ben looked unconvinced. They entered the garage and began sorting through the pile of abandoned material.

"It's a Jaguar XK," Isaac told Ben. "A fifties model. I always wanted one when I were a nipper."

Ben laughed. "Here's hoping it's in good condition and there are people who also wanted one when they were children and now have the money to buy it."

"If it's been dumped here," Ramsay remarked, "it'll be worth nothing. Like all the rest of this junk." He dropped a broken chair onto the pile of discarded items and returned inside for more.

Isaac replied, "Cars like this are worth something even if they aren't working."

Thirty minutes later, they had everything off the car, and they could walk around it.

"Must be the engine that conked out," Isaac said,

opening the hood. A rat scuttled out and under the remaining junk in the building. "Rats have been nesting here for a while, I'd say."

The men gathered around the open engine compartment and stared at the mess inside. "The cables have been gnawed clean of insulation," Ben said.

Isaac nodded. "It's not expensive to replace cables."

"The engine will likely be rusty inside," Ramsay added. "It hasn't turned over since it was abandoned, I'd guess." He walked to the back and opened the trunk, which was empty. The carpets had been torn aside as if someone had searched under them.

Ben tried the driver side door, and it opened. "There's nought much inside either."

"This car was worth something when it was abandoned," Ramsay told them. "It doesn't make sense."

Isaac snorted. "They probably left it cos the ashtrays were full. Rich folk are like that."

Ben looked inside again and, grinning, said the ashtrays were empty.

"Are any of you three going to contribute some work for the rest of the day?" Anne demanded.

"Aye, missus," Ben said, grinning, "but of everything we've seen on this clearance, this is what will likely pay us our bonus."

When the van was full, and Ben and Isaac were preparing to leave, Anne told them she and Ramsay were going to the church. "Look in at the church on your way back to the Hall so we know you're ready."

Before Anne could lock the garage door, Ramsay went back inside to re-examine the car.

"What is it?" Anne asked, coming to peer into the Jaguar as Ramsay sat in the driver's seat and opened the glove compartment and rifled through the storage spaces in the doors.

"I've been imagining young 'wild' Demerlay using this car as the getaway vehicle for that robbery," Ramsay replied. "I wondered if he hid the car in here right after the robbery and was then killed before he used it again."

"That's some imagining," Anne retorted. "Even if he was the getaway driver, he wouldn't use his own car."

"It sounds mad, I know," Ramsay replied, smiling. "That's why I said 'imagining'. But remember, it was a fancy jeweler in the fancy end of town. An aristocrat's son and a fancy car would blend right in. He might have thought that, anyway."

Anne nodded. "I suppose. Are we still going to the church or are we searching the car?"

"It will take only minutes," Ramsay replied. "You look in the boot and I'll finish in here."

They lifted seats and carpets, shone their flashlights under seats and into dark corners without finding anything remotely like a clue. Like the trunk, the carpets in the cabin had been lifted to look underneath. Even the internal door panels had been levered away from the metal. They weren't the first to search the Jaguar.

"I want to look underneath the car, as well," Ramsay said, getting down on his knees and shining his torch in the narrow gap between the car body and the garage floor. The car, however, was too low for casual inspection. "We'll find a garage with a hoist. We'll never see unless we lift it up."

"Isaac can do that," Anne said. "When he isn't working for me, he does odd jobs for people, including car repairs. He has all the equipment a garage has."

"Then lock up and we'll try the church records," Ramsay replied. "We might learn something there."

The church records were spectacularly empty of any references to the events of the time except to note they'd held a memorial service for Jeremy Demerlay. The burial, however. was at the family home in Northumberland.

"Terry Brent is our next stop," Ramsay said, as they climbed back into his car. "I want copies of those treasure hunters' photos. See if anyone can remember names."

Terry didn't have a copying machine so Ramsay, Bracken, Anne and Terry, made their way to the library and bought more copy paper from the helpful Librarian.

"You'll get me fired," the librarian grumbled to Ramsay, as she handed over the pages and he handed over two shillings.

Ramsay thanked her and said, "Maybe suggest to your managers that they could charge for copying. Lots of people would be interested in that service."

"Go on with you," she replied. "Why would anyone want to buy copies of things they can borrow for free?"

Outside, Ramsay asked Terry, "Would you write down on the back of these photos all the names you can remember. I'll ask Ned Wishart if he can add more."

Terry said he would and suggested, "Of course, you can get most of them from the Station Hotel register. Only one or two, the leaders I suppose, stayed at the Hall."

It took Terry barely any time at all to make notes on the photos and hand the pages back to Ramsay.

"Terry," Ramsay asked, "You said the treasure hunters weren't the tenant's family but were they friends of the family?"

Terry's nervousness increased as he struggled to answer the question. "I don't know," he said, at last. "Some stayed at the Hall so they must have been known to the family."

"You didn't interview them for your newspaper articles?"

Terry nodded. "I tried. They weren't very nice." He lit another cigarette from the stub of the one he was just finishing.

"Which is the one who went missing after Saunders did?" Ramsay asked, trying to line up the names Terry had written with the faces. Terry's body language and answers confirmed Ramsay's impression of the 'treasure hunters'.

Terry pointed to a stocky man with a moustache. "That one. Geary was his family name, I think. He wasn't local. He had a northern accent, like you, Mr. Ramsay. They called him Geordie, but that may not have been his name. It could just be a reference to where he was from."

Ramsay nodded in agreement. Just as Welshmen were called 'Taff', or Scotsmen, 'Jock', or people from Liverpool, 'Scousers', men from the north-east were called 'Geordie', whatever their real name may be. "I've been told his name was Oscar Geary, does that ring a bell?"

Terry shrugged. "I just heard him called Geordie. You could ask the landlord at the Demerlay Arms." Then he added. "They drank in there a lot."

"As they should," Ramsay replied, grinning. "And I'll find Ned in there too, I shouldn't wonder. Thanks, Terry. We'll talk again."

As Ramsay, Bracken and Anne drove past the church, they saw Ben and Isaac waiting and signaled them to follow Ramsay's car back to the Hall, where Anne explained the need for some physical assistance to support Ramsay in case the steps gave way as he went down into the tunnel.

"I've the very thing," Isaac said, and brought from the van a harness and rope.

Feeling a fool, Ramsay fastened the harness around his chest and, with the attached rope held tightly by the two workmen, he walked gingerly down the creaking wooden steps. Reaching the bottom without incident only added to his embarrassment.

He shone his flashlight along the tunnel and, so far as he could see, it wasn't blocked. "I'm going to explore," he called up to the others who were peering down the steps at him. "How long is the rope?"

On learning it wouldn't allow him to explore far, Ramsay unclipped it from the harness, saying, "I'll attach it again to come up."

"See you do," Anne called down to him. "The steps took your weight going down, but it didn't sound like they will coming back up."

Ramsay laughed, but he knew she was right. He'd need to be wary on his return.

The tunnel was lined with bricks and, though wet from water leaching through the gaps in the mortar, seemed to be working as intended. None seemed loose and none had fallen out of place, which, Ramsay thought was a pity for loose bricks were where he would expect to find any hidden treasure.

Finally, he came to a mound of earth. Undoubtedly where the tunnel had been filled when they knocked down the old chapel. Although years of dampness had eroded the edge, it still filled the tunnel. If there was another cache of clues or jewels hidden in the tunnel beyond this point, he'd need a team of workers to find it. Ramsay turned and made his way back to the light from the open door.

After re-attaching the rope to the harness, he lightly climbed the steps.

"Well?" Anne asked.

Ramsay told her of the blockage as he took off the harness. "None of the messages we've seen mentioned the chapel, did they?" he asked.

Gold, Greed, and a Hidden Hoard

"None so far," Anne replied. "Beyond the 'mill' and the 'stream', the only other location we've deciphered is 'gargoyle' and the house has plenty of those up on the gutters, so it isn't a help."

Ramsay nodded. "And the trouble with gargoyles is our ancestors used them everywhere. The word may refer to a gargoyle on the Hall, but it could also have been one on the chapel or the mill."

"Or the ones at the end of the stable block," Ben said.

"Where?" Ramsay and Anne cried as one.

"I'll show you," Ben said. "We have to get back to work anyhow, or we won't get a second load shifted today."

The four people and Bracken made their way to the end of the stables where, as Ben had told them, a small gargoyle directed overflow water from the gutters out into a trough, no doubt for the horses. While Ben and Isaac went back to work, Ramsay and Anne studied the stonework.

"What does it say about the gargoyle?" Ramsay asked Anne.

"It says 'below the gargoyle'," Anne replied, carefully examining the stones from the gargoyle to the ground. "But there's no sign of anything loose enough to hide anything behind."

"Let's look at its partner at the other corner," Ramsay said, nodding. He'd also decided this one couldn't be it.

"This one is the same," Ramsay said, in disgust as they examined the stones of the wall. He looked at the trough, before pushing it with his foot.

"You think it's under the trough?" Anne asked.

"Or behind it," Ramsay replied, taking hold of one end and trying to swivel it away from the wall. It was much too heavy and appeared solidly settled in place. Ramsay tried looking behind the stone trough to the ground below, but it was in shadow. He turned on his torch and shone it down the gap.

"The flagstones below the trough could have been lifted to hide something and then the trough replaced," he said.

Anne's expression suggested she thought it unlikely. "Our thieves, if that's who hid the jewels, weren't working men. They could never have moved and replaced this trough quickly enough not to arouse suspicions."

"Maybe the trough was already moved," Ramsay replied. "For repairs or what have you. All they had to do was lift the flagstone, hide the container, replace the flagstone and then the trough was put back on top by the repair workers."

"Now you're clutching at straws," Anne told him laughing.

Ramsay rather sheepishly agreed he also thought he was.

"Different gargoyle," Anne said, "and probably one long gone. Now what?"

"The Demerlay Arms to ask about people in the photos," Ramsay replied, "and talk again with Ned Wishart."

12

THE GARDENER

THE PUB'S landlord was happy to talk about the people in the photos, when Ramsay and Anne ordered their drinks in the Ladies Lounge. He also liked sharing his knowledge about the village's past. It was still early, and the public bar wasn't yet busy.

"I remember them like it was yesterday," he said. "You have to have a good memory in this business."

"Can you put names to the faces?" Ramsay asked.

The man concentrated a moment, then began, pointing to faces and giving first names.

"You don't know their family names?" Anne asked.

He shook his head. "Nay. It's first names or nicknames only in a pub. These two stayed here so they'll be in our register." He pointed to a couple of men standing a little apart from the others.

When he'd finished, Ramsay asked, "Didn't one of them disappear?"

"Two of them did. This one," the landlord pointed to Morris Saunders, "He went first. Then this one," he pointed to a man he'd identified as Oscar, "disappeared later."

"These photos," Ramsay asked. "Are these all of the men you remember?"

The landlord nodded. "That's right. Three came first," he pointed to the men Ramsay had immediately thought of as 'villains' when he first saw the photo. "Then this one, Morris, the one who we later learned was a private detective, then soon after, the two who claimed to be structural engineers," he pointed to the two who stayed at the Demerlay Arms, and finally, Geary, the second one to disappear. Seven, all told."

"And they were all here together?" Anne asked.

The landlord nodded. "It was when that family from Leeds had the place. There was a day or so when they were all here, which must have been when Terry took these photos, Terry was a busy bee in those days writing and capturing our local doings. Then the private detective disappeared. Days later, the first three treasure hunters left, and then Oscar Geary disappeared. Finally, our two engineers left too. That's how it went."

Ramsay interjected, "Was Geary different from the others? We know Saunders was an investigator, which might have made him a target, but was Geary?"

"He wasn't like the others but," the landlord replied. "I don't think he could have been an investigator because of his nature. He was a timid sort of fellow."

"These others don't look timid," Ramsay said, pointing again at the photos. "Do you have any idea why Geary might have been there? Was he a specialist in some way?"

The landlord considered this. "He might have been, though I never heard it said. He was more like a scholar than a digger, that's for sure."

"Had you heard the story of buried treasure at the Hall before any of these people came?" Ramsay asked.

The landlord laughed. "Aye, and the one about the headless ghost in the East Wing, and the crying voice from the well. Old houses have lots of these stories attached."

"Have there been ghost hunters?" Anne asked.

The man shook his head. "They're just stories and there's no money in ghosts." The door to the public bar opened and the landlord looked to see who'd entered. He turned to Ramsay and Anne, saying, "Here's the fellow you should talk to if you want to know about the Hall. Old Ned," he pointed into the public bar to someone they couldn't see from their position, "worked there, man and boy. Still thinks the family will come back and he'll be gardening for them again."

Ramsay smiled. "I'll do that, thanks." He paused, "Would Ned join us here so Anne can hear what he has to say?"

The landlord shrugged. "I'll ask him. He might. He's always looking to share stories of the good old days, and he doesn't get many listeners nowadays on the men's side of the house."

Ramsay and Anne took a table and waited, while Bracken and Rex settled on the floor. The door of the lounge opened and Ned walked in, looking about to find them.

Ramsay stood up and welcomed him. "Remember me?" Ramsay asked.

Nodding, Ned agreed he did and took a seat facing them across the small table.

"We were asking the landlord about these photos," Ramsay began, laying them out on the table. "He says you're the man who knows about Demerlay Hall and we should ask you."

Ned studied each photo in turn. "Aye, I remember them, right enough. They were a rum lot."

"Do you remember their names?" Ramsay asked. "We

have first names, as you see but it's hard to trace people without a family name."

Ned shook his head. "We weren't that friendly."

"There's a red Jaguar in the garage," Anne asked. "Can you tell us about that?"

"It were young Jeremy's car," Ned said. "When he was killed, no one liked to touch it. There were talk of selling it, but the heart had gone out of the old Lord by then and nothing came of it."

"When was that?" Ramsay asked. "Was it before they let the house to tenants?"

Ned shook his head. "They let the Hall to a Leeds man first. Fewster, he was called. A nasty piece of work but friends of the Demerlays through Jeremy. The man's children were trouble and led young Jeremy into bad ways."

"So, Jeremy was still in the Hall during that time?" Anne asked, puzzled.

"They were supposed to be family friends, and he often visited," Ned replied. "I tried to warn the old master about the goings-on here, but it did no good."

"Where was the well?" Ramsay asked. He hadn't seen that on the map they had. "I'm told there was a crying ghost in the well."

Ned laughed. "That old wives' tale. It's behind the Hall, on the hillside. It was closed and covered before I was born, but you can still see where it was. Any ghost down there will be long gone."

"Are there any more old buildings or features we should know about?" Anne asked. "We know of the mill, the stream, and the chapel. We didn't know of a well. Are there others?

Ned shook his head. "There were a lot of old sheds on

the estate, barns, pigsties, and the like, but they're all gone and there's nought much to show for where they were."

"The second man who disappeared," Ramsay asked. "At the time, what did people think of him going?"

"Like the first one," Ned replied. "Some thought he'd found the treasure and run. Others thought he'd been murdered."

Anne asked, "Murdered because he found the treasure?"

"Aye, likely," Ned replied. "Thon engineers left very soon after."

"So, you think there was treasure?" Ramsay asked.

"Not the sort they were looking for," Ned replied. "There were talk of loot from a robbery. I didn't believe that either, until people disappeared."

"Why would the loot be at Demerlay Hall?" Anne asked.

"I don't know but the tenants were from Leeds and their children were tearaways," Ned said. "Then we had that private investigator arrive and he must have had his reasons for coming."

Ramsay nodded. "Anything else you can think of that might help us?"

"What is it you want help with?" Ned responded.

"Who did this to me and why?" Anne retorted, holding up her arm in its sling.

"Someone who doesn't think the treasure was found," Ramsay added. "Any ideas?"

"Yon second-hand shop owner, Nigel whats-his-name," Ned replied. "He's often up there at the Hall. And the fellow who took those photos," Ned nodded to the copies still lying on the table. "He's never given up looking, either."

"You've seen them both at the Hall over the years?" Anne asked. "Not just since I started clearing the place?'

Ned confirmed he had seen them many times, though

he was careful to keep out of their sight. Ramsay offered him a drink in exchange for his information and, when Ned agreed, went with him to the bar.

His refilled glass in hand, Ned returned to the public bar and Ramsay to the table where Bracken and Anne were patiently waiting.

"You know," Anne whispered, as Ramsay sat down. "I wondered at the time if it wasn't Nigel who attacked me. There was something about the man."

"You said you didn't see him," Ramsay said.

"I didn't. I think it may have been his after-shave or cologne that made me suspect him."

Ramsay frowned. "Nigel isn't a likeable personality, but would he really try to murder someone he knew as well as he knows you?"

"That's why I haven't said anything until now," Anne replied. "I couldn't believe it to be true. And yet Ned says he's seen him searching for years. If it's an obsession with him, and we accidentally found clues he hasn't found, maybe it tipped him over the edge."

"He certainly hasn't been around much since the attack," Ramsay suggested.

Anne nodded. "Again, I thought that, but we finished the library clear-out and that was all he seemed interested in, at first."

"Is it possible he thought there was something in a book in the library?" Ramsay asked. "And he found it?"

"He did say he'd found something," Anne agreed, "but he led me to believe it was a rare, valuable book he could sell for a profit."

Ramsay laughed. "Well, if you don't hear of a rare book sale very soon, you'll know why."

"What's next, boss?" Anne asked.

"I'm going to learn more about Oscar Geary and that well," Ramsay replied. "I think you should focus on finishing your contract."

Anne shook her head. "I'm doing both. Tonight, I'm going to re-look for the word 'well' in those messages. It occurs to me that we've been reading the word wrongly all this time. Some of the messages may make sense now we know there was once an actual well."

"Fine," Ramsay replied. "Just don't leave the house without me. Phone any time and I'll be there."

"I have Rex," Anne protested, stroking her dog who'd sat up on hearing his name.

Ramsay shook his head. "Not enough. If Rex, Bracken and I aren't there, you wait until we are."

Anne was still grumbling about his dictatorial ways when he dropped her off at her house and bade her goodnight.

13

THE REGULARS

AFTER A DINNER of a sandwich and a mug of tea, Ramsay too returned to the old documents, his copies of them anyway. *Did any of them mention a well?*

He was engrossed in his research when Bracken growled and sprang to his feet. Ramsay looked where Bracken was staring and saw only the darkness through the window.

"I should have closed the curtains," he told Bracken, and rose to do that when a faint noise outside caught his now alerted ear.

"Do we have a prowler, do you think?" Ramsay asked. He closed the room curtains, and then did the same for all the windows on the ground floor. Returning to his seat, he prepared to continue researching when Bracken again growled a warning, more urgently this time.

"Come on, my friend," Ramsay said, setting out for the door with his flashlight. "We'll see who or what is out there."

Quietly unlocking the door, he swiftly yanked it open and stepped outside. A movement at the bottom of his garden caught his eye and he swung the torch beam that way only to see a figure disappearing over the wall.

Bracken barked and set off in pursuit. Ramsay followed and caught up with Bracken at the wall, where evidence of the intruder's hurry to escape was plain to see. Bracken was standing on his hind legs, front paws on the stone wall, and barking furiously.

"That's enough, Bracken," Ramsay said, taking hold of the dog's collar. "We can't go chasing after him in the dark. We could be ambushed. Remember the scent and you can sniff him out tomorrow."

They returned to the house and Ramsay locked the door behind them. "The good news, Bracken, is he's after us now, which hopefully means he'll have less time to go after Anne. We need to keep it that way."

Ramsay returned to his work. Bracken was too excited to sit and paced the house, sniffing at doors in the hope of another chase.

* * *

NEXT MORNING, as he drove Anne to the Hall, Ramsay recounted his adventure of the night before.

"Did it look anything like Nigel?" Anne asked.

Ramsay smiled. "No, this one looked scrawny like Ned Wishart or Terry."

"That was a thought I had last night when I was going through the documents," Anne said. "Ned told us about seeing the others on the estate, and in a way, told us how often he is on the estate."

"He has the excuse he loves it and goes there in sorrow," Ramsay reminded her.

Anne snorted. "He also suggested the missing people

might have taken the loot, which could be him trying to direct us into stopping our search."

"I'm not really searching for anything other than whoever attacked you and," Ramsay said, "in doing so, stopping them attacking you again."

He pulled up at the Hall's garage, where Ben and Isaac were waiting to start work. "Our homeless friend has already left," Ben told Ramsay and Anne as they exited the car.

"Did you speak to him?" Ramsay asked.

Ben nodded. "He says he's moving on today because we're making his life a misery."

"Would he talk to us, if you asked him?" Ramsay continued.

"If you bought him a cup of tea and a meal, he would," Ben replied. "I know where he'll be. I can ask."

"Go with Tom in his car," Anne said, "Isaac and I will carry on loading the van."

With that agreed, Ramsay, Bracken and Ben set out in search of the tramp. It wasn't long before Ben spotted him.

"He likes this spot during the day," Ben explained, as Ramsay parked. "It faces the sun, and he's sheltered against the wind." Ben got out of the car and went to ask the man to help Ramsay find what was going on at the Hall.

Ramsay watched as Ben and the man talked. Both looked at Ramsay and then back to their discussion. Time passed and Ramsay was giving up hope, when he saw the man rise to his feet and follow Ben to the car. Ramsay and Bracken got out as the two men arrived. Ramsay watched Bracken carefully, but his friend made no sign he recognized the man. *Not our intruder of last night, then.*

Ben introduced the man, and they shook hands.

"What do you want to know?" the homeless man asked.

His face was gaunt, etched with lines, though he was surprisingly clean, Ramsay noted.

"You live at the Hall," Ramsay began. "I wondered if you've seen people coming and going through the grounds in the time you've been there?"

The man nodded. "Aye, lots. But you mean men searching for something, I imagine."

An educated dropout, Ramsay noted. "That's exactly what I mean, yes."

"Three regulars and one or two occasionally," the man told him. "The regulars are local; I don't know their names. I'm not from here."

"What do they look like?" Ben asked.

"One a well-fed man in smart clothes..."

Nigel, Ramsay thought.

"...and two thin. One with horn-rimmed specs and a cigarette hanging from his lips..."

Terry, Ramsay thought.

"...and one looks like a laborer," the man finished.

Ned, Ramsay concluded. *We're right about those three.*

"Thank you," Ramsay said, "that's helpful. The irregular people, what are they like?"

"They don't come often enough for me to describe them," the man said. "They're just people."

"Do they search anywhere in particular?" Ben asked.

"At different times, they have," the man replied. "But then they return to wandering the grounds looking lost."

"Has anything about them struck you as noteworthy?" Ramsay asked. "Something they do that's unusual maybe?"

The man shook his head. "One of them tried using a divining rod once, I recall. Another had a map one time. No, nothing really, other than the hungry look on their faces."

Ramsay handed the man a five-pound note. "For your help to us," he said. "I hope this might help you."

The man looked at him suspiciously. "This is too much," he said.

"Maybe rent a room, buy clothes, get a job?" Ramsay suggested.

The man laughed. "I wasn't thrown out of work," he said. "I rejected it and all your so-called civilization. But I will accept your gift because it'll help in the coming months. The winter is always the hardest time." He turned and walked away, leaving Ramsay and Ben to return to the garage and their fellow workers.

"Did you learn anything?" Anne asked, as Ramsay began lifting broken furnishings from the garage to the growing pile outside.

He recounted what the homeless man had told him about the regular treasure hunters.

"We'd guessed that already," Anne replied. "So, nothing new."

"There are others who are less regular," Ramsay said, "we shouldn't rule them out of our theories."

"I think we can," Anne said. "The people we're concerned with are obsessives who haven't given up after all this time. The ones who come out when the mood takes them are just dreamers. Now, did you have any success with the lost 'well'?"

"Not really," Ramsay replied. "Did you?"

"I did," Anne told him, stopping for a moment. "There's a line that says, 'truth lies at the bottom of a well'."

"Hmm," Ramsay said. "More schoolboy stuff. That's from some ancient Greek philosopher, I think."

"You still think children wrote these?" Anne asked.

"Or people who weren't adept at these kinds of riddles,"

Ramsay replied. "Normally, treasure, or scavenger, hunt clues are riddles set in a rhyme or a clever play on words. These are nothing like that."

"I see what you mean," Anne agreed. Then she smiled. "Which means they are by the robbers, who wouldn't be scholarly people at all, just your average man."

Ramsay laughed. "I hope you're right. However, in my career I met some brilliant people who were criminals."

Anne shrugged. "Well, these weren't that kind of criminal. Why did they do this elaborate game, do you think?"

"I've thought about that and here's how I see it," Ramsay replied. "The gang consisted of three or four individuals. If the loot was brought back here to be hidden until the hunt died down, it might have been split into three or four equal packages and each gang member would get the clues he needed to find his share if anything happened to the person who hid the packages."

"And something did happen," Anne said, nodding. "The man who hid the packages was killed in a motor accident."

Ramsay nodded, and added, "And unfortunately for them, before he'd finished the clues and handed them out."

"Which is why they don't make a lot of sense," Anne said. "They weren't finished."

Ramsay nodded. "Exactly. Now I don't know that's what really happened, but it's the theory I'm working on right now."

"So, not only is the landscape the clues refer to changed out of all recognition, but the clues are no good anyway," Anne said, groaning. "The developer's bulldozers will likely destroy all the packages but the one we found."

Ramsay smiled. "I fear so. Still, there is hope. We have clues, we have witnesses, and we have maps. There's still time to find the jewels before the bulldozers arrive."

14

THE MAID

THEY WORKED FOR A SHORT TIME, before Anne straightened, stretched out her back and shoulder, and asked, "As our hired sleuth, what should we do next?"

"Learn more about Oscar Geary," Ramsay replied. "We learned that Morris Saunders was focused on the icehouse, and we got a package of clues from there. Maybe, Geary was focused on somewhere that will provide similar results."

"The line about the well came from the icehouse pages," Anne said. "Maybe the next cache of jewels is in the well. I want to try there."

"We can do that when Ben and Isaac take this load away," Ramsay replied. "And at lunch visit our friend Terry for more about Geary."

When the van was loaded, and Ben and Isaac had driven it out of the yard, Anne locked the garage doors and they set off to find the well, map in hand. They soon came to the small uphill behind the Hall, sheltering it from the north winds, and began searching back and forth across the face of the incline, Ramsay walking out westward and Anne eastward before returning to the center.

"Anything?" Anne asked, after thirty minutes of pushing her way through briars and bushes had revealed nothing on the eastward side.

Ramsay shook his head, saying, "Not yet but we aren't even halfway yet."

"I've never heard of a well on a hill," Anne grumbled, as they rested a moment.

Ramsay gave her a quizzical look. "Yes, you have," he said. "Jack and Jill went up the hill to fetch a pail of water. You must remember that."

Anne laughed. "I do. Well, we're Jack and Jill and I don't want us to 'fall down' and 'break our crowns' so be careful because it's beginning to get steeper."

They set off again, and Ramsay hadn't gone more than fifty yards when he came across a slab of cemented stones with a rusted metal cover in the center. It was locked. The whole area was bare of weeds, with only mosses growing on it.

"Here," he called, and Anne was soon at his side.

"Isaac will easily open that," she said.

Ramsay agreed but cautioned. "If Isaac can easily open it, others will have done so before now. This was hard to find but I'm sure every treasure hunter of the fifties found and searched it thoroughly."

"We said that about the icehouse, remember?"

Ramsay grinned. "I'm just saying don't get too excited."

They returned to the garage and began sorting the last pieces into the 'keep' and 'discard' piles ready for the return of the truck.

"I know who might help us learn more about Oscar Geary," Anne cried. "Old Alice Greystoke."

"And who is Alice?" Ramsay asked.

"Like Ned, she worked at the Hall all her life," Anne

explained. "She's even older and dottier than Ned, which is why I'd forgotten about her."

"She still lives nearby?"

Anne nodded. "In the old Almshouses. She was given one years ago by the Demerlays and has lived there ever since."

"All good information," Ramsay replied, smiling, "but I repeat, nearby?"

Anne laughed. "Beside the church. We can go there at lunch time."

"Not if we're opening the well at lunch time," Ramsay reminded her. "Maybe after we finish here."

Their conversation was halted by someone calling from the front of the Hall.

"It's Nigel," Anne told Ramsay, looking concerned. "Why is he suddenly back?"

"Maybe he thinks they threw some old books in the garage," Ramsay replied, smiling.

"Round here," Anne shouted, as hard as she could. It was obviously enough because, in a few minutes, Nigel appeared around the corner of the building.

"I hear you found a car," he said, by way of greeting.

"Are you interested in cars too?" Anne asked, as Nigel peered into the garage and the Jaguar, which now Isaac had cleaned and polished, looked immaculate.

"I wanted one of those so badly when I was young," Nigel said, staring at it in awe. He held a box camera in his hands and clicked photos as he walked around the car.

"Apparently every little boy did," Anne retorted.

Nigel nodded. "It's true. Does it run?"

"We don't know," Ramsay said. "Isaac is going to take it to his shop and strip it down to see if it will run. How did you hear of it?"

"Word gets around," Nigel replied vaguely. "You can't keep secrets in a village, you know."

"You didn't already know there was a car in here, did you?" Ramsay asked.

Nigel shook his head. "The whole place has been locked and boarded up since the last tenant left. I don't believe anyone has been in here since then."

"There's been a homeless man living in the garage for some time now," Anne said. "Even he didn't seem to find it. The junk they'd piled in here was worse than in the cellars. We only began to see it when we shifted all the stuff near the doors."

"It's infuriating," Nigel told them. "A car like that abandoned here and no one with the knowledge to bring it to light."

"Isn't that how you make your living?" Ramsay asked. "Buying what people think is junk and selling it at its true price?'

Nigel laughed. "Of course. That's what makes this so upsetting. It, sitting right here, and nobody telling me about it."

"Have any of the books turned out to be worth their weight in gold?" Anne asked, trying to break the fixed stare that Nigel was continuing to bestow on the car.

Nigel came out of his trance. "Not gold but one is definitely silver."

"Are any of them about the Hall?" Ramsay asked.

"One was," Nigel replied. "A historian in Victorian times wrote a book about the Hall. I didn't keep it because no one would be interested now. Even the family left it behind."

"It might tell us where to find the Civil War treasure," Ramsay said, chuckling.

"I'm sure the historian wouldn't have wasted time on

anything as silly as that," Nigel said, "except maybe to make the book more interesting. It's in Anne's warehouse, if you want to read it."

"We should," Anne said. "It might help explain the mysterious tunnels."

"There's no mystery about the tunnels," Nigel said. "There was one to the chapel and one to the icehouse, which I find odd."

"Why odd," Ramsay asked.

"Because who cares if the servants have to walk out in the rain or snow to get ice?" Nigel said. "I've never heard of anyone going to that much trouble."

"I see what you mean," Ramsay agreed, nodding. "Maybe we should look in there in case there are more treasures hidden there."

"Treasures?" Nigel asked.

Ramsay laughed and pointed to the pile of discarded junk they'd removed from the garage.

"Oh, I see," Nigel said, smiling.

He seems relieved, Ramsay thought. "Maybe that's where the Civil War treasure is hiding," Ramsay continued.

Nigel shook his head. "Those treasure hunters knew all about the tunnels. If there was treasure there, they'll have taken it."

"Two of them did disappear quickly," Anne said, "as we've discovered."

"There's nothing in the car, I suppose," Nigel asked, changing the subject.

"Nothing," Anne replied. "Not even a 1950s road map book."

Nigel nodded. "Well, when you've decided what to do with the car, let me know. I'd be happy to take it off your hands."

"How kind," Anne replied. "We'll certainly keep you in mind. We think auctioning it will bring us the best price."

"It may," Nigel said, as he turned to leave, "however, there are costs, even if an auction house does the work. I could save all that with a reasonable price." He didn't wait for an answer and walked off with a cheery wave.

"What do we make of that?" Anne asked Ramsay.

"We need security on this car," Ramsay replied. "We can't leave it here alone." As he was speaking, the van with Ben and Isaac pulled into the yard, reversed and drew up to the doors. The two men jumped out, and Isaac asked, "What was that fat waster doing here?"

Anne was about to reply that Nigel wasn't really 'fat', he just looked it beside her two workers, when Ramsay replied to Isaac, "He was here after your car."

"He can't have it," Isaac growled. "I'd take it to pieces and throw the pieces in the sea rather than let him have it."

"We need someone to stay with it until we can move it," Anne said. "Any ideas?"

"Yes," Isaac said, "me. And if he comes looking for it, he'll leave in an ambulance."

"I get the sense there's something between you and him, Isaac?" Ramsay asked.

"He robbed my old mam of the one decent thing she had," Isaac replied. "Gave her a pound for it and next thing we see, it's on sale for fifty pounds."

"He's a sharp one, all right," Anne told Ramsay. "The morals of a weasel, though I suspect weasels would be outraged to hear me say that."

Ramsay shrugged. "The antiques business has always been a sewer. But we have a more interesting job for Ben and Isaac. The well." He explained what they'd deciphered and how effectively the well they found was sealed. "By the way," he continued, "did either of you mention the Jaguar to anyone?"

Isaac retrieved a crowbar from his toolbox in the van and, after locking the garage and backing the van against the doors, they set off for the well.

"Did you?" Ramsay asked again.

"Of course not," Ben replied, as he and Isaac shared disbelieving glances. "You don't get far in this business telling the world what you've found in a house clearance. There'd be nothing left when it came time to sell the stuff."

"We didn't either," Ramsay replied. "He's been watching us closely, it seems."

They arrived at the well, and it took no more than a minute for Isaac to break the lock and lever open the cover. *I don't fancy Nigel's chances if he comes after the car when Isaac is on guard*, Ramsay thought, grimacing.

Ramsay and Anne shone their flashlights down into the well and saw nothing but the reflection of light beams on water, yards below the surface.

"We need your harness again, Isaac," Ramsay said, "and a frame to hold steady the rope as I go down."

Isaac unclipped a tape measure from his belt and measured the size of the hole. "We'll close this up and put a boulder on top to keep it secure tonight. I'll make up a frame and pulley block for tomorrow. You can't go down there with just us holding a rope."

Looking down the narrow tube going on into the darkness, Ramsay agreed. "I only hope it's worth it."

After closing and securing the lid, they returned to work in the garage. Thanks to the work Ramsay and Anne had done earlier, they were finished quickly and moved to the second garage.

"Not too bad," Ben said. "Have you looked in the third?"

Anne opened this last one and groaned. "It's worse than the first."

Ben shrugged. "We can empty the second today and start on this in the morning. We still have days to go."

Ben was right. The pieces in the second garage were soon sorted into the 'take' and 'leave' piles and the van filled. As the two men prepared to leave, Isaac said, "Don't leave until I get back, missus. I'll be quick." He jumped into the van, and they were gone.

Ramsay laughed. "Well, that's us told. Why don't we lock up the garages and go find that tunnel to the icehouse. Provided we don't leave the premises, Isaac can't be too mad at us."

The tunnel led from an underground pantry below the kitchen and, like the one to the chapel, was filled with earth part way along its length. "I don't remember seeing a door to this tunnel in the icehouse, do you?" Anne asked, as they returned to the kitchen. "I think we missed something there."

"How could we?" Ramsay said, puzzled. "We examined the wall all around the room and the floor too."

"Maybe this doesn't go to the icehouse," Anne suggested.

"It has to, there's nothing else out that way," Ramsay replied. Before he could continue, they heard the van returning.

"I hope Isaac has brought food and warm clothes for the night," Anne said, as they hurried out to the garages to meet him. "Otherwise, he's a long cold night ahead of him guarding that car."

"If he hasn't, I can bring some when we leave here," Ramsay told her.

"He's my employee," Anne said. "We'll both come back. After we've talked to Alice."

Isaac hadn't stopped for anything, so they explained their plans and set out for the almshouses and Alice.

Alice was a small, sprightly woman despite her ninety-one years, as she informed Ramsay when Anne introduced them.

Anne explained the reason for their visit and when Alice appeared to have taken it in, asked her if she could give them any information about those unsettled times at the Hall in the mid-nineteen-fifties.

"I blame it on the war," Alice replied. "The old families having to sell or rent to 'Flash-Harrys' who were no better than guttersnipes."

Anne smiled. "It must have been painful for you, serving such people after an old family like the Demerlays."

"It was more than painful," Alice replied. "What was worse, they dragged young master Jeremy down to their level. He'd gone to school with the son of these tenants. One bad apple ruins the barrel, they say, and it was never truer than what happened."

"You mean Jeremy's death?" Ramsay asked.

Alice frowned. "*Master* Jeremy never drank much until they plied him with it, day and night, when he stayed with them. Him staying with them, what an outrage! They were entertaining him in his own house -- and laughing at him behind his back." Her anger grew hotter, the longer she spoke.

"Were you there in the days before Jeremy died?" Anne asked.

Alice nodded. Her eyes were bright with tears. "He'd been staying with them for a week or so and growing wilder every day."

"Was something happening that was upsetting him?" Ramsay asked.

"I couldn't say, sir," Alice replied. "He was nervous the day he arrived. He hardly spoke to me at all and that wasn't like him. Then he stayed in his room with the son. I could have murdered that boy any time, him and his father."

"He stayed in his room for the rest of the visit?" Anne asked.

Alice shook her head. "Only for a day or so. He was so excited, I thought he wasn't well. Then, only days later, he drove his car into the railway bridge just outside the west gate. I blame myself for not seeing how unhappy he was." She began to sob, and Anne moved to sit beside and hug her.

Ramsay waited until Alice began drying her tears with her handkerchief, then asked, "You say 'he drove *his* car' into the bridge but there's a red Jaguar in the garage at the Hall we've been told was his car."

"The one he crashed was a new one bought for his birthday," Alice explained. "That's why they think he crashed. He always drove like a race car driver and, because it was new to him, the coroner decided it got away from him on the curve."

"Did you ever see him writing messages on scraps of paper?" Anne asked. "For a scavenger hunt or something like that?"

Alice shook her head. "Never. To be honest, he wasn't a great writer of any kind, or reader either. He thought both too dull."

"Were you there when the treasure hunters came?" Ramsay asked.

"They were a rum lot, sir," Alice replied. "I liked them even less than I liked the tenants. To be honest, it was them that made me begin thinking I should leave the Hall."

"Do you remember a Morris Saunders?" Anne asked.

Alice shook her head.

"Oscar Geary?" Ramsay suggested.

"Him I do remember," Alice said. "He stayed at the Hall. Better than the others, he was, more polite, like."

"Do you remember him leaving?" Anne asked.

"I do. He was there in the evening and gone the next morning with all his things," Alice told them. "I can't say I blame him. The others picked on him something rotten."

"You didn't hear why he left?" Ramsay asked.

Alice frowned in concentration. "The father, I can't remember the name, I've blotted them out of my mind. Anyway, the man of the house said Geary had decided they were on a wild goose chase, and he, the head of the household I mean, had driven Geary to the station for the first morning train." She looked uncertain as she said this.

"You don't think that was true?" Ramsay asked.

"That man never did anyone a good turn," Alice replied, "and the first train in those days wasn't so very early. I'm sure I would have heard the car go out."

"You didn't say this to them, of course." Anne said.

"I didn't. I was too frightened of them all by this time," Alice replied. "I was waiting to talk to Lord Demerlay about leaving, he often visited when master Jeremy was there, but he didn't come again until that family were gone. I think he blamed them for master Jeremy's death. I know I did."

Ramsay could understand why Alice blamed them. In his mind, the theory he'd been formulating seemed proved. "And when you spoke to Lord Demerlay, what did he have to say?"

Alice's expression became guarded. "He thanked me for trying to warn him about his tenants, which made me feel brave enough to say I wanted to retire."

"And that's when he let you have this house?" Anne guessed.

Alice nodded. "He said after my ordeal, his very words, it was the least he could do. The family pays me a pension and I have this house until I die."

"I agree with him," Ramsay said. "You do deserve it. Two people disappeared among those treasure hunters. That must have been frightening. Did you ever hear them talking about what they'd found or anything of the kind?"

"I tried not to listen," Alice said. "Their language wasn't what I was accustomed to in Demerlay Hall. They searched everywhere I think." Her expression lightened. "Even master Jeremy's room, would you believe?"

Ramsay would believe it. "You saw them?"

"Oh, no, sir. What I saw was everything in the room moved, when I came to pack his things for sending back to his parents," Alice said.

"Was anything taken?" Alice asked.

"Nothing I could see," Alice replied. "Of course, there may have been things I didn't know of."

Ramsay asked, "Has anything occurred to you in the years since that time that you now think strange?'

"It was *all* strange, sir," Alice replied. "The talk of treasure and then the structural engineers saying there was subsidence under the Hall, which there never was. The two men disappearing. The Leeds family that arrived with talk of buying the Hall and left after master Jeremy's death. None of it makes sense to me, even now."

Ramsay smiled and nodded. "I imagine it didn't. Thank you for talking to us, Alice. You've cleared up a lot of things for me."

Alice beamed with pleasure. "It was a pleasure to talk about the old days, even though it brought back the bad times too." She walked slowly with them to her door and watched them leave.

Ramsay looked back to wave and saw she was puzzling something out. "What is it, Alice?"

"That Geary chap," she said. "He had a journal, one of those thick ones that had a clasp to fasten it. I saw it open one day. He was writing in it as I was doing his room. He was writing about the old well, which was odd because the well was shut up even before my time. It wasn't used and you couldn't get in."

"Then I expect it was just an idea he had," Ramsay told her. "Good night and thanks again."

As they drove away from Alice's home, Anne said, "Sounds like you were right about what happened back then. No wonder she was scared with two people gone like that."

Ramsay nodded. "From what Alice said, I'm guessing they killed Geary because they took away his things and gave a plausible story of him leaving. My friend Baldock should be able to discover if there's any record of Oscar Geary after his disappearance."

"And Saunders?" Anne asked, puzzled.

"I think we, or the developers, will find his bones," Ramsay replied. "I think he got into a hole or tunnel he couldn't escape from."

Anne grimaced. "You mean the two blocked tunnels?"

"Possibly," Ramsay said. "Or one we haven't found yet. The chapel crypt or the mill's cellar, for example."

"Do either of those exist?"

Ramsay laughed. "No idea. And they must wait until after we inspect the well tomorrow."

* * *

Gold, Greed, and a Hidden Hoard

ISAAC WAS ALREADY WORKING on the frame to carry the block and tackle, when Ramsay and Anne brought him food and blankets.

"Good to see you aren't wasting your time," Ramsay teased him, when they entered the garage. "We thought you might already be asleep."

Isaac grinned. "I look after my own," he said. "And I regard that car as my own. I have my toolbox and a pile of useless wood, what more could I want to fill the night?"

Anne placed the blankets on the car and asked, "Did you ever hear of the chapel or mill having cellars?"

"To be honest, missus," Isaac replied. "I didn't know they had a chapel or mill here. Before my time."

"The two tunnels we found have piles of earth in them," Ramsay said. "Not full, just dumped through a hole in the roof and left, I'd guess. How would you move them quickly?"

"Water," Isaac said. "Something like a firehose pumped down the hole in the roof, provided the tunnels aren't blocked in some way."

"We can't hire the local fire station for the job," Anne said. "Anyway, they were probably blocked before the treasure hunters arrived."

Ramsay nodded. "Probably. Thanks, Isaac. Anything else you need?"

"Put your weight on the frame," Isaac said, gesturing to Ramsay. "Let's see if it's going to hold you."

Ramsay pressed down on the crossbar with both hands, lifting himself off the ground when it felt safe.

"Sit on it," Isaac ordered.

Warily, Ramsay did as he was asked, slowly increasing his weight on the bar until he was able to lift his feet off the ground.

"Good," Isaac said, as Ramsay stepped off. "I'll add some more strength and then make you a chair to sit in. It'll be easier to search that way."

Leaving Isaac the door key, Anne and Ramsay left him to spend the night with his car and his tools.

"I'm not going to be able to sell that car, am I?" Anne said, chuckling, as they drove away.

"To be honest," Ramsay replied. "It would be better in the hands of a loving owner than some rich man who collects them just to look at."

15

THE CRYPT

THE FOLLOWING morning was cold and wet, a steady rain poured down soaking everything and leaving puddles in all the low ground.

"I shouldn't go into the well today, Mister Ramsay," Ben said, as they stared out from the garage at the water running down the courtyard. "It'll be too dangerous."

Ramsay nodded. He'd come to that conclusion himself. "Ben, did you ever hear of a crypt under the chapel?"

Ben thought a moment. "My father told me there were coffins brought out of the chapel before it were pulled down. They'd likely be in a crypt, wouldn't they."

"They would," Ramsay replied, hope soaring in his heart. "You folks work here. I'm going to find a way down into it." He pulled his raincoat tighter around himself and said, "Coming, Bracken?"

Bracken was eyeing the rain dubiously. He was always pleased to follow his friend, but this jaunt didn't look at all pleasant. However, when Ramsay walked out into the rain and across the courtyard, Bracken reluctantly followed.

They pushed through the overgrown shrubs, which

added even more water to Ramsay's sodden coat and Bracken's fur, until they reached the bare space that Ramsay knew had once been the floor of the chapel.

"Last time it rained," Ramsay told Bracken, "You found that biscuit box. See what you can find this time."

It took Bracken no time at all. He ran straight to the place he could hear water spilling down into the earth and barked at Ramsay, who was as usual looking in all the wrong places.

Ramsay arrived at Bracken's side and whistled. "I knew you were the man for the job." Over the years, water had cut a channel down the side of the old floor. Grass and weeds covered it from casual observation but in the rain, they were pushed aside, and it was laid bare.

"Can Isaac open that to man-size, do you think?" Ramsay asked Bracken. Then he noticed Bracken was shivering. "Time for us to get dry, my friend. We've done a good morning's work."

They ran back to the garage and using the blankets they'd brought Isaac the previous night, toweled themselves dry. Ramsay told the others what they discovered and asked for ideas on how to get through the gap.

Isaac laughed. "If it's a gap in concrete, we need serious equipment. Did you notice?"

Ramsay admitted he hadn't thought of that.

"We'll finish loading the van and maybe we can look at it before we leave for the auction rooms," Ben said. "That way, we can pick up anything we need before we return."

The rain had eased off by the time the van was loaded and the whole group ran quickly to the site of the old chapel to stare at the hole in the ground, now drying. Ben pulled the grass and weeds away to reveal old, crumbling bricks.

"No problem," Isaac said. "A pickaxe will soon shift them."

They returned to the van and Isaac asked anxiously, "You two won't leave here before I get back, will you?"

Ramsay replied, "Cross my heart and hope to die if we do," which seemed to be the right response because Isaac nodded and jumped into the van and drove off.

"Cross my heart and hope to die," Anne exclaimed, laughing. "Are we in a Boy's Own comic book now?"

"It feels like it to me," Ramsay replied, and a sudden pain struck his heart as he realized why he felt as he did. He'd read a story just like this to his sons at bedtime all those years ago, before they were killed.

"Are you alright?" Anne asked, seeing his face turn white.

"I'm fine," Ramsay replied. "Someone walked over my grave, that's all. Now, we should carry on sorting that garage or Ben and Isaac will be cross with us when they get back."

They worked steadily while Bracken and Rex enjoyed chasing the last few rodents from the premises. With most of the rubbish removed, the old stables were beginning to look liveable again.

"There was nothing in your coded messages that mentioned stables or garages, was there?" Ramsay asked, when he saw Anne resting on an old desk that was missing a leg.

"Nothing," Anne said. "Anyway, this would be too close to the package we found in the basement don't you think?"

"I wondered if all the packages might not be around the Hall," Ramsay replied, straightening up to stretch. "The clues may have been spread around the grounds, but the actual jewels might have been kept where they would be safest."

Anne stood and turned to examine the desk. It was a roll top affair with drawers down each side of the place where a person's legs would be when sitting at it. A common enough design. She'd already mentally marked it for the dump because, while well-made and attractive in its own way, it was factory-made and therefore not interesting to collectors.

She tugged at the roll-top, but it didn't move. "Another job for the boys' toolbox," she said to Ramsay. The drawers opened and were stuffed full of papers that had long been used as nesting by mice.

Ramsay came to look at the desk. He pulled the papers out of the drawers to see if any were still legible. They were but in so many pieces it would be a life's work to re-assemble them. He too tugged at the top and found it immovable. He took out his penknife and slid the blade under the edge and pressed hard against the latch. The blade bent and threatened to break so he stopped.

"As you say, another thing for our friends to open," he agreed.

On Ben and Isaac's return, the desk was levered open immediately by Ben while Isaac went off to work on the chapel crypt wall.

As with the drawers, the desktop was stuffed with papers, but this time mice had failed to get inside, and the words were readable.

Ramsay and Anne shuffled through the pages hoping for more coded messages.

"Anything?" Anne asked Ramsay, as Ben walked off to help Isaac.

"Not yet," Ramsay replied. "Still, I think we should take them with us and study them at home tonight."

Anne agreed. She took the handful that Ramsay was reading, scooped up the remainder from the desk and carried them out to Ramsay's car, dumping them in the backseat.

"And don't you two make a mess of them when we drive home," she told Bracken and Rex, who'd come out to see what she was doing. Anne locked the garage door and the whole group made their way to the chapel, where Isaac had opened a hole big enough for an adult to enter.

Inside the crypt empty shelves and water on the floor were all that could be seen in the dim light from the opening. Ramsay shone his torch inside, examining the walls for possible hiding places.

"I'm going to go in," he told the others. "I can't see clearly enough from here."

"You don't know how deep the water is," Ben pointed out. "Best wait to let it dry out."

"It could rain again," Ramsay protested. "I'll wear the harness, and you can hold the rope up here. If there's a deep spot, you can pull me out."

The ever-willing Isaac ran off and returned moments later with the harness and rope they'd used yesterday.

Ramsay, barefoot and pantlegs rolled to his knees, was soon being lowered into the crypt and he began working his way around the walls, as far as the rope would allow him. The smell in the crypt was nauseating. Years of dead creatures and rotting vegetation combined to fill the room with a gas that made him ill and soon fainting. He called to them to pull him up and was soon back into the fresh air, where he gasped and reeled.

"We have to let the crypt clear before we go back in," Ramsay said, when he could speak again.

"The well will be the same," Anne added, agreeing.

Ramsay climbed to his feet, dusted himself down, unfastened the harness, and said, "Back to the real work then."

When the van was carrying the next load of furnishings off to the warehouse, Ramsay and Anne made their way back to the icehouse. Once inside, they returned to their inspection of the walls, where once again they found no evidence of the tunnel.

"It's here somewhere," Ramsay said, "or that tunnel from the kitchen pantry is a nonsense."

"I don't see where, do you?" Anne asked.

Ramsay considered the icehouse and its orientation to the Hall. When he had fixed it in his mind, he walked to the wall where, in his mind, the tunnel should be and looked again.

"I think the entrance was bricked up before the tunnel was filled with soil," Ramsay said, as Anne joined him. "See here," he pointed to where the bricks seemed different to their neighbors.

Unconvinced, Anne replied, "We will see similar places around the walls, if the icehouse walls were repaired over the years."

"Maybe," Ramsay agreed, "and the grime and mold covering it all doesn't help We need Isaac's pickaxe."

"He's going to want a separate contract for all this extra work he's doing for me," Anne grumbled.

Ramsay laughed. "We'll just rent the pickaxe. That'll keep the costs down." Before he could say more, Bracken and Rex, who were hovering near the entrance began barking and running.

Ramsay and Anne chased after but once outside could see neither dogs nor their quarry. Bracken barking told Ramsay where they were and the two set off in pursuit. The chase ended at the old estate wall, which here was still standing high enough to be a barrier to the two dogs, but not it seemed to who they were chasing. Ramsay clambered up the wall to see a heavy-set man running through the trees toward the road.

"Well," Anne asked.

Ramsay frowned. "I could only see him from behind. He looked like Nigel, only I don't think it was Nigel."

"I've never trusted Nigel and this kind of sneakiness is well within his scope I'd say," Anne told him.

Ramsay grimaced. "Like I said, I can't be sure. Nigel's the one person we know is interested in what's going on here and who is, well 'portly' as they say."

"That's good enough for me," Anne retorted. "I say we have the police investigate Nigel for the attack on me."

"We already told them about the attack and who it might have been," Ramsay said. "Nothing I saw today adds anything to it being Nigel."

They returned to the icehouse, closed it, and returned to the Hall to await the return of Ben and Isaac.

"I'm going to measure the distance from the pantry to the blockage and the same for the Priest hole to the blockage," Ramsay told Anne. "Then walk the same distance on the ground to see how big these blockages are."

As they made their way to the first tunnel entrance, Anne said, "You know when this last garage is empty, my contract is finished. There are no other buildings for me to clear. The crypt, tunnels, and any cellar below the mill, weren't included."

"I know," Ramsay agreed, "but the developer doesn't know you're finished. Don't tell him and we'll have the last few days for just treasure hunting."

Anne shook her head. "You can. I must get the pieces I've selected appraised, repaired, and ready for sale. And everything else, carted off to the dump."

"You do that, and I'll continue searching," Ramsay

agreed, as they reached the start of the first tunnel. "Now, quiet while I count steps."

Ben and Isaac still hadn't returned when they'd recorded the distance to the blockage in both tunnels, so they counted the steps over the ground.

"There isn't much soil down there on either of them," Ramsay said, as he noted the steps in his book. "Just a few wheelbarrow loads, I'd say. This was done on the cheap." He examined the ground between his estimate of where the blockage began and where he thought the icehouse wall would be. His search was soon rewarded. "Here's where they poured it into the tunnel," he said to Anne, pointing to a sunken pit covered with vegetation. "This is dangerous. After heavy rain, I can imagine a man falling through that and into the mud below."

"You think Saunders?" Anne asked.

Ramsay shook his head. "I think the earth would have been firmer when he was searching. I just mean someone walking this way today."

They heard the van returning and set off for the Hall, where the whole crew continued clearing the last garage until they were all too tired to continue. Ramsay drove Anne and Rex home, after sharing the newly found papers between himself and Anne, before returning to his own home, where he phoned Inspector Baldock.

Baldock groaned. "You want to know about your two missing treasure hunters, I assume?"

"I do," Ramsay replied, smiling to himself. His conversations with Baldock were always drawn-out affairs. He suspected Baldock had no other friends.

"Morris Saunders was ex-army, ex-police, and a private investigator," Baldock said. "He was on the trail of those missing jewels we discussed last time. There was a search at the time, but no body was found. He either found the loot and ran for it under a false name or he was killed, murdered likely. Certainly, he doesn't appear in the tax records after then."

"That's the local gossip," Ramsay said. "I've come to the conclusion he died in an accident and his body was just never found."

"Whatever happened to him, I don't care," Baldock retorted. "It's over ten years ago and not my case. Do you want to hear about Oscar?"

"Of course," Ramsay replied, chuckling.

"There was no search for Oscar Geary because there was no suggestion of foul play. He left and that was that. However, I had the lads check the files and there's no record of him from that time. I think you can assume he was murdered."

"That confirms my suspicion about him too," Ramsay said. "Now there's a murder you could clear up and improve your local standing."

Baldock snorted derisively. "Nobody today has heard of the man and nor do they care what happened to him. If you want to keep getting help here, you'd better come up with something current."

"There's the attack on Anne Watson," Ramsay reminded him. "That was attempted murder."

"That was an assault, and the local bobby is looking into it," Baldock responded. "Something for the investigation branch is what I'm looking for."

"When we find the jewels," Ramsay said, "you can clear that up."

"Will any of the people involved be alive?" Baldock asked. "The last two names you gave me aren't."

Ramsay had to admit, he also wondered if those

involved in the robbery would be alive. After all, Jeremy Demerlay wasn't.

"It's not so long ago," Ramsay replied. "Some will be alive. We just have to find the jewels and then we'll find the crooks."

At this, Baldock laughed. "Your persistence is only exceeded by your optimism, Ramsay. Admirable qualities, I'm sure, but ones likely to lead to misery in the end. Your misery, I can live with; mine, I won't."

"Did your men learn anything about Oscar Geary?" Ramsay interjected as he sensed Baldock was about to hang up. "Did he have a family? What was his occupation? Anything that might help understand why he was murdered, if he was murdered?"

Baldock sighed dramatically, and replied, "He was a single man, worked as a clerk until he was laid off some weeks before, and a founder member of something called the Northern England Psychic Research Institute, who have since gone dormant, apparently."

Ramsay laughed. "A ghost hunter, not a treasure hunter. That explains his preference for the well." He quickly explained to Baldock about the noisy ghost in the well.

"Why are you wasting police time with this nonsense?" Baldock asked and hung up the phone.

Ramsay went into his living room, poured a glass of his favourite whisky, Glenfiddich, and began reading through the new papers they'd found.

16

THE WELL

BRACKEN AND RAMSAY stepped outside next morning to one of those glorious warm, almost summer, days that the north sometimes gets late into autumn. As he sipped his tea, and Bracken investigated the scents of their nightly visitors, Ramsay considered his day ahead. Rubber boots were going to be a requirement at the very least. There'd been no rain overnight so the water in the crypt and well should have abated enough for a proper search in each.

Bracken began searching furiously in the blackcurrant bushes at the foot of the garden so, calling for Bracken to stop, Ramsay hurried across the lawn to where his friend was intensely digging. Bracken was too apt to eat things he shouldn't, Ramsay knew, and he needed to stop that before the dog poisoned himself someday.

He took hold of Bracken's collar and pulled him back. "What is it, you silly dog?" Ramsay asked. Bracken remained fixated on whatever it was in the tangle of branches that he desired but couldn't reach. Peering through the stems, Ramsay could see what looked like the fur of a small creature and scolded Bracken. "It's dead, Bracken, and you don't know why so you don't eat it. Do you understand?"

Bracken, however, was beyond rational thinking in this matter and continued straining against the collar. Ramsay tugged harder and Bracken thrust himself even more urgently at the dead animal. Realizing his friend wasn't going to stop until the animal was out of reach, Ramsay put down his mug of tea and thrust his hand into the bushes. The dead animal felt cold and unpleasant in his hand, but he grasped and drew it out, sending Bracken into wild ecstasy.

Ramsay examined what he held and found it wasn't an animal at all, but the skin of an animal wrapped around a piece of what looked like chicken. He grimaced in disgust and was about to throw it into the field beyond when he stopped. This may well be meant to poison Bracken. He returned to the house holding the baited skin and wrapped it in waxed paper.

"We're taking this to my friendly chemist in Scarborough, Bracken," Ramsay told his dog. "This may have been meant for you and there may be others around the village. In a way I almost hope it's just some crank who hates dogs." He placed the wrapped meat in a paper bag and placed it well out of Bracken's reach.

"I'll rescue my mug, get ready, and we'll go," he told Bracken. "After I've phoned Anne and told her I'm going to be late."

It wasn't until he was putting on his jacket and hat preparing to set out, that he noticed the papers on his dining table were gone. For a moment, he thought he'd tidied them away before he remembered he hadn't.

"Someone took quite a chance there, Bracken," Ramsay said, locking up as he left the house. "They expected us to go on our morning walk, I imagine." He paused, as the idea they also expected Bracken to be taken ill while on that morning walk came into his head. "They know our morning routine, whoever they are," he concluded, slamming the car door and starting the engine. *This is the second time they've targeted me away from the Hall*, he thought as he backed out of the drive onto the road.

His friend the chemist, like Baldock wasn't pleased to see him. "I have a business to run," he complained when Ramsay handed him the bag and its contents.

"I think it will be drugged," Ramsay explained, ignoring the man's grumbling, "either to kill or tranquillize a dog. Can you tell me which and where someone might get it?"

"I don't have a laboratory here, you know," his friend complained. "Just a small compounding shop. You need Scotland Yard or something to do these things."

"It's the kind of challenge a professional man like you will relish," Ramsay replied. "I'm sure you're bored handing out aspirins to malingerers. As soon as you can, Jim. Thanks." He hurried out of the store before his friend could say no.

"I may have to start giving him a retainer, Bracken," Ramsay said, as they drove out of Scarborough and back to the Hall. "If the Agency continues getting these tricky cases, having a team of experts helping with the technical stuff will become important."

Ben had picked up Anne on his way to the Hall and they were both working with Isaac, loading the van, when Ramsay arrived. Bracken joined his friend Rex to go hunting rabbits and Ramsay joined the others in clearing the garage.

"Nice of you to join us," Anne said.

"I'm paid to investigate, not move furniture," Ramsay reminded her, and then told her of the morning's alarm.

"You've lost the papers?" Anne retorted. "That's the gist of it."

"There wasn't anything beyond long ago bills and invoices in what I had," Ramsay replied. "What about yours"

"The same," Anne said. "Not worth carrying home, let alone reading."

Ramsay placed an ugly but whole ceramic dog ornament in the back of the van and addressed the group, "It's been dry since midday yesterday. I'm ready to try the crypt and the well. Who wants to help?"

Lugging furnishings had lost its allure it seemed, for they all did. They set out for the chapel first.

Inside, the floor was inches deep in clinging, oozing, mud but solid to his rubber-clad feet. The walls, however, unlike the icehouse and tunnels, had too many possible hiding places. The mortar had been washed out between almost all the bricks and, in Ramsay's view, made the structure unsafe. He was determined to be out of it the moment he knew there was nothing to be found. Unfortunately, the crypt was of a size that would take time to inspect so he was glad when he heard a heavy thud behind him and saw Isaac with a flashlight looking about himself.

"You start at that end, and I'll start here," Ramsay told him. "We can both finish at the entrance."

"The shelves make it awkward," Isaac said, his voice echoing through the chamber.

"If there's anything hidden in the walls," Ramsay reminded him, "it would be where the person hiding it could easily reach. I shouldn't worry about the walls behind the stone shelves. There would have been coffins on them at the time, I think."

More time passed before Isaac called, "Got it."

After marking where he'd reached, Ramsay hurried off

to Isaac's side. It was another metal box like the last only much smaller.

"Where was it?" Ramsay asked, examining the empty shelves where coffins had once been placed.

Isaac asked, "Don't you see it?"

Ramsay shone his flashlight across the two shelves in front of him and said, "I don't see anything."

"Here," Isaac said, stooping down and lighting the underside of the shelf where a square hole could be seen partially obscured by the thick support on which the shelf rested. "Whoever hid the box knew this slab of limestone had a fault in it. They chiseled out enough to hide things inside."

"But it would fall out?" Ramsay objected.

Isaac lifted a thin wooden cover and fitted it to the hole. "The hole goes back about halfway across the support so the box sat on that. My guess is Jeremy found this fault as a youngster and made it big enough to hide things from his older brother. All children hide things. Later, when he had this to hide, he plastered over the cover to make it even more invisible."

"What made you look under the shelf?" Ramsay asked.

Isaac pointed to the lower shelf. "The plaster has grown wet and has fallen away. As you see, it looks nothing like the other dust laying on the shelf."

"I'm going to start again," Ramsay said. "I might have missed a hiding place just like this."

"I doubt it," Isaac said. "These shelves are solid stone. It's unlikely two would have faults like this."

Ramsay shook his head. "If one did, others could. Anyway, hand it up to Anne," Ramsay told Isaac. "We should finish our inspection to be sure there's nothing else."

When they met at the entrance with nothing more

found, Ramsay was hauled up and out by Ben and Anne before the rope was thrown for Isaac, who nimbly swarmed up it, grinning. "Like being back in the army," he said.

The box had been left closed until they were all assembled. Ben deftly opened it by banging the edge of its lid on the corner of an exposed brick.

Isaac groaned. "All that for papers."

Ramsay could understand Isaac's frustration. He too was covered in foul-smelling slime and all he had to show for it was two pages from an old book. But they did have two more coded sentences!

"Does ought of this mean anything to you two?" Ben asked, looking at Anne and Ramsay.

"We're decoding the gibberish you see here," Anne said, pointing to the symbols along the bottom of the sheets, "but we haven't got it all yet and the ones we have decoded aren't helpful."

"Maybe the well will make everything clear," Ramsay said, hoping Isaac's disappointment wouldn't prevent him helping there.

Isaac laughed. "You're on your own down there," he said. "There isn't room for two of us."

They tested the frame and chair in the garage before hauling it up the slope to the well. Even though the chair had passed its strength test in the garage, Ramsay couldn't help but feel queasy as they lowered him down into the darkness. He was also wearing the safety harness and rope as a second line of defense.

As his feet touched the water, which was still higher than it had been when they'd first looked down the shaft, he called on them to stop lowering. Looking up, he grinned at the sight that met his eyes. A pale circle of light with the faces of Anne, Rex, Ben, Isaac, and Bracken peering down anxiously at him.

Methodically, he began inspecting the walls of the well. They were in much better condition than those of the crypt, he was relieved to find. Slowly, they raised him and at every stop, he swung the torch around the full circumference of the wall and signaled to lift again. The obvious answer, of course, was that whatever was placed here wasn't in the wall at all. It would have been lowered in and let fall to the bottom. No one would have willingly done what he was doing to loosen a brick or two and hide another box, before bricking it back up again. Nevertheless, he continued all the way to top without finding anything.

As he climbed off the chair, Ramsay had another thought. "Two ideas for us to consider," he told the others. "One, whatever it is, is at the bottom of the well and we need a hook to lift it out. And two, as at the icehouse, maybe it isn't *in* the well but *at* the well. We need a spade to dig around the outer edge."

"After lunch," Anne said. "You and Isaac need to go and change, and I'm starving."

* * *

RAMSAY WAS DRIVING BACK to the Hall, after bathing and changing his clothes, when he saw a large van turning out of the gate of Demerlay Hall. This puzzled him as it wasn't Ben and Isaac's van. It turned toward him, and he could see the three men in the cab, Nigel, Ned, and Terry. The van passed him, and he drove on, turning into the entrance of the Demerlay estate where he stopped, reversed, and set off in pursuit. Only when he was following the van did it occur to him that Anne and Ben may be injured or dead.

The van halted in the village center and Ramsay saw Terry and Ned jump out. The van set off again and, maintaining a distance that should keep him out of Nigel's sight, Ramsay followed. He had to hope Isaac would arrive at the Hall soon and get help, if Anne and Ben needed it. Nigel driving off with what was undoubtedly the Jaguar, was the best thing to happen in the investigation so far.

The van ponderously rolled through the narrow lanes onto the moors, heading in the direction of York, and Ramsay prayed he had enough fuel to last until the destination was reached. He hadn't anticipated this additional, and extended, journey.

At the outskirts of York, the van followed a lane that led to a leafy suburb with large houses. It slowed, Nigel wasn't sure of the address Ramsay guessed and they crept on another half mile before the van turned into a driveway of an older house with high walls and a substantial gate that swung closed behind the van.

Ramsay parked on a side street that gave him a view of the house and gates. Looking about, he saw a telephone box nearby and, collecting all the change in his pockets and the car, he hurried across the lane to phone Baldock.

It took some time before he was connected to the inspector. "What now?" Baldock demanded.

Ramsay explained quickly and Baldock growled, "I have no jurisdiction in York."

"I know. Phone someone in York and get them here," he read out the address. "And have someone go to Demerlay Hall, it's likely Anne and Ben may be injured."

"We have someone there already," Baldock replied. "Isaac phoned some time ago."

"Are Anne and Ben alright?" Ramsay asked.

"They were drugged, nothing worse. It was in their

flasks, probably in yours too, if you'd been there and not touring our beautiful Yorkshire countryside."

Ramsay ground his teeth and said, "We have him. He was probably the one who dislocated Anne's collarbone and he's the sort of fancy dresser who'd wear his old suit to do it."

Baldock laughed. "York have just confirmed they have cars on the way. You should see them soon. I told them to talk to you so be outside the gate when they arrive. Now buzz off."

"Buzz off?" Ramsay asked, incredulously.

"We've had a memo about being nice to the public," Baldock replied, chuckling.

Shaking his head in disbelief, Ramsay hung up and walked quickly to the gate, arriving only minutes before two police cars pulled up beside him.

"Mr. Ramsay?" A sergeant asked, winding down the window.

"That's me," Ramsay replied and, when asked to provide details of the crime they were about to stop, he explained.

The sergeant stepped out of the car and began deploying his men. "There's another team at the rear of the property," he told Ramsay. A crackling on the radio told them the other team was in position, and they began.

From the safety of his own vehicle, Ramsay watched Nigel and another man being led from the house to the police cars and a driver backing the van containing the precious Jaguar out onto the road. He followed the convoy to the police station and was able to give the people there more background to the case. He rather hoped he'd be allowed to stay but, after giving his statement, he was politely shown the door.

Back at Demerlay Hall, he found Isaac working on the

pile of selected furnishings and asked about their two friends.

"They've taken them to the cottage hospital," Isaac replied. "There were nought I could do so I came back here to move another load. When will I get my car back?"

Ramsay laughed. "It's the property of Watson's House Clearance company and it will be returned once it isn't needed any longer as evidence."

"They won't leave it outside, will they?"

Ramsay didn't know how to answer that. He suspected the police would indeed leave it in an outdoor pound. "I don't know," he said. "If I help load this van, will you help me dig around the well?"

Isaac shrugged. "Spades and shovels won't go through the roots of those gorse bushes. You need a mechanical shovel for that."

"Where could we get one?" Ramsay asked.

"Scarborough and it'll be too big for the job. It'd wreck any box the size of the others."

"Then how am I going to find the box by the well?" Ramsay asked.

"I'd try the hook on a rope first," Isaac replied. "Best rule out the well itself before tackling the ground up there."

"After all this time," Ramsay said. "What are the chances of the box being down there? Anyway, it would be a crazy place to hide papers. What if the box leaked."

"Whoever hid these things wasn't expecting them to be hidden long, I reckon. A few weeks at most. The papers may be no good but finding the box would save a lot of work for a lot of strong men."

"You have the rope," Ramsay said. "Do you have a hook?"

"I do," Isaac replied, grinning. "And a new lock to put on the cover. We can't leave that open for children to climb in."

With the van once again full and ready to roll, the two men set out for the well. Isaac with the rope coiled around his shoulder and Ramsay carrying an assortment of hooks and a shiny lock.

Cast after cast snagged nothing and they were on the brink of giving up when Ramsay, looking down the shaft said, "The water is very low now. I'm going down there to root around with my hands."

They brought the frame and seat Isaac had made, along with the safety harness, from the van and Ramsay was slowly lowered down into the darkness. He found holding his flashlight tricky while wearing the large rubber gloves Isaac had found for him and more than once, he almost dropped it. When he was at the water, he called on Isaac to stop. Sliding off the chair he felt for a bottom through the dark water. It was as he'd hoped. It hardly came to the ankles of his rubber boots, and he stepped down from the chair, his feet sinking into the murk on the floor of the well. It too wasn't as deep as he'd feared and he began casting about across the bottom with one hand, while grasping the torch tightly with the other. It didn't take long to find what he was looking for. He pulled the square metal box from the goo and shook it gently in the water to wash off the worst of the dirt.

Ramsay sat on the chair, perched the box on his lap and called for Isaac to start lifting him up. Out again in the bright sunshine, they examined the box and Ramsay tried to open it. It wouldn't move so he repeated Ben's method on the bricks of the well, and the top broke in half. Inside was remarkably dry and the papers were still readable. One was a hand sketched map of the grounds and the others more cryptic coded notes.

"I'm tired of our incompetent puzzler," Ramsay grumbled, as he read each sheet. "If this was *master* Jeremy, as I suspect, he's no credit to his school, no matter how much they paid for him to go there."

"He was generally liked in the village," Isaac told him. "I were only a bairn at the time, but the old people spoke well of him."

"They don't have to make sense of these hopeless messages he's left," Ramsay replied. "If it was him."

After locking the well, they returned to the garage, which, as Isaac said, looked depressing without the Jaguar.

"You'll get it back," Ramsay said. "Now, show me the way to the cottage hospital on our way to unloading the van."

17

STOLEN JAG

RAMSAY AND BRACKEN didn't have to visit the hospital because the two patients had already been sent home with orders to sleep it off and not drive until the next day. After they emptied the van, Ramsay drove to Anne's house to discover what happened.

"It's no use asking me," Anne grumbled, when she'd ushered them in, and Bracken and Rex were back resting in front of the fire. "Ben and I started our lunch the moment you two set off for home and next thing I knew was I was in an ambulance on my way to hospital."

"Baldock says it was a Mickey Finn in your Thermos flask of tea," Ramsay told her. "Our friends Nigel, Ned, and Terry must have dropped the drug into our flasks while we were at the well."

Anne considered. "They got in the same way the homeless man did, I expect. We should have boarded that up properly. Anyway, you got them?"

Ramsay nodded. "Well, the police did. I only helped. I'll phone Baldock tonight, when I get home."

"We need to interview them too," Anne said. "Why do

they believe the jewels are still buried on the estate, for instance. Everyone else gave up years ago."

"I'm sure they'll all get bail," Ramsay replied. "We can grill them then."

"And these are the new papers?" Anne asked, pointing to the pages Ramsay had in his hand.

Ramsay nodded. "They are and there's a map." He handed over the map.

Anne studied it carefully, moving the page back and forth. "My eyes are still a bit woozy."

"It seems to show four packages of one kind and four packages of a different kind," Ramsay said. "I'm guessing that means four lots of messages, and we've found three, and four packages of jewels, of which we've found one."

"Seems odd to give the location of all four packages to whoever finds this map," Anne said. "After all, the first one to find it could take the lot."

"I suspect it's another red herring, if I may borrow a phrase from mystery novels," Ramsay told her. "Our puzzling person still makes me think of children's stories. Still, we should dig at those locations just in case."

"When?"

"I'm going there with a spade the moment I leave here," Ramsay said.

"I'll get my coat. I can't dig, but I can supervise."

When they arrived at the Hall, they found only one of the three locations marked on the map where the ground was open enough for digging. Ramsay set to work, and he'd dug a wide hole a foot deep by the time the light was gone, and Anne was lighting the area with a flashlight.

"You were right," Anne said. "A joke by our mapmaker, it seems."

Ramsay nodded. He put on his jacket, picked up the spade and they returned to the car.

"Alice liked young Jeremy, and Isaac says the old people liked him too," Ramsay growled. "I don't."

"Is it possible that when he began doing this he'd come to his senses and realized what he'd allowed himself to be part of?" Anne asked. "These clues and the map were revenge, if you see what I mean."

"That would only work if he wasn't going to be around when they began searching," Ramsay replied. He paused, "which, of course, he wasn't."

Anne nodded. "Not an accident, suicide."

"If that's true," Ramsay said. "We shouldn't waste any more time on these *clues*."

"The necklace and earrings were here," Anne reminded him. "I think the others are too. Finding them will be a huge boost for my company. You don't know how 'hand-to-mouth' it's been since Dad died."

"What you have, the necklace and the car, must already be a good day's work for you all," Ramsay said.

Anne nodded. "It is, but the rest of that haul would be even better."

"You're not concerned someone will try to kill you again?"

"Now we know it was Nigel, I know he wasn't trying to kill me," Anne said. "And nor would Ned and Terry. No, I'm safe now and we still have three days to search the estate from one end to the other."

Ramsay shook his head. "We don't know it was Nigel, and I'm sure it wasn't Nigel who stole the papers from my home earlier today. I'll continue investigating until this new villain has been unmasked." He didn't feel kindly disposed toward people who threatened Bracken.

* * *

Baldock was happy to tell Ramsay all he knew about the arrest. His colleague in York had been waiting some time for an excuse to search that particular house and they'd found many 'items of interest'.

"I have some favors to call on now," Baldock said. "And that makes me a happy camper. What do you want to know?"

"First, has Nigel been bailed?" Ramsay asked. "I want to speak to him as well."

Baldock's voice returned to its usual tone. "He will be and if anything happens to him, I'll have you in mind as a suspect."

"I mean him no harm," Ramsay replied. "Though I hope he goes to prison for stealing that car. Poor Isaac is distraught."

"It's just a car," Baldock said, "and an old one at that."

"You have no soul," Ramsay told him. "Now, how did they steal the car?"

Baldock chuckled. "They watched you as you worked and learned your routine. They rented a furniture removal van, he often uses them in his business, and he saved up his sleeping pills for days to knock you all out."

"Me and Isaac going away must have seemed like the gods were smiling on them," Ramsay remarked.

Baldock grunted his agreement. "That's what he said, they couldn't believe their luck. They'd known about the window so getting inside and lacing your lunches with the Chloral Hydrate was easily done. They just had to wait for you all to come back to the garage for lunch."

"Isaac even moved the van away from the door for them when he went to wash and change," Ramsay interjected.

Baldock laughed. "If you'd been in on it, you couldn't have made it better. Anyway, when the coast was clear, one of them crept through the window, tied up the two sleeping beauties, opened the door, and they rolled, and winched, the car into the van. It was all over in fifteen minutes."

"All told, rather more," Ramsay said, "Because I was returning as they were leaving."

"Oh, they gave your two colleagues time to fall fast asleep," Baldock replied. "That was where the time went."

"Was there anything else?"

"Not really," Baldock said. "They're considering the legality of ownership of the car, but that won't get them far. It isn't theirs, even if a court decides it doesn't belong to Miss Watson's company."

"Did you ask about the attack on Anne Watson?" Ramsay continued. He'd suggested that to Baldock in the phone call that started the whole chain of events.

Baldock replied, "Yes and he denies hurting anyone. But he would, wouldn't he."

Ramsay asked. "It's what I'd expect, that's true. Were the forensic people able to match the cloth and button to anything in Nigel's wardrobe?"

"No, or he wouldn't be bailed," Baldock replied. "I think he's telling the truth about that attack. It wasn't him. Anyway, he's not the type. Great soft tub of lard. Even hitting a woman would be too frightening for him."

Ramsay laughed, grimly. "On a different thought, can you confirm Fewster was the name of the tenants who were in Demerlay Hall when that robbery happened?"

"It was Fewster," Baldock replied, nodding. "I recognized the name when I was searching for the missing treasure hunters."

"Thanks," Ramsay said. "Their name didn't come up in

the newspaper articles and Alice couldn't remember it either."

"Alice?" Baldock queried. Then seeing he wasn't going to get an explanation, shook his head and said, "Oh, never mind. Anyway, it wouldn't come up because they weren't the kind of people you upset, even if you were a journalist. The father and his eldest son are both in prison now doing life for murder. You're lucky they aren't hunting for the loot as well."

Ramsay considered this for a moment. "You said 'eldest son'. Are there other sons?"

"Just one and he's only free because nobody's been able to pin anything on him," Baldock said.

"Do you have a photo?" Ramsay asked. "Or know where he is right now?"

"I have photos," Baldock replied, "but he's not on our patch so I don't know where he is."

"I'm coming into Scarborough tomorrow," Ramsay said. "Can I get a photo from you?"

With that agreed, they hung up the phone and Ramsay phoned Anne to tell her he'd be late in the morning, and she should get a ride to work with Ben and Isaac. With the arrangements for the morning complete, he settled himself down to decipher today's cryptic sentences.

* * *

THE FOLLOWING morning was a satisfactory one for Ramsay, though less so for Bracken who found his morning walk curtailed. Ramsay's chemist friend confirmed the meat in the skin was laced with a sedative, enough to knock out a dog Bracken's size for hours.

Baldock was interviewing Nigel, Ned and Terry,

concerning their administering drugs illegally to people and stealing cars, but he'd left a photo of Conn Fewster for Ramsay to collect.

The only Fewster still at large, Conn Fewster, was as Ramsay had thought he might be, a stocky man wearing a tailored suit that, however hard it tried, couldn't make him look like a gentleman.

"Things are coming together nicely, Bracken," he told his friend as they drove back to the Hall for what was expected to be the last day's work.

His disappointment as he turned into the yard blew away all his optimism. The piles of unwanted furniture and equipment that had been piled outside the garage were strewn across the ground in front of the garage doors and his three companions were clearing up the mess.

"We had visitors during the night," Anne said, when he joined her. "It'll take much of the day just to get into the garage again. Whoever it was, knew where we were working."

"Obviously they didn't get inside," Ramsay remarked, seeing the lock still in place on the garage door. He lifted an old bedframe and put it down again, choosing to haul it away instead. "Many of these pieces are heavy," he said, when he'd cleared it from the doors. "Whoever it was, had some strength. It couldn't be Nigel because he isn't strong enough and he's still in custody."

"That's why we think 'visitors'," Anne replied. "There's too much for one man alone to do in one night."

Ben said, "My question is why they did this? It slows us down, but how does that help anyone?"

"More likely vandals," Anne replied. "They came to see what was happening, couldn't get in to steal anything so made a mess. Just spite, I think."

Ramsay said, "Could be or..., it could be this man." He showed them the photograph. "His name is Connor Fewster, Conn to his friends, and we need to be careful going forward. He's the sort of person who doesn't mind hurting people, by all accounts."

"I've seen him around the village," Ben told them. "A holiday visitor, I presumed."

"A visitor, certainly," Ramsay replied. "We need to find and watch him. He must have friends nearby, if he did this."

Ben shook his head. "Why would he do this? If he's looking for treasure, he should be helping us, not getting in our way."

"Or if he did this," Anne said, lifting her arm, which was still in its sling. "But I take your point, Ben. In the minds of those who are watching us, we're making progress toward finding the loot. The sensible thing for them to do is let us find it, then pounce, steal it from us and get away sharpish."

Ben looked anxiously at Ramsay who nodded, saying, "We must be ready for that, if we find anything because they won't want to leave witnesses behind to identify them."

This left an uncomfortable silence in the air as they began again removing the junk.

18

THE CELLAR

"Did you decipher any of the new notes," Anne asked Ramsay, as they worked.

"Some," Ramsay said, "but there were new symbols in my pages that we haven't seen before. I remain convinced they aren't clues or pointers at all. What about you?"

Anne gave him a broad smile. "I got more clues about the mill and the stream, which suggests they are important, even if they're no longer there."

"I think we have to approach this from a new direction," Ramsay said. "I'll leave you to dig those up. Look how much we got from the icehouse and the well. It wasn't worth the time we spent."

"It has to mean something," Anne persisted, "otherwise why bother?"

"A smokescreen," Ramsay replied. "When we understand what Jeremy was like, we'll know what he would do if he had to hide something he didn't want found."

"Or he did want found," Anne retorted. "It's only a guess he suddenly found a conscience."

"Did you two finish examining the cellar?" Ben asked

Anne and Ramsay. "It's empty now, that might be a good place to start."

Ramsay nodded. "I agree, and also the icehouse where we can't find the tunnel from the Hall."

"Nobody's doing anything until we have this garage doorway cleared," Anne reminded them.

Ramsay laughed. "I'm an investigator but I'll hold off starting my new investigation after the door is cleared."

By lunch time, the last garage door was again open, and they sat down to eat. Each of them unwrapped the sandwich they'd bought and paused, suddenly realizing they'd been so busy they hadn't watched the vehicles, and their lunches may once again be laced with sedative or poison.

"Madge would make us something fresh," Anne told them, as she looked around at the group. "Maybe our investigator could make that his first interview?" She looked at Ramsay, who nodded.

Madge's tearoom wasn't busy. It was mid-week and out-of-season. Only local women meeting friends and taking a rest from shopping occupied the tables, which left Madge time to answer Ramsay's questions, while her helper made up Ramsay's order.

"I was a girl when all the treasure hunting hullabaloo happened," she said, in answer to his question 'did she remember the events at the Hall'. "I remember some of it because me mam had this teashop before me. I'm the second Madge. Mam died two years ago, or you could have asked her."

"Nothing sticks in your mind from anything your mother said?" Ramsay continued.

Madge shook her head.

"What about this man?" Ramsay showed her the photo of Conn Fewster.

Madge studied the picture, before saying, "He looks a bit like a man I've seen around the village, staying at Dora Petrie's place."

"Where?" Ramsay queried.

"The 'White Rose' bed and breakfast, on Howard Street," Madge told him. "Mind you, I can't say it is him. I've never seen him close to. He's a birdwatcher, Dora says. Out all hours of the day and night looking at birds and such. Got a fancy camera for taking their pictures."

His order of sandwiches and pop arrived. Ben and Isaac had been unhappy at a choice of only Dandelion and Burdock, Lemonade, or Orange Squash, but with no beer being sold at the teashop, they'd agreed to Dandelion and Burdock as the next best thing. None of them wanted to use their Thermos flasks again until they'd thoroughly washed them out.

Ramsay thanked Madge for her information and took the order back to the Hall, where the hungry crew were grumbling about the time he'd taken.

After he'd finished his ham and pease pudding sandwich, armed with a broom, Ramsay set off once more for the icehouse where he hoped to find the tunnel entrance. Leaving Bracken on guard, he once again set himself the task of solving the mystery of where the tunnel and the icehouse connected.

After closely examining them, Ramsay decided the walls were solid. There was no sign of a door anywhere. *It must be the floor. After all, the tunnel starts below ground at the kitchen end.*

They'd cleared the rubble and shelving from the floor at their earlier inspection, but a layer of debris and dust remained. Apart from their footprints, it looked level, without any sign of dips or bumps to mark a hatch. He'd remembered this as being the case, which accounted for the broom. Beginning where he anticipated the tunnel should be, Ramsay began sweeping. The layer of dirt was, unfortunately, wet and sticky and made his progress slow. The cleared area grew larger until he almost finished the floor when he heard Bracken barking.

"What is it, Bracken?" Ramsay asked, as he joined his friend outside staring into the shrubs. There was no sign of anyone, and Ramsay closed up the icehouse door, while scanning the surrounds.

Disappointed, and relieved, Ramsay and Bracken made their way back to the garage where the others were hard at work.

"We could use a third able-bodied man," Ben told him, when he appeared in the door. "We've an old wardrobe the missus says she wants and it's awkward for just two of us to lift."

As he helped them lift the heavy oak wardrobe onto the dolly, Ramsay told them of his lack of success.

"It seems to me," Anne said, "we know all the places where there's no treasure hidden."

"I'm taking Ben's advice and re-doing the basement next," Ramsay told her. "I only came back to rinse the taste of slime from my mouth."

"That's all pop is good for," Ben commented.

Ramsay laughed, rinsed and spat out some of the fizzy liquid before drinking some properly. "For energy," he told them. "It's hard work exploring. And if you don't mind, I'll take one of your clean brooms. This one," he pointed to the one he'd been using, "is thick with muck."

"Which you'll wash off at the end of the day," Ben told him, as Ramsay walked off with Bracken and a new broom.

The Hall's cellar was as he remembered it, full of

cobwebs and dust. There were windows in some of its many rooms that allowed small pools of light, which made the rest seem even darker than night. Ramsay returned to the safe, its door still standing open. He examined the inside in case they missed a second compartment, but there was only the one. Now that Ben and Isaac had emptied the cellar, he could see there were rooms that once had special purposes. One, with a high round ceiling, he imagined once held a beer barrel, another, a wine rack. Would a young man newly introduced to the pleasures of alcohol choose these as hiding places? After all, with barrels and bottles filling the space, the walls would have been invisible to anyone entering the cellar. Another high-ceilinged room had hooks in the ceiling, and he guessed it was where they hung the game they shot. Here the walls would be always visible, but the bodies of dead animals may deter all but the butchers in the house.

When his cursory exploration of the rooms' walls was over, he began on the floor. Unlike the icehouse and crypt, here the floor was dry. Only dust covered it and not in sufficient quantities to hide any trace of a hatch. The floor seemed intact, and he decided it need not be closely examined. He'd do one room's walls in detail, so he didn't have to carry any more furniture, before returning to the others and seeking their assistance for the rest of the cellar walls. It seemed only fair. He'd helped with the wardrobe.

After an hour, he'd finished the beer barrel room and found nothing. "Come on, Bracken," he said, as he climbed the steps out of the cellar to rejoin his friend who was guarding the door, "We'll join the others."

When he arrived at the garage, however, he found them huddled over a large map and holding various pieces of paper.

"They fell out of the wardrobe when we moved it to get more stuff in the van," Anne explained. "It looks more like a plan for gardening than a treasure map."

Ramsay agreed it did, and the sheets of paper were planting guides.

"Did you find anything?" Anne asked.

Ramsay shook his head. "Nothing but there are lots of possible hiding places down there. I'm going to need help."

"We saw someone out there," Ben said, pointing to the bushes across the courtyard. "Rex went after them, but the missus called him back."

"I don't want him killed," Anne retorted. There'd clearly been some discussion about this. She turned to Ramsay, "It looked like the man in the photo."

Ramsay said, "Madge said the same thing, when I showed her the photo. The holiday visitor in Grassmount 'looked like the man in the photo' and that bothers me."

"Will you phone Baldock tonight?" Anne asked.

Ramsay nodded. "With luck, he'll tell us he's broken Nigel down into confessing it was him who attacked you. Then we can relax. This other interested party is likely just another treasure hunter, and an innocent one at that." He hoped his words would reduce the tension he could feel among the group, but he was soon disabused of that hope.

"Pigs might fly," Ben retorted.

19

BAITING A TRAP

BEN'S gloomy prediction was correct. When Ramsay phoned Baldock, he confirmed that none of the three men admitted to attacking Anne and were adamant they'd never hurt anyone. The car, they felt, was their just reward for all the time they'd spent searching for the jewels and finding nothing. In their minds, the car was 'first come, first served' and they were there first, long before Watson's House Clearances came on the scene.

"Then I suspect we have a problem on our hands, and you have a villain on your patch," Ramsay told Baldock.

"You mean Conn Fewster. It would be nice to send him to join his brother and father," Baldock said, rather wistfully, Ramsay thought, "but unless he does something villainous, he's just another member of the public as far as the police are concerned."

"You want to use the house clearers as bait," Ramsay replied.

"I want everybody to get along and not bother the police," Baldock replied. "If, however, Fewster does do something illegal, I want to nick him."

"I have a plan," Ramsay said, and laughed.

Baldock warned him, "Don't do anything that gets anyone hurt or gets you on the wrong side of the law."

Ramsay promised he wouldn't and hung up the phone.

* * *

INSTEAD OF DRIVING Anne straight to the Hall, they went to pick up Judith on the way. As they drove, Ramsay told Anne what Baldock had told him. Nigel and the others were not her attackers.

"I found it hard to believe anyway," Anne said, nodding. "They're each strange in their own way but none of those ways are violent ones."

"That leaves us with the very real danger of Conn Fewster," Ramsay said, "and he has a direct link to the events of that time. What that tells me is they never did get their share of the loot, and they've waited a long time for someone to find something that gives them hope."

Anne's expression became concerned. "If this is true, Nigel, Ned, and Terry can thank their lucky stars they never came close to finding anything."

Ramsay laughed. "True but more importantly, you finding something places you in great danger. That's what we need to keep in mind. Now, why are we bringing Judith along?"

"She's finished the code's alphabet and written out all the messages she and I have," Anne told him. as they parked and waited for Judith to lock up her shop. "She can do the same for the pages you have, maybe even the new pages with the different symbols, now she knows how the coder's mind worked."

Judith opened the rear door, told Bracken and Rex to 'move over' and settled in the back seat. "Has Anne told you?" She asked.

"That you've finished the alphabet and can finally decipher all the sentences, yes," Ramsay replied.

"They're no more sensible when I can read them, than they were when I was guessing at their meaning," Judith told them as Ramsay drove away.

"We decided the coder wasn't the best at this kind of game," Anne told her. "Did anything new jump out at you?"

Judith said, "No, but it's clear they're talking about the real stream, mill, and icehouse. One mentions the cellar too, though you'd never find the safe from what it says."

"Has Anne told you about the new threat in town?" Ramsay asked Judith. When she said Anne hadn't, Ramsay explained.

"I'm not sure now that I want to come with you today," Judith said, laughing.

Her laughter felt forced to Ramsay. "I can take you home and bring my new pages to you, if you'd prefer. The fewer of us on this man's radar, the better it will be."

"Tom's right, Judith," Anne said. "You should keep away until the police catch this man."

"Is he wanted by the police?" Judith asked.

"Not at present," Ramsay told her.

"Then they can only catch him if he does something wrong," Judith said. "None of us is safe until that happens. Remember, I was there when we found the safe, Anne."

"He may not know that," Ramsay replied. "It would be best…"

Judith interjected, "It's nice of you to care, Tom, but I was there at the beginning and I'm in this to the end."

Ramsay nodded. "Then here's how I suggest bringing this to a close quickly. I want us to 'find' some new pages today and make sure anyone watching sees that's what we've done. We'll put them 'somewhere safe' while we work and always have that place watched. This is our last day with Ben and Isaac on site with us. Today is our best hope of catching him red-handed when we have numbers on our side."

"What if he doesn't bite?" Anne asked.

"Then I take the 'new pages' home with me, and wait for him there," Ramsay replied.

"I don't like that at all," Anne cried. "He's younger than you and looks like a thug. That isn't a fair fight."

Ramsay chuckled. "I plan to invite Inspector Baldock to be on hand."

"What if this Fewster fellow brings friends too," Judith asked.

"I'm sure the inspector will have support nearby," Ramsay replied. "Don't worry. He'll go for the pages today, particularly when we add the 'new pages' to this pile of papers you've brought with you, Judith."

"Much good they'll do him," Judith replied. "We've found the boxes at the well, the chapel, and the icehouse. And the mill and the stream are gone."

"He doesn't know these papers are useless," Anne reminded her. "And if he watched us find things where we did, he'll assume it was the papers that led us to find the next lot of papers."

"If he watched us find things, then he must know some of the jewels have been found," Judith said, as Ramsay parked the car alongside Ben and Isaac's van.

"He may not have been there at the beginning," Anne

said, "and we were careful not to carry the necklace where it could be seen. I think he's only seen the papers." Anne stepped out of the car more easily now, her shoulder and arm being almost healed.

"Quiet," Ramsay warned them, before greeting the two men who were yawning and checking their watches.

"Afternoon," Ben replied. "We could have been finished by now, if we'd started on time."

"Good morning," Anne said, and unlocked the garage door. "We'll finish today and that's what matters." She led the way inside and signaled the others to join her. "Tom has something to say."

Speaking softly to the group, and as far away from the door as he could get them, Ramsay outlined his plan.

"Oh, aye," Isaac whispered, when he finished speaking. "I signed up for house clearing, not fisticuffs with felons."

"Isaac's right, missus," Ben said, addressing Anne. "This is a police matter. Fights with local idiots is one thing, this man will likely be carrying weapons of some sort."

Ramsay interjected. "We'll watch him come to the bait. If he has a gun or a knife, we simply witness what happens and phone the police."

With this agreed, Ramsay said, "I've taken some of the pages Judith brought today and hidden them in my jacket. While you work, I'm going to continue my search of the cellar. I'll return, waving the papers excitedly and you all gather round to be excited at what I've found." With that, Ramsay and Bracken left for the Hall and its cellar.

Leaving Bracken on guard, Ramsay entered the cellar and began examining the bricks of the wine cellar. He hadn't gone far before he saw what he was after. Near the back wall of the room, and behind where a shelf was once attached to the side wall, the bricks — though level with the others — had clearly been replaced at some time. The mortar surrounding them was newer than that of the walls themselves.

Using that useful stone-removing device on his penknife, he scraped and picked away at the concrete. It was soft and easily scraped out. He suspected all the mortar was like this in the basement where damp and age had worked their decay. Soon he had the six bricks that made up the suspicious section moving as he pulled and pushed at them. He levered them forward with his penknife and eased them out. After placing them on the floor, he shone his flashlight beam into the cavity. Another box reflected the light back to him. He pulled it out and examined it on the floor. It was in much better condition than the others they'd found, and he was able to force the lid open with his fingers.

Inside, a black cloth bag, tied neatly with a cord, lay on a bed of papers. He groaned inwardly. *More of those idiotic clues, Judith could work on them. He wasn't wasting another minute deciphering such nonsense.* He undid the knot and tipped the bag into his hand. Even in the dim light from the torch, the stones flashed, and the gold gleamed. Five gold rings, *like the song*, two bracelets of gold and emeralds, and a brooch of gold and diamonds, lay in his palm and even Ramsay was impressed. He'd always been scornful of 'sparkly stones and shiny metals', as he phrased it, but these took his breath away. He replaced them in the bag, retied the cord, and put it in his jacket pocket. No one need know of this new find until after their trap was sprung.

With the box in one hand and papers in the other, he hurried to show the others, doing his best to look like a man who has just discovered Eldorado. His performance was enough to energize the work group, and they too were suitably excited. Pages were passed hand-to-hand, the box was examined, and Ramsay was enthusiastically questioned about his find, which he answered in a way he hoped sounded natural to any eavesdropper.

The fact Bracken and Rex weren't registering any strangers nearby was disappointing, Ramsay thought, but he proceeded as if they were being watched. After everyone's excitement had abated, and they were wandering back to work, Ramsay placed the box and papers on his car seat, slammed the door shut, and walked into the garage to help load the van.

Whispering instructions to Anne, he took her place in the conga line that passed small ornaments from the garage to be placed by Ben into soft walled containers in the back of the van. Anne took up a resting spot that allowed her to see Ramsay's car in a mirror on an old cabinet and chatted to the others as they worked. The van was finally filled, and Ben and Isaac set off for the auction house, where these smaller items could be bought by people who simply loved old things.

"Nothing so far," Anne whispered, as Ramsay and Judith began arranging their lunch, and that of the two dogs.

"Bracken and Rex would have told us if anyone was here today," Ramsay replied.

"I hope they don't come now," Judith whispered, as she sat beside Anne and offered her a sandwich.

Ramsay sat across from them and poured tea from his flask into the cup. "Tonight, it is, then," he whispered.

"We shouldn't have brought the dogs," Anne replied. "Even gangsters wouldn't want to be attacked by dogs."

Nodding, Ramsay settled down to eat his lunch. "Trouble is," he whispered, "if they didn't see us find these papers, they won't know to come looking for them at my house tonight."

"We could do the whole performance again tomorrow," Judith replied softly.

Anne shook her head. "There's only one more van load and that will go this afternoon."

"We can try again without Ben and Isaac," Ramsay suggested. "For now, we continue as planned." He was still speaking when Bracken and Rex began to growl.

Ramsay stood quickly just as a stranger walked in the door, smiling and bidding them 'good afternoon'.

Ramsay responded, before saying, "This is private property. What are you doing here?"

The man, much younger than Conn Fewster and much lighter in build, walked further into the garage, smiled and said, "I heard you had a Jaguar XK here and I came to look at it." He looked about the almost empty space.

"It's not here right now," Anne told him. She too had stood to face the man who was approaching Bracken and Rex who were no longer growling. They seemed happy to have him approach and stroke them.

The man straightened and said, "Can I see it? I'm a collector of classic cars and I hear this one is in mint condition."

"Where did you hear this?" Ramsay asked.

"Nigel someone," the man responded. "He phoned me, and I imagine others, a few days ago and asked if I was interested. I said I wanted to see it. I live down south and I'm a busy man so I may be too late. Am I?"

"Did you see Nigel on your way here?" Anne asked, fascinated by the man's amazing air of confidence and ease.

He shook his head. "I phoned him and called in at his shop, but he seems to be away. Why?"

Anne glanced at Ramsay who said, "The car is being kept at a safe place right now. Maybe you could leave us a card or a number where we can reach you?"

"You want to sell it behind Nigel's back, is that it?" The man said, grinning. "Well, here," he handed Ramsay a stylish business card, "it's always good when there are two sellers undercutting each other."

"There aren't two sellers," Anne retorted. "My company owns the car, not Nigel."

"He's your agent. I see," he responded. He looked at his watch and said, "I have an appointment. Goodbye, and tell Nigel I'm sorry to have missed him." He strolled out of the garage as calmly as he'd walked in.

The three humans and both dogs followed him out and watched him walk to the end of the stable block, turn the corner, and out of sight.

Ramsay looked at the card. "He claims to be Billy Tempest, whoever that is."

"He's a pop star," Anne and Judith cried. Judith added, "I thought he looked familiar. I should have asked for his autograph."

"I thought it was all groups now," Ramsay said, failing to keep his derision in check.

"Oh, he was before the groups. He was like Marty Wilde and Adam Faith," Anne said. "Do you even read the papers?"

Ramsay laughed. "Not the entertainment section, obviously." His smile froze. "The car," he cried, and ran to open its door. Everything was gone.

The others arrived at his side and peered round him. "Was Billy in on it?" Anne asked.

"A decoy, you mean?" Ramsay asked. "I don't think so. They couldn't have put together such a convincing performance in the time they had. Especially this business card?"

Judith said, "But they could have used this trick many times before. I only thought it was Billy Tempest when you read the name on the card. What if he was just a, what's the word, a doppelganger?"

"A look-alike and now we've lost everything you found today," Anne moaned, "and what Judith brought with her."

"Not everything," Ramsay whispered.

Judith interjected. "And I only brought copies. Our village librarian jumps for joy every time I go in there nowadays. Your bill for copies, Anne, is going to be higher than my fee."

Ramsay added, "If it's true it was a trick, and I think you're right, Judith, then there are two of them staying nearby. Maybe more. We only knew of one."

Anne and Judith considered this, before Anne said, "It's odd. In the summer, you wouldn't notice two extra men around the village, but at this time of the year even one stands out, as we know."

The arrival of the van with Ben and Isaac brought their conversation to a close. And the two men's laughter when they were told about the lost papers, promised to sour the final afternoon of work for the team. It took some time to calm Anne and help her see the funny side of the incident.

The final load was packed and ready by mid-afternoon and the van drove off for the last time. Anne locked up and the group climbed into Ramsay's car for the drive back into the village.

"What did you mean 'not everything'?" Anne asked Ramsay, suddenly remembering his whispered words earlier.

"I'll show you when we're indoors and no one can see," he replied.

"Then we should go to my house first," Judith told them. "I'll make tea and then pop over to the library and make new copies of the deciphered sheets. While we have tea, Tom can show us what didn't get taken."

"I feel like a child on Christmas Eve," Anne grumbled. "I want to open my presents now."

20

A TRICK

WHILE JUDITH and Anne bustled in the kitchen with kettle, teapot, and slices of cake, Ramsay kept watch from Judith's living room window. It gave a fine view to the lane leading into the village, with a hawthorn hedge on a high embankment across the lane. The late afternoon sun was sinking down behind it. Ramsay didn't like that at all. Anyone could be hiding behind the hedge with binoculars and would see right into the living room, while they would be hidden by the leaves and, even if seen, would be a silhouette to an observer in the living room. He joined the ladies in the kitchen.

The kitchen window was worse. A short garden and then a field with an open view of the kitchen to anyone out there.

He left the kitchen and found the cottage's 'best room', as he guessed he would. Everyone in the north had a room reserved only for special occasions or special guests. Rarely used and furnished with the best furniture, this room also looked out to the field but had net curtains across the window.

Gold, Greed, and a Hidden Hoard

"In here," Ramsay called, when he heard Judith on the move with a tray of clinking crockery.

Judith arrived and said, "Oh, it will be cold. I don't normally keep a fire lit in here."

"It has advantages," Ramsay explained, taking the tray from her and placing it on the table. While she went for the rest of the tea things, he drew the drapes tight shut and laid out the jewels on the crocheted tablecloth. Switching on the room's one light he adjusted the stones, making sure the light played on them. The stones sparkled as if newly cut.

The effect was so mesmerizing, Anne who was carrying a plate of scones forgot to put the plate down, standing, staring in awe.

"They're even better than the necklace," she murmured, as Ramsay took the plate from her hand.

Judith entered the room, and her eyes followed their gaze to the jewelry. "They're beautiful," she whispered.

"I thought you'd like them," Ramsay said, smiling. "Even I do and I've no time for such nonsense."

"How many more caches of stones are there likely to be?" Judith asked.

"We don't know for certain," Ramsay replied. "We know from the newspaper reports what was claimed to be stolen and, if they're accurate, I suspect not many more caches."

"Exactly," Anne cried. "We can make an educated guess. We know what was taken. We know what we have. It should be easy to guess how the remaining items we don't have could be divided up to equal the value of the two packages we've found."

Ramsay agreed, saying, "if we can get an educated guess from someone who knows jewelry as to the rough value of these packages we'll know how many packages. The gang members would expect roughly equal value. Honor among thieves doesn't go very far. Do you have any jeweler friends?"

Judith laughed. "In my business, they're ten a penny."

"It has to be one we can trust, Judith," Anne replied. "And one who can work from the description of the haul. We're not showing anyone the real things."

Judith nodded. "I have someone in mind. I'll phone while we have tea. We must put these in the bank tomorrow first thing."

"I'll phone Baldock when I get home," Ramsay told them. "I want to know how old that photo is of Fewster and also if he works with a known con man pretending to be an aging pop star…"

"Hey, less of the aging, if you don't mind," Judith cried. "Billy Tempest was the love of my life only ten years ago." She took her cup and saucer out to the hall where the phone sat on a table.

"Sorry," Ramsay called after her, grinning, then continued, speaking to Anne, "and finally, I want to visit Alice again. I don't understand what was happening at Demerlay Hall in the days following the jewel robbery."

"What about it don't you understand?" Anne asked.

Ramsay explained. "If the Fewster family was at the Hall while Jeremy was hiding the jewels, why didn't they know where the jewels were after he was killed? And why hide them at all, if they were all there?"

"I see what you mean," Anne replied. "Alice did make it sound like they were all there, didn't she."

Ramsay nodded, unhappily. "I've just realized if they were, then my whole theory is nonsense. None of what I've been imagining happened and we're on completely the wrong track."

Judith returned to the room and told them her contact

was willing to give them what they were looking for, if they provided the full list of the missing items and any information they had regarding the quality of the pieces.

Ramsay nodded. "As I thought, they'll want more than we can provide to do a good job."

Anne shrugged. "We just want a guess."

"I can already guess," Ramsay replied. "A job like that robbery would need three people or four, at most. Any more than that and it wouldn't have been worth doing."

"Then there is one, or maybe two, caches like the two we've found," Judith replied. "They're likely in the bank of the stream or in the basement of the mill. The first can't be found because the stream is buried now and the second will need days of digging, you said, Tom. We should just stop now."

"It is tempting," Ramsay replied. "The difficulty I see is the people watching and waiting won't stop and, if we do, they'll likely want to know why. Things could get ugly at that point because they'll assume we've found the loot."

Anne frowned. "You know these kinds of people better than we do, Tom. I think we must be advised by you. What do you suggest?"

"They have the papers and I'm sure they can decipher the new pages using the alphabet," Ramsay replied. "If they're like the ones we've read so far, they're useless. Our competitors in this search, if I can call them that, will assume we understand these things better than they do because we've had them longer and keep finding new ones..."

"All you're saying is one of us is likely to be abducted and tortured for the information," Judith interjected. "That isn't something we can live with."

Ramsay agreed, and continued, "I propose we stick

together to prevent them taking one of us and we draw these people into a place they can be caught, like the cellar or the icehouse."

"The icehouse door isn't secure enough to hold two grown men," Anne said.

"We need to make it so, or we use the cellar," Ramsay told them.

Anne and Judith exchanged glances and then Anne said, "Sooner the better. When do we start?"

* * *

THE THREE SLEUTHS and their canine companions first call that evening was to Alice's cottage. As before, she was happy to have visitors and welcomed them inside.

Ramsay explained this new visit and asked her to explain once again the events of those last days in Demerlay Hall before mister Jeremy was killed. "For example, was he there alone or were the Fewsters there as well?"

"The Fewsters," Alice repeated nodding. "That was the name. I don't recall so well nowadays and nothing that was bad, if I can help it."

Ramsay smiled. "Understandably. But can you remember if Jeremy was alone in the Hall at the end?"

Alice continued nodding. "He was, yes."

"Isn't that a bit odd?" Anne asked. "After all, the Fewsters were tenants then. Jeremy could hardly just walk in any time."

Alice looked at Anne in a puzzled fashion. "The rich aren't like you and me. They have houses they visit. They don't really have homes like we do. And the Hall was Master Jeremy's more than theirs."

"You're sure they were elsewhere at this time?" Ramsay asked.

"Oh yes," Alice replied. "They came back in a big rush when Master Jeremy had his accident."

"Last time we were here," Ramsay said, "You told us Master Jeremy and the Fewster boy were together only days before the accident?"

Alice concentrated before saying, "That's true, sir. They were. Then they left for a day and Master Jeremy came back alone."

"Do you know where the others were?" Ramsay continued.

Alice shook her head. "It was a long time ago. Probably they were at their house in Leeds."

"And they came to the Hall when Jeremy had his accident," Ramsay re-iterated.

Alice nodded. "Yes. Well, the old man and the oldest son, Master Jeremy's friend, came. Not the mother or the younger son."

"And what did they do?" Anne asked.

"There was nothing they could do," Alice replied. "Lord Demerlay came down to collect his son's body soon after. He traveled with it back to Northumberland. There wasn't anything for those two to do." Her contempt for 'those two' was evident.

"We thought they might have searched for something?" Anne asked.

Alice shook her head. "They searched Master Jeremy's room, as I told you. It was later when the treasure hunters came, not the first days after the accident."

"You said, the last time we spoke, the Fewsters left?" Ramsay suggested.

"They did," Alice replied, "but they didn't leave by

choice. After the funeral, Lord Demerlay canceled their lease. He came down here and told us himself."

"And that's when he offered you the almshouse?" Ramsay added.

Alice nodded. "Yes, but I didn't stop work right away. I moved into this house and traveled into the Hall each day. Ned Wishart had a small car then, a Morgan three-wheeler, and he gave me a lift."

"You were at the Hall when the treasure hunters came?" Anne asked.

"I was. The first group came when the Fewsters were still there. It was about the time of Jeremy's funeral. The father and oldest son went up north for the funeral while these treasure hunters combed the house and gardens."

"They didn't have long to search if Lord Demerlay canceled the lease right after the funeral," Ramsay suggested.

Anne considered this, before saying, "It was more than a week, I think. It's hard to remember exactly but it was some time. I know the first man who disappeared left the day before Lord Demerlay arrived to throw them out. Ned and I thought his lordship had learned of their influence on Jeremy from someone more important than us." She paused, lost in thought.

"What happened then, Alice?" Anne asked.

"The Hall was empty for a while, not long, then the family from Bradford took the Hall and they brought the second lot of treasure hunters in. That family were no better than the Fewsters," Anne told them.

"Did they know the Fewsters?" Ramsay asked. "Maybe they were friends or relations?"

"I couldn't say, sir," Alice replied. "If they told me, I don't remember now."

"And you were working there throughout their tenancy?" Anne asked.

Alice nodded. "Yes. It was horrible. Ned had a couple of shouting matches with their children because of what they did to the garden. Then the second treasure hunter disappeared, and the police asked Lord Demerlay questions. Lord Dermerlay wasn't having that and they were gone. He stopped their lease. Sadly, it was the end of the Hall too. I stayed on some months keeping the place nice in case new tenants came and Ned stayed on tending the gardens too. There were no more tenants. I think the Hall had a bad name after those two families."

"You and Ned retired, and the Hall was closed?" Judith asked.

Alice grimaced. "I did. Ned stayed on for a time but the Hall's stood empty ever since. It's ten years or more now."

"Have you been back to see it?" Judith asked. Alice only lived a mile from the Hall, and she might have seen someone if she had gone that way.

Alice shook her head. "It would break my heart to see what it has become. Ned wanders up there, and he tells me what it's like." She looked about to break down crying, so Ramsay brought an end to the interview. "You've been most helpful, Alice. Thank you. Now we should stop pestering you so late in the evening."

Alice walked them to the door and thanked them for dropping in. 'I don't mind, sir. Talking of the old days brings them back, the good as well as the bad."

"Was there any good in those last days?" Ramsay asked.

"Oh, yes. The night before he died, mister Jeremy and I talked for ever so long. He was as happy as he had been when he was a boy, and we talked upstairs when the grown-ups were dining and drinking below."

"Did he say why he was so happy?" Anne asked, glancing at Ramsay.

"Not exactly, Miss," Alice replied. "He said he'd played a trick on the Fewsters that he thought would be a good joke. He never got to see if they agreed with him or not. Personally, I never saw an ounce of humor in that family. The only time I saw them laugh was when they were treating something or somebody cruelly."

They thanked her again. Anne and Judith promised to visit more often and the three drove away in quiet thoughtfulness, until Anne said, "Your theory must be right, Tom. He did double-cross them at the end."

Judith said, "I don't like the sound of the Fewsters and what Alice said scares me. If that man we've seen is Conn Fewster we can't fall into his hands."

"Could you extend Ben and Isaac's contract to include following the man at the bed and breakfast until we know who he is?" Ramsay asked Anne.

"I don't even like the idea of getting someone Ben's age mixed up with a sadistic thug, to be honest," Anne replied. "Particularly, now we believe there are two of them."

Ramsay nodded. He couldn't argue with that.

21

THE MILL

When Ramsay phoned Baldock later that evening, the inspector couldn't confirm that the man staying in the village was Conn Fewster, or that Fewster ever worked a confidence trick with a Billy Tempest look-alike, because, whatever Ramsay may think, the police were fully occupied managing their own case load.

"Just have the constable on the beat chat to him," Ramsay pleaded, but to no avail. "How old is the photo you gave me?"

"About two years," Baldock replied. "His last court appearance hence the suit and tie. Why?"

"The man in the village could be the man in the photo but we aren't certain," Ramsay admitted.

"Then I'm even more certain I'm not giving you a private army to harass potentially innocent people with."

Changing his argument, Ramsay told Baldock of his plan to trap the person or people who were after the stolen jewels and who'd attacked Anne.

"How long do you think you could hold them in the cellar?" Baldock growled. "The door must be a hundred years old. Even if you phoned us the moment you turned the key in the lock, we couldn't be there in less than an hour. It's madness."

"There are piles of junk I can use to barricade the doorway even if they get the door open," Ramsay told him. "And the door is only wide enough for one person so I can push them back down the stairs one at a time."

Baldock's frustration could be felt through the phone. "If they haven't done anything wrong, other than trespassing in a building that hasn't been occupied for a decade or more, and you injure them, it's you who'll be arrested for assault, not them."

"I can't leave Anne and Judith alone with these kinds of people around," Ramsay protested. "You can be sure he knows them by sight and they're not safe living there alone in the village."

"You've heard my advice," Baldock said. "Now, until you can show me good reason why I should assign men to watch this man you think may be Conn Fewster, I can't do anything."

"What was the court case about?" Ramsay asked, hoping it wasn't for murder or similar.

"Fraud," Baldock said. "He was an impresario who managed acts, and some of them accused him of stealing their earnings."

"And had he?"

Baldock chuckled. "The court said not. They accepted his argument that he was trying to keep their careers going. It seems, the acts he was managing were of the past and they couldn't see that the world changed in 1963. No one wanted old-fashioned people like ventriloquists anymore."

"Was the court right?"

"How should I know?" Baldock retorted. "I don't go to

shows. I've no idea how you sell jugglers in an age of Rolling Stones."

"Is he still an impresario?" Ramsay asked.

"I don't know that either," Baldock replied. "I imagine not. Would you sign up with a man who'd been taken to court for fraud?"

Ramsay agreed he wouldn't and thanking him, hung up the phone.

He wasn't surprised Baldock wouldn't loan him any police constables. In fact, he'd expected it. He'd just hoped their successes together this past year would have bought him some small gesture of support, but it seemed not.

* * *

ANNE HAD STAYED the night at Judith's house, and it was there she was picked up next morning by Ben and Isaac. She hoped in another day or so to be able to drive her own car to work. The three and Rex sat squashed together in the van's cab, when Anne saw the man that she believed to be Fewster on the street.

"Pull over slowly and park," she told Ben.

When they were stopped, she pointed the man out to Ben and Isaac.

"This is the one in the police photo?" Isaac asked.

Anne explained that he looked like the man in the photo, only they weren't sure.

"If he is, we should be watching him and not labeling vases and other such stuff," Ben said.

"If he is, we should keep well away from him," Anne responded sharply. "All I want us to do is recognize him again if we see him."

"Why would we," Isaac asked. "Now we're done at the Hall, he can be up there all day without us bothering him."

"He may think we have what he's looking for in our warehouse," Anne replied, "and come looking."

"Ramsay can watch him," Isaac said. "Or has he finished his contract now?"

Anne shook her head. "I've kept his contract going because he and I feel with someone like this watching the Hall, there must be something hidden there. He's hoping to lure the man into a trap."

Ben laughed. "If that pop star yesterday wasn't real, like Judith said, then we must trap the two together. I doubt they're so stupid they would let that happen."

Anne bit her lip. She thought the same. And the problem grew worse if there were more than two.

"Drive on," she told Ben, when the man had turned a corner and was out of sight. "We need to get to work. I've promised the better pieces to Robertson's Auction House by Friday."

Isaac opened the van door. "I'll see where he's going, missus. You two drive on." He jumped down, slammed the door and walked away too quickly to be called back.

Ben looked at Anne, who nodded, and they drove on to the company warehouse, which was a grand name for an old barn. Isaac rejoined them in short time.

"He bought a newspaper and went to Madge's for breakfast," he told them.

"No one joined him?" Anne asked, hoping he might have been meeting the pop star look-alike.

"Not when I were there but I didn't stay long," Isaac replied. "There's nowhere to hide across the street from Madge's Cafe window."

Rex growling focused their minds. The barn was far enough out of the village to be spared people walking by.

Isaac strolled out to the door and stroked the tense, staring dog. "What is it, Rex?" Isaac followed Rex's gaze but there was no one to be seen among the trees in the wooded area opposite.

"Anyone?" Ben asked, when Isaac returned.

"I didn't see anyone," Isaac said, "but Rex doesn't usually growl at squirrels."

"Could be a fox," Ben suggested, but turned himself so he could watch the door as he worked.

* * *

AFTER THEIR MORNING WALK, Ramsay and Bracken made their way to Demerlay Hall and, using the keys Anne had given him, let themselves in. Ramsay locked the door behind them.

"Alice said Jeremy's room was the one in the East Wing looking out to the moors, Bracken," Ramsay told his friend as they climbed the stairs. "I've got a notion he never left the Hall to hide the gems, only to hide those silly clues he thought were such a good joke."

Ramsay spent an hour examining the walls and floors of the room for secret compartments, rapping on the wood panels and stretching his hand high up the fireplace chimney. Nothing remotely interesting came to light.

"Let's try the Master's bedroom," Ramsay said. "After all, it would be a laugh to hide the gems where the big man slept each night."

This was more promising. Almost at once Ramsay found a hidden cupboard that opened when he pressed on a wooden boss among the scrolled decorations of the paneling.

"Where there's one," Ramsay told Bracken, who by now was lying at the window soaking up the morning sun and yawning exuberantly, "there may be another."

A loose floorboard gave Ramsay another burst of excitement, but it too proved not to be hiding any precious objects. "Still, that shows we have the right idea," Ramsay began saying to Bracken when Bracken sprang to his feet and padded swiftly to the door, which Ramsay had closed.

Ramsay, moving as quietly as he could across the bare loose planks, opened the door and peered out. There was no one in the corridor and the two sleuths left the room. Now Ramsay too could hear sounds from down below and they slowed as they reached the top of the stairs. At a ground floor window near the main door, he could see a man peering in. Ramsay stepped back, pulling Bracken with him.

"I think it's Ned Wishart," Ramsay told Bracken. "He has a nerve, considering he's on bail. We'll go and surprise him." Returning to the top of the stairs, he looked again and saw the window was clear of anyone. Ramsay practically ran down the stairs and, unlocking the Hall door, set off to find Ned. The man wasn't in sight, so he ran back to the door, only to find Ned in the lobby of the building.

Grinning at the old man's impudence, Ramsay closed the door behind himself and greeted Ned.

"What do you want?" Ned demanded, in reply.

"I want to know why you're trespassing."

"Same reason as you, I guess," Ned replied. "To find the loot."

"Any ideas?" Ramsay asked.

"Nay, but it must be in here somewhere," Ned replied. "We've searched everywhere outside."

"But not inside?" Ramsay asked.

Ned shook his head. "It hasn't been easy to get inside since it were all boarded up."

"Now things are happening here again, it is, I suppose," Ramsay agreed.

"Aye. With you lot leaving the doors open all day, and the boards off the windows, there's more opportunities."

"We found a safe in the basement during the house clearing," Ramsay told him. "I thought there may be more down there. Want to help look?"

Ned was clearly suspicious at this invitation but finally agreed. "Only we leave yon door open the whole time," he said, pointing at the cellar door.

'You don't like closed spaces," Ramsay said. "I can understand that. Agreed, cellar door left open."

Ramsay began by showing Ned the safe and the hidden compartment in the wall. "That's the sort of hiding places we've found the coded messages in."

"Haven't they led you to the jewels?" Ned asked.

"Not yet," Ramsay replied. "But we think they will when we have more of them."

Ned grunted, as he began peering at the brick wall. "You're further ahead than we got, anyway. We've been wandering around in the dark for years now."

"I can understand Nigel and Terry wanting the loot," Ramsay said. "They're young enough to enjoy the rest of their lives spending it. But what's your reason?"

Ned chuckled. "When I began, I were younger and saw myself retiring somewhere warm. Now, it just keeps me busy. It's a quest. Like the Knights of the Round Table and the Holy Grail. They weren't planning to sell the grail if they found it, were they?"

"I suppose not," Ramsay agreed smiling. "And the car?"

"That was part of it," Ned told him. "The place was abandoned, which means everything here was abandoned. It was ours, after all the work we put in."

Ramsay laughed. He could see he wasn't going to convert Ned over to the legal way of regarding things.

As they examined the walls and floor of the remaining rooms of the cellar, they chatted about the Hall and its history, without Ramsay learning anything new.

"That's it, we're done," Ramsay said, when they'd finished everywhere in the cellar. "And I have to get the keys back to Anne."

They returned to the ground floor where Bracken was waiting, and then out of the main doors of the Hall.

"Where next, Mr. Ramsay?" Ned asked, as Ramsay locked the outer door.

"For me," Ramsay replied, "it's the old mill. Two of the coded messages referred to it and that must mean something. I could use some help digging." Ned could rush back and start digging before Ramsay returned, but the risk of him finding anything was so low, Ramsay thought it one worth taking if it meant he could have a second shovel at work in the afternoon.

"The mill's gone now," Ned protested. "And it was almost gone when the gang would have hidden their loot."

Ramsay nodded. "Which means if it is still there, it must have been buried in the foundations or the wheel pit or somewhere."

"More likely somebody found it years ago," Ned grumbled.

"True but that hasn't held you back these past ten years," Ramsay reminded him.

"I'll be back with my spade," Ned replied, and wandered off down the drive.

Gold, Greed, and a Hidden Hoard 221

When he was gone, Ramsay drove to Watson's Clearance warehouse, where he found Anne and Judith cataloguing the next items to go for auction.

"I wish you weren't here alone," Ramsay said, when he entered the door.

"Ben and Isaac have just gone and now you're here," Anne retorted, "and we always have Rex." Hearing his name, Rex, who'd gone to welcome Bracken, returned to Anne's side.

"Have there been any alarms here today?" Ramsay asked, leaning against a bench that wobbled as he did so.

"None," Judith replied. "You?"

"I was at the Hall and in the cellar," Ramsay told them, "working with Ned."

"But were there any alarms?" Judith persisted.

Ramsay grinned. "I think Ned was the one causing alarm," Ramsay said, and told them how he caught Ned peering through the window before inviting his help.

"So, it's just Ned," Anne suggested. "And not Fewster, or his look-alike?"

"Could be," Ramsay agreed. "Particularly, if this holiday visitor is just a lonely birdwatcher photographing migratory birds and enjoying the last good days of the weather."

"What are your next plans?" Judith asked.

"I'm returning to the Hall and the old mill," Ramsay told them. "I've seduced Ned into helping me dig."

"We got something new from our papers last night," Anne said. "It was confirmation of a set of numbers I found earlier and forgot because they seemed meaningless. Then Judith suggested it was a library reference."

Ramsay laughed. "We would find that after we cleared every book from the library."

Anne smiled. "I thought that too, but it wouldn't have

mattered. Most of the books were on the floor or had been turned into mouse nests. It was Judith who recognized it as a library number."

"Would the Hall's library have been organized using modern library reference numbers?" Ramsay asked.

"The Demerlays let a professor work in, and reorganize, the library in the late Victorian period," Judith said. "If he wanted to demonstrate how 'modern' he was, I expect that's how he'd have done it. The Dewey Decimal System was the latest thing back then."

"I'll look at the shelves when I go back," Ramsay replied. "Maybe it was the shelves or the wall behind the shelves rather than the books on the shelves."

Anne shook her head. "Shelves are down too, and we could see the walls behind them as we worked. It had to be a book."

"What a killjoy you are," Ramsay retorted. "Tell me the number and I'll look anyway."

Judith removed a notepad from the jacket pocket and read out to him, "364."

"Any idea what it means?" Ramsay asked. When they shrugged and shook their heads he continued, "We'll ask our helpful librarian on our way home. We've bribed her enough to be given some free information."

22

THE LIBRARY

Ramsay was making a note of the library number when Ben and Isaac returned. He chatted with them briefly before setting out for the mill, where he found Ned was already digging.

Ramsay laughed as he saw Ned turning the earth. "Found anything?"

Ned shook his head and replied, "Early days." He wasn't joking. He'd dug a six-foot arc of a circle inside the remains of the wall. At least ten times that remained to be dug.

"I'm going to start in the wheel pit," Ramsay said, pointing to the dip in the ground where, in his mind, the old wheel had turned as the stream ran by. He froze, remembering 'where the water ran free' was one of the phrases they'd deciphered. "Which way does the stream run, Ned?" he asked.

Ned straightened up and pointed toward the Hall and grounds. "After the mill, it ran down there to fill an ornamental lake where those bushes are now. Apparently, some child in Victorian times drowned in it and they filled in the lake. And covered the stream too, for good measure."

Ramsay stepped down into the pit and plunged his spade into the bank at that end of the pit. Bracken stood on the lip of the depression, perplexed. "Where the water runs free, Bracken," Ramsay said, softly, hoping Ned wouldn't hear. "This is where the water left the water wheel and ran freely down the stream."

Bracken watched for a moment then leapt into the hollow alongside Ramsay and began digging the bank with his claws.

"I need all the help I can get," Ramsay said, grinning, and patting his friend.

Ramsay's spade made a bigger hole in the bank than Bracken's claws, but it was Bracken who yipped first. His claws scratched metallically across another box.

"You have a nose for this, Bracken," Ramsay said, watching as Bracken's paws flew like rotors, scratching away at the earth around the box, which finally, slid out, and down, to land at Bracken's back paws. He stopped to sniff at the box. It had no interesting scents, so he let Ramsay take it.

Ramsay looked above the bank to see where Ned was and saw him working diligently with his back turned. Using the edge of his spade, Ramsay forced the lid off the box. More papers and what looked like a diary. Inwardly, he groaned. Replacing the lid, he called Ned over.

"We found this." Ramsay showed Ned the box, before going through the motion of levering off the lid again with the spade. "This is what we keep finding," Ramsay said, handing a page up to Ned.

"These squiggles?" Ned asked, pointing at the row of symbols along the bottom of the page.

Ramsay told him how they'd deciphered the alphabet and could now read almost every page they'd found.

"And they don't help?" Ned asked, incredulous.

"The one that said, 'where the water runs free' helped me find this one," Ramsay said. "And these will tell us where to look for another one. To be honest, I'm losing patience with it. We go round in circles."

"What about the mill?" Ned asked.

Ramsay shrugged. "That was a different line, so I imagine there's still one to find here at the mill. I'll come and dig on the outside of the wall. It's not lunch time yet." He took the page from Ned and returned it to the box. That done, Ramsay laid the box on the ground where they could both watch it as they worked.

It was past lunchtime before they'd each finished a single trench around the inside and outside of the mill's wall foundation. "I'll come back later," Ned said, as they walked back to Ramsay's car. "I want to know what those pages say, when you have them worked out."

Ramsay laughed and agreed he would be told when Ramsay returned from lunch. "I'll translate it as I report back to Anne and Judith. This is their mystery really."

"It's been mine since the Hall was abandoned," Ned reminded him. "Thon women only joined in a month ago."

Ramsay dropped him at his cottage and drove back into the village, watching in his rear-view mirror to be sure Ned didn't see him return to the Hall. He took the box inside with him and he and Bracken hurried to the library.

Anne was right about the shelves. Those that were still in place were numbered with number 700 and above. He searched the ruined wooden shelving on the floor and found 364. There was a notch under the number that wasn't on any other numbers he could see.

"It really did mean something," he told Bracken. "But we don't know where it fell from." He scanned the existing shelves to gauge the distance between the numbers and measured back along the wall. He stood where he estimated 364 would have been and studied the wall intensely. There was a hole, at least three inches across, where the shelf would have been attached to the wall. It was too high for Ramsay to reach, and he looked around the room for a step. The library's moveable steps had been taken to the warehouse, he remembered that. *Surely, there must be something he could stand on.*

There wasn't anything safe to stand on in the library, so he went out into the entrance hall where he saw a pile of planks that had fallen from wall panelling. Lifting as many of these he could carry, Ramsay returned to the library and stacked them against the wall. He put his weight carefully on the pile to test it before stepping up to shine his flashlight into the hole. There seemed to be a cloth stuffed deep into the cavity, but his hand was too big to reach it. Heart thumping, he stepped down and went in search of wire. He knew where he could find coat hangers, many bedrooms had them strewn across the floor. It was the work of only a minute to twist the coat hanger into a hook, step back up to the cavity, and a moment later, draw out another felt bag tied with cord.

"We have number three, Bracken," Ramsay told his friend, who was watching the bag as glittering jewels tumbled into Ramsay's open palm. "Now, here's the sixty-four-thousand-dollar question. Were there four of them in the gang or only three? What I mean is, do these jewels equal the value of the other two packages added together? If so, they were for the boss. If they only equal the value of one of the other packages, then there's one more to find. I wish I knew more about gold and stones and could make an educated guess."

Bracken didn't know the answer any more than Ramsay did, so Ramsay replaced the jewels in the bag and stuffed them in his pocket. "I'm sure now that all the loot is in the Hall," he told his friend as they returned to his car and drove away, "and there's one more package to find. In fact, I'm almost sure of it because what I have in my pocket can't equal those other two. It just can't. Do we tell anyone this, or not?" This question was one Ramsay had pondered more than once.

At the warehouse, the gang were wrapping up their lunches when Ramsay arrived. He handed Judith the box and said, "How soon can you have these deciphered?"

"Five minutes," Judith told him. "I have the alphabet in my diary ready for when we find new pages." She took the pages Ramsay handed her and sat at a bench with a pencil.

"Well?" Anne asked, as Judith finished scribbling on the first page. Judith handed it over.

Anne's disappointment was written on her face. "More about the icehouse. We've done that to death."

"Unfortunately," Ramsay said, looking over her shoulder, "the coder didn't know which ones would be found first, nor I suspect, did he care. I think he was playing games with the searchers."

The second sheet was ready, and Judith handed it over. It too referred them to a place they'd dug -- the well.

"Did you have any success in the Hall's library?" Anne asked Ramsay, as they waited for Judith to finish the next sheet.

Ramsay grimaced. "As you'd guessed, 364 was lying on the floor. There's a hole in the wall close to where I think that shelf would have been, but it's only where the shelving was bolted into the wall."

The next sheet referred them to the cellar. "I think,"

Anne said, "we can say beyond any doubt that we already know all the places where the *clues* are hidden."

Ramsay agreed. "This last one," he pointed to the one Judith was working on, "will mention the stream, you can be sure of it."

It did. The dejection of the group was palpable. Every face was a long one. "Back to work," said Ben, "at least we can make an honest living."

The group returned to their benches and continued sorting and labeling items in silence. A gloom so deep, it made Ramsay feel guilty about hiding the jewels he'd found.

"I'm returning to the mill," Ramsay told them. "Ned's years of gardening and my poor efforts will have the place turned over by nightfall."

Ramsay's first stop was Ned's cottage where he expected to see Ned waiting for him. He parked and knocked on the cottage door. There was no answer.

"He's having his afternoon nap," Ramsay told Bracken, as he walked across the lawn to the living room window. Ned wasn't asleep on the couch, so Ramsay made his way the back of the house and the kitchen. Looking through the window, past shabby net curtains, he saw Ned's back. He was sitting in a chair, his chin slumped on his chest and a hat pushed over head. "What did I tell you, Bracken," Ramsay said, as he rapped loudly on the window. Ned didn't respond.

"I've worked him up to a heart attack," Ramsay muttered, horrified. The kitchen door was also locked, and he raced around the house to find an open window. As was usual, the small toilet window above the pebbled lower pane was open and Ramsay climbed onto the sill to reach through. He couldn't reach the lever for the lower pane with his hand, so he removed his tie, formed a loop and lifted the lever that way. He pushed it open and climbed inside. Running through the house, he reached the kitchen to check Ned for a pulse.

He saw Ned's head was covered in a sack bag and then Ramsay realized he was also tied into the chair. There was a cigarette burn on his hand.

"Please tell me he has a phone," Ramsay pleaded with himself as he quickly untied the cord around Ned's neck. Drawing off the bag and throwing it aside, he checked for a pulse. It was faint but noticeable. Ramsay ran into the hall and living room. There was no phone.

His fingers fumbling on the knots that held Ned in the chair, Ramsay thought desperately where he'd seen a phone box in the village. He lifted Ned to his feet, the man groaned, which was a welcome sound, and carried him through to the couch in the living room. When Ned was laid on his side, head on the arm of the couch, Ramsay brought a glass of water and tried to revive him. Ned remained unconscious and Ramsay said, "If you can hear me, Ned, I'm going to get help. I'll be back as soon as I can."

There was no response, so Ramsay returned outside the way he'd come in, closing the windows behind him. He didn't want anyone else getting in.

He drove back into town and screeched to a halt outside the rail station where a red telephone box stood empty. He dialed '999' and asked for ambulance and police, giving the operator Ned's address. With that done, he phoned Baldock who was out of the office. "Radio him and tell him to come to…" Ramsay practically yelled Ned's address at the Desk Sergeant who'd taken the call. When the man confirmed he'd do that, Ramsay ran across the street, Bracken alongside him, to the doctor's surgery.

Telling his waiting patients there was an emergency, the doctor followed Ramsay and Bracken outside. Ramsay began saying Ned's address, only to be told the doctor knew where Ned lived. They arrived together at Ned's cottage and Ramsay once again climbed in through the window to open the front door.

The doctor was still measuring Ned's breathing and pulse when the sound of the ambulance arriving sent Ramsay outside to lead them through to where the patient lay. In minutes, Ned was in the ambulance and the doctor in his car. The small convoy set off for the nearest hospital. As the two vehicles disappeared down the road, the police car arrived, and Ramsay explained events to the officers inside.

"They went that away," Ramsay said, quoting from some old movie he'd seen in the mists of time. The officer radioed it into headquarters. Then he too left Ramsay to wait for Baldock.

Baldock, when he arrived had only bad news. "Ned Wishart died on the way to hospital," he told Ramsay. "I've just heard it on the radio."

"Somebody must have seen us digging this morning and me showing Ned the pages I'd found," Ramsay said. "I never thought they'd go this far."

"Ned, by what I hear, was an old man," Baldock said. "They probably didn't take that into account."

"It's still murder in my eyes," Ramsay growled.

Baldock nodded. "You think it's Conn Fewster?"

"Who else could it be?" Ramsay said. "No one local would do this and leave Ned alive or he'd identify them."

"My forensic boys will be here in a minute," Baldock told him. "If there are fingerprints or even footprints, it might be enough to bring him in for questioning."

Ramsay watched as the team set to work but he could

see from their body language there was nothing to identify the killer.

"I told them to bring Fewster's prints with them," Baldock said, as they watched the men work.

"They haven't found any prints, I'm guessing," Ramsay said. His prediction was borne out when the man dusting the chair and table looked at Baldock and shook his head. "He or they wore gloves."

Baldock shrugged. "Everyone does nowadays. Every criminal, anyway."

Ramsay ran his hands across his face. "I should have taken him to the warehouse with me."

"You'd have only gained him another few hours of life," Baldock replied. "They'd have done this tonight when he got home, and he wouldn't have been found for days."

"Inspector," a forensic officer called from the garden. "There are footprints here."

Ramsay and Baldock hurried outside. Ramsay said, "those are mine. I was looking for a way in."

Another call, this time from the road outside finally provided a clue. "A car stood here, and its tracks don't match yours, Mr. Ramsay, or the ones I've been told were the doctor's car and the ambulance."

"Any ideas?" Baldock asked.

The man shook his head. "It's a Dunlop tread pattern and a narrow wheel. A motorbike or a small car. Something like a mini, I'd say."

"If our man drives such a vehicle, it might be enough," Ramsay offered hopefully.

Baldock considered the possibility and said, "Let's go and ask him." The two jumped into Baldock's waiting car and drove back to the village.

23

MEANWHILE...

"I wish I was digging at the mill," Judith grumbled, as she handed yet another ornament to Ben for packaging. "I'm tired of this."

Rex, who'd been resting beside Anne's feet, suddenly barked and raced out of the warehouse with Isaac after him.

Anne too, leapt up and ran, terrified Rex would be killed if Fewster was the man she'd heard he was.

"Rex," she called as she arrived on the track outside the barn and couldn't see him anywhere.

"He went into the woods," Ben told her. He was still holding the ornament given to him a minute ago.

"I'll go, missus," Isaac said, running past her and diving into the undergrowth.

They heard Isaac calling Rex for some time before the two emerged out of the bushes.

"Did you see him?" Ben asked.

"Saw his car," Isaac said. "Nice little MG TD roadster. I'd settle for one of those if I can't have my Jag."

"Never mind that," Anne cried in exasperation and taking Rex's collar. "Did you get its number?"

Isaac shook his head. "I was trying to stop Rex here from chasing it and it was around the corner before I had the chance."

"You know the color and year, though," Ben asked.

"Of course," Isaac said, scornfully.

"I wonder what that man in the White Rose bed and breakfast drives?" Anne murmured.

"We can ask Dora the moment we finish here," Judith said, excited at the chance for more entertaining activities than labeling old furnishings.

When they arrived at the White Rose, Dora didn't know what sort of car her guest drove, and he was out so they couldn't look for themselves.

"Trust a woman not to know," Isaac grumbled.

"Well, not everyone cares about cars," Anne responded. "You're just mad about them."

Isaac, however, was trotting across the street where two boys were playing marbles. He spoke to them briefly and trotted back.

"A red MG TD," Isaac crowed. "I knew it would be."

The others hadn't time to reply before Ramsay and Baldock arrived and parked outside the White Rose.

"He's your man, Inspector," Isaac told them as the two men joined the group.

"What makes you so sure?" Baldock asked.

"We saw a red MG TD drive away when we chased a man who was spying on us," Anne interjected quickly.

"And this lodger," Baldock said, gesturing at the White Rose, "drives such a car?"

"Yes," Isaac stated bluntly.

"You've seen it and him driving it?" Ramsay asked.

"Well, no," Isaac replied. "I saw the car drive away from

the warehouse and the boys over there say the lodger drives a red MG."

Baldock said, "It isn't a common car, it's true, but there will likely be more than one in the county. We need something more than this."

"We need to match the tread print your forensic people have taken at the scene to this car," Ramsay responded. "And we need to see what name this man is registered under at The White Rose."

Baldock nodded. He turned to the group and suggested they return home or to their place of work. When they objected, he shook his head, saying, "If he returns and sees you standing here, and if it was him spying on you, he'll drive away, and I need to talk to him before he does that. Now go."

"Not until we know what 'scene' you're talking about," Anne retorted, suddenly picking up on Ramsay's earlier words. "What haven't you two told us?"

"Ned was injured," Ramsay replied. "We've just come from his cottage. There was a nice clear tread mark in the mud outside Ned's gate." He glanced at Baldock, before continuing, "and we've just heard Ned died on the way to hospital."

"Happy now?" Baldock said, glowering at them. "Now go. We have work to do and I'm sure you folks do as well."

"I'll bring you up to date later," Ramsay told them. "Don't worry."

Grumbling, the Watson's House Clearance crew left and Baldock and Ramsay went into the guest house.

"His name's Connor Fewster, Inspector," Dora told them, handing over the guest house register. "He lived in the village, at Demerlay Hall, when he was a boy. It's something of a sentimental journey for him."

The idea of any member of the Fewster family harboring a 'sentiment' seemed to amuse Baldock but the tone of his voice remained neutral. "How long does he intend to stay?"

"He's not sure," Dora replied. "When the weather turns, I expect."

"He doesn't have a job he needs to get back to?" Ramsay asked.

Dora shrugged. "I don't know. He didn't mention it."

Baldock's request to see the man's room made Dora unhappy. "Shouldn't you have a warrant to enter people's private places?"

"Of course," Baldock replied. "And I shall get one, if you insist. However, if you accompanied us to see we don't remove or add anything, perhaps you could save us all some time."

Dora agreed and led the way to Fewster's room, which she unlocked and let them enter. She stood at the door watching them both as they gazed about them. The room was Spartan in its emptiness. The bed was made, the floors clear of shoes or other signs of habitation, the drawers and wardrobe doors closed with nothing peeking out.

"A neat, tidy man," Ramsay commented.

Dora responded, "I've just cleaned, but it's true, he's tidy. I thought maybe time in the armed forces."

Baldock nodded. "Possibly," he said, smiling.

"Has he spoken of his family or friends?" Ramsay asked.

Dora shook her head. "Only what I told you." Her eyes never left Baldock as he opened and closed all the spaces in the room.

"And you haven't seen anything in his possessions that alarmed you?" Ramsay asked.

Dora's expression was frankly incredulous. "I've seen

what you can see. He's a single man, with few possessions, who is here remembering better times in his life."

Ramsay asked, "Do you remember the Fewster family at the Hall?"

Dora shook her head. "I bought this place only a few years back," she said. "When my husband died."

Baldock and Ramsay exited the room and waited while Dora locked it.

"As I said, we have to eliminate him from our enquiries," Baldock told her as they descended the stairs. "An awful thing has happened today, and a car stood near the spot it happened. A car that's maybe like the one your guest owns. Thank you for your assistance."

"I will tell Mr. Fewster you called," Dora said. "I'm sure he'll want to re-assure you of his innocence."

As they walked back to their vehicles, Ramsay remarked, "I think she likes Fewster."

Baldock nodded. "If all she knows about him is in that room and in his manner toward her, why wouldn't she? Imagine, a tidy man."

Ramsay laughed. "I like to think I'm a tidy man too."

"Army or prison?" Baldock asked, grinning, as he got into his car, slammed the door, and drove off.

Ramsay also drove away, to Alice's cottage. He doubted anyone would have told her about her old friend and colleague's death.

* * *

ANNE, Rex, Judith, Ben, and Isaac made their way to Anne's cottage for tea and consultation. Ben and Isaac, after hearing from Ramsay and Baldock why they were searching for the red MG, wanted to arrange shifts to guard the two women in one of their cottages.

"We don't need guarding," Anne retorted. "Anyway, I have Rex."

"Aye," Ben said, "and who does Judith have?"

"Judith can stay with me, if she thinks it best," Anne said, glancing at her friend.

Judith nodded. "After hearing what happened to Ned, I do think it best. Thank you."

"But you two," Anne told Ben and Isaac, "don't need to sit outside on guard."

Ben and Isaac exchanged glances that suggested they didn't agree, but Ben replied, "It's your funeral, missus." He sipped the mug of tea he'd been handed.

"Oh!" Anne cried. "Who will organize Ned's funeral? He doesn't have any family I know of."

"We'll ask the vicar," Judith suggested. "He'll know. And if there is no one, we can organize it."

Ben chuckled. "It'll be a small affair. He were a surly old so-and-so."

"Nevertheless," Anne replied. "Somebody must." She crossed the room to the telephone on a side table and dialed the vicarage.

The others listened as Anne and the vicar discussed what should be done and by whom. When she hung up, she said, "You heard all that but so you know, the vicar isn't aware of any relatives. Ned wasn't a regular churchgoer and avoided the vicar when he could. He thought the vicar a foreigner, and didn't hold with such folk."

Judith laughed. "I've been here for years and I'm still a foreigner too."

"Why don't we finish our tea," Anne said. "Then Judith and I can break the news to Alice. She won't know."

When they arrived at Alice's cottage, they found Ramsay had beaten them to it. Alice and Bracken let them in, and Alice offered them tea, which they declined.

"Mr. Ramsay kindly came to tell me the news about Ned," Alice told them, as they sat down. Alice sat back in an armchair and Bracken sat beside her, while Alice stroked his head.

Anne explained about funeral arrangements, asking, "Do you know if Ned had any family?"

Alice shook her head. "He was the only surviving child, and his parents are long gone."

"Then we must do something," Judith said, looking at Alice and Anne. They both nodded.

"I'll let you folks talk about details," Ramsay said. "But I do want you to hear what Alice just told me before you arrived."

Alice looked puzzled.

"About Connor Fewster as a young man," Ramsay prompted her.

"I didn't say much," Alice replied. "Only that he was the best of a poor lot."

Ramsay smiled. "Alice didn't like any of the family, however, she remembers Connor as a young man of about twenty at the time and she saw no harm in him."

"Not much of a recommendation," Anne remarked.

"It wasn't meant to be," Alice replied.

Ramsay grinned. "I'm just suggesting we need to exercise caution. We don't know he's done anything wrong here." He rose and, bidding Alice farewell, made his way outside, Bracken trotting alongside.

"And we don't know he hasn't," Anne called after him, before turning to Judith saying, "If, as we're told, his father and older brother are serving life sentences for murder then

I think we're entitled to treat Conn Fewster as a dangerous man until we know different."

As Bracken got into the car, Ramsay said, "You're much better at condoling with people than I am, Bracken. I honestly don't know what I'd do without you some days."

Bracken nodded his agreement. He often wondered the same thing.

Ramsay had planned to stop at the police house on his way home but saw the constable talking to Conn Fewster outside the guest house. They were both staring at the red MG parked beside them. Ramsay turned his car and drove back to park behind the MG.

"Mr. Ramsay," the constable greeted him in a chilly manner.

"Constable," Ramsay replied. He could understand the man's dislike of having a third in this delicate discussion. "I don't want to take up your time, only I want to introduce myself to Mr. Fewster and arrange to talk sometime soon."

Fewster's face was flushed, but with anger or embarrassment, Ramsay couldn't decide.

"And who are you?" Fewster asked.

"Tom Ramsay." He held out his hand and Fewster shook it unconvincingly. "I've been working with Watson's House Clearing and I think you've been watching us work."

"Mr. Ramsay," the constable interjected. "I'm sorry but the police have questions for Mr. Fewster that must come first."

"Quite right," Ramsay said, "may I drop by this evening, Mr. Fewster?"

"If these people haven't locked me in a cell," Fewster replied, and turned his attention back to the constable.

Ramsay left them talking about where Fewster had been all day and could anyone vouch for him. While he'd spoken to Fewster, Ramsay had taken the opportunity to look carefully at the car's tires. They were Dunlop tyres, and he was sure the tread was the same as the marks in the wet earth outside Ned's house. Unless Fewster could convincingly explain how that came about, he wouldn't be available to talk to Ramsay for some time.

For Ramsay, the wait until later that evening was interminable. At seven-thirty, he phoned the White Rose guest house, only to be told that Mr. Fewster wasn't available. He'd left with a police constable some time ago and wasn't yet back.

Ramsay phoned Anne to ensure they were safe and told them his news.

"Now he's locked up," Anne said, "we can all feel safe. Still, Judith is staying with me tonight, just in case they let him out."

"I'm going to phone Baldock at home later," Ramsay told her. "I'd like to be sure he is being held."

"You seemed unsure after what Alice told you," Anne reminded him.

"There are no other credible suspects," Ramsay said. "And yet, her opinion is unsettling."

"We're also not forgetting there was an accomplice," Judith shouted, in the background, making Anne laugh nervously.

"The Billy Tempest look-alike," Ramsay said, smiling. "That's true. Keep the doors and windows locked and phone me if you even suspect someone's outside."

As Ramsay made and ate his evening meal, he compared the jewels he'd found that day with the list of those stolen in Leeds all those years ago. The brooch was easy to identify, the others were described only generally and so an exact match was difficult.

"Still, the brooch makes it certain these are from the robbery, Bracken," Ramsay said to his friend who lay on the hearthrug in front of the glowing fire. The evenings were cold now. Occasionally, Bracken jumped as a coal crackled and sparks flew. He still didn't fully trust the fireplace screen that protected the rug from the burning fragments.

"What I do now know," Ramsay continued, "Is that there were four in the gang. And I know that because we have found three-quarters of the haul, leaving only one quarter missing." He glanced at Bracken who was ignoring him. "So, who were they, my friend? I say, Jeremy was the get-away driver, though they don't seem to have needed him, if the reports are to be believed. Then Jeremy's school friend, the oldest Fewster son. And I'm guessing old man Fewster wouldn't have let his son do something this big without supervision so old man Fewster is my guess for the third man, (*wasn't that a book and a film*), and that leaves only one, the safecracker. Who was he?"

Bracken didn't know that either. He yawned and settled further into the rug.

"Jeremy is dead," Ramsay continued, "the two thugs are in prison, which is good, but the safebreaker is where? Is he alive? The good news is they generally aren't thuggish brutes. Does that mean the person who killed Ned isn't the safecracker?"

BY TEN O'CLOCK, Ramsay decided he'd find Baldock at home and he dialed the inspector's number. The phone rang for some time and Ramsay was about to hang up when he heard Baldock's aggressive, "Yes?"

"It's me, Ramsay. Where are you with Fewster?"

"None of your business," Baldock retorted.

"If it wasn't for me..." Ramsay began.

"That's right," Baldock growled. "I have you to thank for another night of interviewing a suspect without a lot to go on."

"Did the treads match?" Ramsay asked.

"Course they did," Baldock said, chuckling. "I wouldn't be interviewing him if they didn't."

"What's his side of the story?"

"A week or two ago, he heard on the radio about the development of the Hall and the house clearing and thought he'd have one last look for the stolen jewels," Baldock replied. "He and his," Baldock paused, "friend, took rooms. Him in Grassmount; his friend in Sleights."

"The friend is the look-alike?" Ramsay guessed.

Baldock chuckled. "More than a look-alike. He actually performs on stage doing a Billy Tempest act. Before you ask, we're interviewing him too."

"Are you holding them?" Ramsay asked. Thinking of Anne and Judith alone in the house.

"We are," Baldock said. "They've asked their lawyer to be there for tomorrow morning."

Ramsay continued, "How did he explain the tread marks outside Ned's house?"

"He went there to talk to Ned," Baldock told him. "Ned had provided information that helped them get started on their search and Fewster had more questions for him. He knocked on the door, looked through the living room window and when there was no answer, he left."

"Plausible," Ramsay replied. "That's what I did too. Have the forensic people found anything to link Fewster or his friend to Ned's house?"

Baldock said, "Not yet, but they have previously been in the house, if I'm to believe them."

"Do you believe them?" Ramsay asked.

There was a long pause. Baldock was clearly considering his reply carefully. "I can't make sense of him. Fewster, I mean. Apart from some childish misdemeanors, he has no criminal record. I wonder if he was swapped at birth in the maternity hospital."

Ramsay was tempted to tell Baldock what Alice had said but decided that would be counterproductive. He wanted Baldock at his bulldog best on the following day.

"Just means he's cleverer than the rest," Ramsay said.

"Maybe, and we have no one else with a reason to torturing the old man so for now, I'm working on breaking them down," Baldock replied.

"I'll leave you to it, then. Good night," Ramsay rang off and returned to his fireside armchair.

"Baldock has doubts about Fewster, Bracken," Ramsay murmured, "and after what Alice said, so do I. In the morning, we'll talk to Terry and Nigel again. If anyone saw Mr. Conn Fewster around Ned's place or anywhere else, they'll know."

24

ALIBIS

The morning air was crisp, with a hint of frost when Ramsay walked up the path to Terry's house and knocked on the door. There was no answer.

"Does he work, Bracken?" Ramsay mused. "I had the impression he didn't." He knocked again and waited, before going to the bay window that looked out to the road. He had an uncomfortable feeling of déjà vu as he did this. It was so like his experience at Ned's house. Like Ned's house, he could see no one in the living room.

"Did they do the same to Terry, Bracken?" Ramsay asked, as he made his way around the house to look into another window. He breathed a sigh of relief when he could see there was no one tied to a chair in the kitchen.

He returned to the front door and hammered on the door. *Loud enough to waken the dead* he thought and immediately wished he hadn't. It seemed like tempting fate.

"Maybe we should try Nigel," Ramsay said. "He can't be away at work; he lives above the shop."

Ramsay drove through the village, where people were

already beginning their day, hoping he might see Terry on the street, but he didn't.

Nigel also failed to answer his doorbell and couldn't be seen through windows of the shop and house either.

Ramsay laughed. "I'm slow this morning, Bracken," he said. "They'll be searching the house and grounds at Demerlay Hall, you can bet on it."

Bracken yawned. This mad rush into Grassmount instead of his morning walk was a grave disappointment, and he felt Ramsay should be made to understand that.

"We'll drive out there and catch them at it," Ramsay said, hurrying back to his car.

Bracken got the sense that something may be happening and trotted quickly after him, leapt into the car and prepared to be entertained.

When they arrived at the Hall and Ramsay found no parked vehicle his dismay was quickly transmitted to Bracken, who slumped down into the passenger seat and glared at Ramsay.

"They might have walked here," Ramsay said, at last. "We'll take a look around before we do anything else." They exited the car and began a tour of the locations where they'd found hidden notes. Apart from the calls of pheasants and blackbirds, they heard nothing. No people were nearby.

Returning to his car, Ramsay mused, "One of them missing from home, I could accept but not both. But you heard no one in the icehouse or the Hall, so they can't be here." He unlocked the car, and they returned to their seats. "Has Baldock pulled them in again for more questioning?" Ramsay asked, as he drove down the drive. The idea cheered him considerably.

Rather than drive home, he went to Watson's warehouse

where he found Anne and Judith patiently inspecting small items for future sale. "I'd like to borrow your phone," he asked.

"Why?" Anne asked.

When Ramsay explained, she shook her head, and said, "Nigel will be at the Scarborough salerooms today. You won't find him at home until tonight."

"Any idea where Terry may be?" Ramsay asked.

"None," Anne replied. "He does occasionally do odd jobs for people. So maybe he's something on today."

Ramsay said, "I'll wait until later then. I was hoping they would have seen Fewster and his friend, if they spend as much time spying on us and the Hall as we think they do."

"Dora at the White Rose might know," Judith said. "After all, it's possible the man was at his lodgings at the time you want him to be killing Ned."

Ramsay nodded. "I should ask." He wasn't happy doing this, it was the sort of work he'd have set the beat coppers doing only a year ago.

Dora could only say Mr. Fewster had left early yesterday and not returned until he was questioned by Constable Heyer, which Ramsay should remember because Ramsay had spoken to both men at the time. Ramsay did remember. This confirmed Fewster could have hurt Ned, which wasn't what Ramsay was hoping to learn. He thanked her and drove away.

"We'll try Terry again, before we let it rest, Bracken," Ramsay told his friend.

This time, even before he parked, Ramsay saw smoke rising from the chimney of Terry's house. "Now we'll see what our friend, Terry, has to say," he told Bracken as they walked briskly up the path to the door and knocked on the door.

Terry's face appeared briefly at the bay window and soon Ramsay heard him at the other side of the door.

"Good morning, Terry," Ramsay called, when the door didn't open. "Can we talk?"

"I don't want to talk to you," Terry replied.

"It will only take a minute," Ramsay said.

"No."

"Did you know the police have a man in custody over what happened to Ned?" Ramsay asked.

"No," Terry responded.

"I'm sure the police will be looking for witnesses who might have seen this man near Ned's house early yesterday afternoon," Ramsay said. "I know you're often out and about, particularly at the Hall, and wondered if you might have seen something."

"We saw no one," Terry replied.

"You mean you and Nigel?" Ramsay asked.

"I mean I saw no one," Terry cried. "I wasn't anywhere near the Hall or Ned's house yesterday."

"Where were you?" Ramsay asked.

"None of your business," Terry yelled.

Ramsay heard him moving away from the door and he strode quickly to the bay window. Terry wasn't to be seen. Circling the house, he didn't see Terry in any of the lower windows.

"Gone to hide in his bedroom, Bracken, that's my guess." Ramsay said, returning to his car with Bracken alongside. "I think it's safe to say he and Nigel were at the Hall yesterday, desperately searching for the jewels before the developers arrive." The difficulty for Ramsay was that Ned's house wasn't so close to the Hall that they might have seen anything accidentally. His hope had been they would have gone seeking Ned to further their search and that way they might have seen what happened.

"Of course," Ramsay continued as he drove away, "that still could be what happened. Neither Terry nor Nigel would want to testify against Fewster if they had witnessed anything."

Bracken yawned and placed his head on his front paws. This was becoming an extremely boring day.

* * *

RAMSAY SPENT the day knocking on doors of the very few homes near Ned's, asking if anyone had seen anything. The answers were all the same. They hadn't and they'd already told the police that and what business was it of his?

By evening, he was as tired of this as Bracken was. "Anne said Nigel wouldn't be back until evening," Ramsay told Bracken as they waited outside Nigel's shop. "It shouldn't be long now."

It wasn't long, though it seemed like a lifetime. Nigel's car pulled into the narrow drive that ran beside his shop to the garage behind. Nigel wasn't out of the car before Ramsay and Bracken were at his side.

"Good evening," Ramsay said, hoping a cheerful tone would set the man at ease.

"Not with you about, it isn't," Nigel growled, closing and locking his car door uncertainly.

He's been drinking, Ramsay noted. *Good, it might loosen his tongue.* "When you and Terry were at the Hall yesterday, did you call in to pick up Ned?"

"What? No! Now get away from me. I've nothing to say to you." Nigel walked stiffly to his back door, fumbled with his keys and the lock, before turning to say, "Haven't you done enough harm already? Go away."

As it seemed he was to get nothing from the man, Ramsay said, "I'll go, but I'll be back tomorrow. Someone must know something, and my guess is you and Terry are the most likely to know. Ned was your fellow treasure hunter, and you would want him involved."

Nigel shook his head and slammed the door shut behind him.

As Ramsay drove away, he could see Nigel watching from the window. "I'm tempted to watch his house tonight, Bracken, but I can't honestly see him leaving it. Did you see how many times he fumbled the key in the lock? He'll be flat out on his couch before we've left the village."

25

ROBBED

IT WAS dark when Anne and Judith set out on Rex's evening walk, but the night was clear, a crescent moon shone brightly in the sky and the air was still warm enough to be pleasant.

As Rex trotted on ahead of them, Judith said, "I'm glad it's all over. I didn't like to say so before, but I was beginning to feel scared."

Anne agreed, adding, "When we heard about Ned, I was trembling. Those two must be monsters."

"I suppose they are *both* in custody," Judith replied, looking around. The hedgerow at the side of the track was bathed in moonlight but dark shadows could be seen on the field side.

"I'm sure they will be," Anne said. "No one suspected of behaving as they did to Ned could be let out, I would think."

Judith nodded. An owl hooted nearby, and she twitched. "We used to make owl hoots when we were children playing wide games in the girl guides."

"We did too," Anne said. "We'd hoot to each other when we sneaked up on the other team." She laughed. "The silly thing was, we all did it -- both teams. So, we never knew who was hooting to who."

Judith laughed as well. The owl hooted again, closer this time. She glanced at Anne and saw her alarm. She felt the same.

"Maybe we should get back," Anne said, and called Rex, who was no longer in sight. She called again. "Bother. We must find him." She began hurrying down the lane in the direction Rex was last seen.

A turn in the lane showed only an empty track ahead of them. "Maybe he's in the bushes hunting rabbits," Judith suggested, her voice breaking.

"Rex," Anne called. There was no answering bark.

"We need to get back inside and quickly," Judith said, tugging at Anne's sleeve. "If Rex can't reply, someone already has him. We're next." They began running back down the lane.

"How could someone get Rex?" Anne gasped. "He's wary of all strangers."

"Then it isn't a stranger," Judith replied, like Anne speaking through gasping breaths.

"I have to rest," Anne said, walking and holding her sides. "If we get out of this alive, I'm going to exercise every day of my life from now on."

Judith tried to laugh but was also too busy gasping for breath.

They walked on as quickly as they could. Anne's home was still some distance when she said, "I didn't leave the kitchen light on."

They stopped, staring at the lighted windows shining over the hedge. "Are you sure?" Judith asked.

Anne nodded, too numb to speak. "I think the front door is open too."

Judith squinted. "I don't have my glasses," she said.

"If someone's there," Anne told her, "We should go straight past and bring Constable Heyer from the police house."

"They will be gone by the time we got back," Judith told her. "Let's look in the windows and at least see who it is. It may be a neighbor."

Anne drew a finger across her throat in a graphic reminder of the possible outcome. "If we're seen...," she said, leaving the sentence unfinished.

Slowly now, they approached the house until they were at the garden gate. The front door was open, and they could hear things being thrown about inside.

"Looking for the jewelry or the coded messages," Judith whispered.

"Do you think it's Fewster?" Anne replied.

Judith shook her head. "Even if they did let them go, they wouldn't be loose like this. Fewster would be watched, wouldn't he?"

"What about his partner, the phoney Billy Tempest?" Anne asked. "I wish we'd accepted Ben and Isaac's offer to stay."

"I wish we'd walked into the village instead of out," Judith told her. "What are we going to do?"

"Look in a window and then run to the police house," Anne said.

"We didn't last two minutes of running to get here," Judith whispered. "We'll be caught long before we get to the police house."

"What do you suggest, then?" Anne retorted.

"Look in the window and if we aren't seen, hide among your currant bushes."

"And if we are seen?" Anne demanded.

"Then we run. One of us might get away, if there's only one of them."

"But someone must have Rex," Anne retorted, "which means there's two of them."

Before they'd made better plans, the noise inside the house stopped abruptly and they dived down behind the hedge hoping not to be seen when the intruder came out of the gate. They scurried farther around the corner of the garden wall when a door slammed shut. Time ticked away and still no one came out of the house. The silence now was unbearable.

"Did they go out the back door?" Judith whispered.

Anne signaled her to move farther along the wall, which they did keeping as low as they could. Anne grabbed Judith and stopped her. She signaled she was going to look over the wall. Judith grimaced. Anne slowly rose until she could see the kitchen and rear door of the house. It was shut, which didn't answer Judith's question.

"It's all quiet now," Anne said. "I'm going inside. You stay out until I call. If I don't, you run for help."

Judith nodded and they crept back to the garden gate, where they stopped. It was still quiet.

"Ready?" Anne asked. Judith nodded and Anne stood upright and walked swiftly up the path to the open front door.

"Hello," she called. "Is there someone in there?" She hoped a confident tone might be effective, if it was simply children. There was no reply, and she continued inside. The floor of every room on the ground floor was strewn with her belongings. In the kitchen, the binder where she'd kept the coded messages and maps was empty and cast aside. She returned to the front door and called Judith in.

"Phone Tom," Judith said, looking around at the mess. "He'll know what to do. What to look for."

Anne nodded. She phoned Ramsay who told her to phone the police and keep the doors locked until he got there. Judith had already locked the doors and windows by this time so all that remained was to dial the emergency number.

Ramsay, when he arrived, inspected the mess, being careful not to touch anything. "You couldn't tell from the noise if it was one or two people?" He asked.

"I couldn't," Anne replied, and glanced at Judith who shook her head.

Ramsay mused aloud. "What made the intruder leave in such an abrupt way? Something he heard, or was there a lookout who saw you both?"

"We didn't hear or see anyone," Anne reiterated. "Why do you think there was?"

"Someone was dealing with Rex while someone was breaking in here," Ramsay continued, still working it through in his mind. "They can't have been the same person. I suspect that the one dealing with Rex saw you as they came to the house and they warned their partner."

"We must find Rex," Anne cried. Ramsay's reminder of Rex hurt her.

"Two people?" Judith queried. "Did the police let Fewster and his friend loose?'

"Finding Rex must wait until morning or sufficient police to arrive for a thorough search," Ramsay told Anne, and then added, "I think this tells us we were wrong about Fewster because I can't believe he was released."

"But there is no one else!" Anne protested. "Unless there was more than two of Fewster's friends here."

A rapping on the door knocker ended the conversation.

Ramsay let in Constable Heyer, who told him the 'Whitby lot' were on their way. Ramsay smiled at the way he said that.

Ramsay, Bracken, Anne, and Judith spent an uncomfortable night answering questions and being ordered aside by forensic officers in white coats, who, after fingerprinting them, made it clear they were always in the way. Dawn was well advanced when Ramsay escorted Anne and Judith to Judith's house and he and Bracken made their way home.

26

WAITING

Even before he'd parked his car, Ramsay knew what he would find. The people who'd ransacked Anne's home had seen their opportunity when he arrived there, and they'd come straight over to his house.

He didn't bother looking about. He knew what would be missing. After phoning the police, Ramsay sat on the only unbroken, upright chair to await their arrival, clutching the jewels safely hidden in the pocket of his Tweed jacket with his left hand, and stroking Bracken's ear with the right.

Baldock arrived with the same forensic team that had been working at Anne's home. They didn't look pleased.

"What were they looking for?" Baldock asked, as they watched the team working.

"Same as they've taken before," Ramsay said. "The coded messages and maps we keep finding around the Demerlay estate."

"It can't have helped them so far then," Baldock replied, chuckling.

Ramsay explained his belief the messages were just

nonsense, done by Jeremy Demerlay as revenge, or maybe just as a prank.

"No wonder he killed himself," Baldock retorted. "He was clearly mad."

Ramsay nodded. "We followed the suggestions in the messages and what we found were more messages pointing us back to the places we'd already found."

"Somebody believes in them," Baldock said, gesturing to the wreckage of Ramsay's home.

"Which is how we're going to catch them," Ramsay replied. "Soon, and it must be soon, because the developers move in next week, our intruders will be on the estate, maps in hand, following the clues. We have to be there too."

"They wouldn't be that stupid," Baldock said. "They must know we'll be waiting."

Ramsay smiled. "I'm not sure they care at this point. Ned said yesterday that he did it because it was 'a quest', and I think that's what it has become for all these treasure hunters -- an obsession, a compulsion. They must find the treasure before it is destroyed when the building is demolished or remodeled."

"I'll have someone hide themselves on the property this morning with a radio," Baldock said. "You may be right."

"I'm going to do the same," Ramsay told him. "After some sleep. It's been a long night."

"I'll let my man know," Baldock said. "And don't try to arrest the culprits yourself. We want solid evidence before we move in."

Ramsay laughed. "I'll be a model member of the public. On a different subject, did they get into Ned's place using a key?"

"Maybe, or a picklock," Baldock replied. "The lock wasn't forced."

Ramsay nodded. "That's how it looked to me as well." He paused before saying, almost to himself, "They had a key, or they can pick locks." He shook himself awake and continued, "There's one more thing you could have someone look into today."

Baldock groaned, and retorted, "Model members of the public *provide* information; they don't demand it."

By mid-morning, the police were gone, and Ramsay had returned most of his unbroken furniture to its proper position. He made breakfast and phoned Judith's house. There was no answer. He found them when he phoned the warehouse and told them about his house being burgled too. They were sympathetic, which he brushed aside, and asked if Rex was found.

"He was drugged," Anne said. "He's fine now."

"Good," Ramsay replied, "Has Rex or any of you seen or heard anyone today?"

"Nothing. They got what they wanted at our houses last night, I assume," Anne said. "Much good it will do them."

Ramsay agreed and explained his plan for sleep. "I may go up to the Hall later."

"You'll see Ben and Isaac there. They're carting away the rubbish and taking it to the dump. We must leave the site clean."

Ramsay laughed. "I won't disturb them. They have their work cut out to have that done by tomorrow night."

"You could earn your keep by helping," Anne retorted.

Ramsay refrained from saying 'if his advice had been heeded last night, he'd have earned his keep twice over' and instead said, "Good night."

* * *

Gold, Greed, and a Hidden Hoard

AFTER LUNCH at Madge's Teashop, Ramsay drove to the Hall, where Ben and Isaac were nowhere to be seen. "Taking the first load to the dump, I expect, Bracken," he told his friend, who seemed even more tired than he was.

"Where is the man Baldock promised?" he asked Bracken, who just looked puzzled. "We'll walk the grounds until we trip over him," Ramsay continued and set out for the mill, where he and Ned had been digging only a day or so ago.

Where they'd dug was as they'd left it. No one had continued the work, which gave Ramsay hope that he was here before the remaining treasure hunters. The open space, however, brought the scent of tobacco on the breeze.

"The idiot," Ramsay fumed. "If I can smell it, so can the people we're hoping to catch. Find him, Bracken."

Bracken trotted across the mill floor and into the bushes beyond, leaving Ramsay struggling to keep up. When he did, he found Bracken sitting on the ground staring at a policeman in a tree, screened effectively by evergreens.

"You must be Mr. Ramsay," the officer said.

"And you aren't thinking," Ramsay retorted. "We could smell tobacco smoke from across the estate."

"Relax. There's no one here," the officer replied. "I can see the Hall and its buildings. Since the two workmen left, you're the only person around."

Ramsay gritted his teeth and nodded. "It will probably be later anyway, when the workers are gone for the day."

"I reckon you're right," the man replied, his tone gloomy. "All the action will be on the evening shift and I'll miss it."

Ramsay said, "The person or persons we're expecting have caused the death of one person and severe injury to another. Missing the action might be for the best."

"Best you go on with your walk, sir," the officer told him. "You're giving away my cover."

Ramsay agreed that was good advice and left the man to watch while he returned to the Hall by way of the well. It too, showed no signs of any recent activity. The icehouse and chapel were the same. The makeshift doors they placed across the entrances to both were untouched.

He was making his way to the stable block when he heard a truck pulling into the drive and then saw it heading up to the yard, with Isaac in the passenger seat. By the time he arrived, Isaac was operating the small crane to load the bundles of discarded furnishings into the bed of the vehicle. Ben, who'd driven them here, considered that gave him time for a rest and was sitting watching Isaac's masterful handling of the crane.

Ramsay greeted them and asked if they'd seen any strangers around the Hall. Ben said the strangers were likely in bed after their night shift spent ransacking Anne's house. Ramsay laughed and told them about his home.

"There you are then," Isaac said, halting the crane long enough to speak. "You won't see them until tomorrow."

Ramsay nodded. "I think I'll do the same," he told them, "Rest I mean." Jumping into his car, Ramsay and Bracken drove away.

"It was always the same before a big operation," Ramsay said to Bracken, who was curled up in the passenger seat trying to sleep, "I hate the waiting." Ramsay glanced at his friend and laughed. "I wish I could nap the way you do."

He couldn't sleep. Later, with Bracken, who was now rested, Ramsay drove over to Anne's house to see if they were recovered. His arrival was perfectly timed, for tea had just been made and he was able to join them for pastries.

Rex still seemed groggy from his experience and

Gold, Greed, and a Hidden Hoard

Ramsay was glad he'd been able to save Bracken from such a fate. The house was restored to be livable, though there were noticeable gaps where furniture had been.

"They're going to the dump with the Hall's old junk," Anne told him, when she saw him noticing the gaps around the room.

"I spoke to Ben and Isaac earlier," Ramsay said. "They hadn't seen anyone loitering around the place."

"After their busy night," Judith replied, "the thugs will have been resting. Anne and I were planning to look out at the Hall tonight."

Ramsay explained about Baldock's man on guard, and they said that was good because it made them feel safer.

"You haven't recovered from the last attack," Ramsay told Anne. "You should stay at home and continue your recovery." He knew this advice too would be ignored, but he felt he had to give it.

"We're only going to observe," Anne explained, as if to a rather slow child. "They won't see us, and we won't confront them. We just want to be witnesses when it's all over."

"See you stick to that," Ramsay told them, giving them a stern look, which only made them giggle.

"We assume you will be there too," Judith said.

Ramsay nodded. "Like you, I'm only there to observe and be a witness when the trial comes."

"I've been assuming I own the jewels I found because of my contract for house clearing," Anne asked. "Judith thinks the insurance company that paid out the Jeweller's claim own them. What's your opinion?"

"I'm fairly certain the law would say they belong to the insurance company, if they paid out for the loss," Ramsay replied. "That's what would happen if you didn't have your contract to own everything you found in the house."

Anne's expression darkened. "What you're saying is my lawyers and their lawyers would argue about this for months and the whole value of the jewels would go into the lawyers' bank accounts."

"I'm afraid so, yes," Ramsay said.

"What about a 'Finder's Fee'," Judith suggested.

Ramsay nodded. "If the company is a reputable business, I'm sure they'd be agreeable. However, opening negotiations would be tricky and if they aren't a company that prides itself on its reputation and they offer nothing, you'll have no recourse in law."

"I can see Nigel walking off with the only book worth selling, the insurance company walking off with the jewelry and the rest of the bric-a-brac from the Hall only just covering my costs," Anne cried.

"I don't imagine the insurers paid out anything on the car," Ramsay suggested.

"If we get that back from the police, and after Isaac has put in the hours and costs to refurbish it," Anne grumbled. "It won't be a money-spinner, will it."

Ramsay had no idea what the costs and value of any of these items were so he couldn't provide much comfort. He changed the subject.

"Are Ben and Isaac coming with us tonight?"

"We haven't spoken to them," Judith replied, as Anne was still pondering her gloomy thoughts. "They'll be here soon. We can ask them."

"I think the fewer people there, the better," Ramsay suggested.

Anne nodded. "I agree. I can't afford the overtime."

She looked so miserable that Ramsay wanted to give her hope, but he also didn't want a wildly excited woman fidgeting for hours as they waited for their quarry to arrive. It was much better she remain subdued.

Ben and Isaac arrived, told Anne they would finish tomorrow and not to worry. They were in good spirits despite the long day lifting and hauling loads of rubbish to the dump. Nothing was said about the evening and the two men left, promising to call in on their way to work in the morning.

When the truck was out of sight, Ramsay said, "We should get ready and go. Warm clothes, blankets, hot sweet tea for that middle of the night low, and flashlights everyone." He rose and left them to get ready while he returned to his own home to prepare.

He'd advised Anne and Judith to park in a field entrance some distance from the Hall driveway entrance and he did the same. The walk back to the Hall under the clear starry sky was exhilarating in its freshness, which he knew would be finger numbing cold by midnight.

Ramsay didn't go in by way of the driveway, he climbed a fallen place in the boundary wall near where the constable of the morning had been watching. He reasoned the evening shift would likely be in the same place.

As he neared the trees, he heard the faint crackle of a radio and knew he'd guessed right. The man was easy to see, a dark figure against the bright sky. He whispered to the officer and grinned when he saw him jump. *Serves him right*, Ramsay thought. *A sentry who is this easily crept up on would be a dead man in the army.*

"Mr. Ramsay?" the officer queried.

"That's me, constable. Is all clear?" He watched as the man swept binoculars across the land in front of him.

"There are two women approaching the house," he whispered back.

"I'll head them off," Ramsay said. "It's the owner of the House Clearing Company and friend. I shall watch from the other side of the Hall. Don't mistake us for the villains." With that, Ramsay moved quickly to intercept Anne and Judith before the real villains appeared and were frightened off.

He found it hard to make progress among the undergrowth, the bushes, and uneven ground, even with the light of the moon and stars. He began to fear he'd fall in a hole, and no one would find him until it was too late. Remembering Morris Saunders went missing somewhere on this estate didn't make him feel better.

It was Bracken who told him they were near when his low growl was answered by Rex appearing out of the trees ahead of him.

"Anne, Judith," Ramsay whispered, and was relieved to hear them equally quietly answer.

"Where's Baldock's man?" Anne asked and, when Ramsay told her, continued, "Then we should be on the other side, so we have everything covered."

Ramsay agreed, saying, "If you watch near the icehouse, I'll watch at the mill." He reasoned that the people who killed Ned had seen Ned and Ramsay digging there and likely would choose that place to begin.

As Anne and Judith had passed the path to the icehouse, they turned and disappeared back into the trees. Ramsay turned in the other direction for he too had passed the quickest path to the mill. He'd picked out a place to hide earlier when it was daylight and found it again. Throwing a waterproof sheet on the ground, and a thick tartan blanket on top, he sat down, arranging his Thermos flask, gloves, and flashlight around him in easy reach.

27
CAUGHT

BRACKEN WAS asleep and Ramsay struggling to keep his eyes open when he heard the hooting of an owl. He checked his watch. After midnight. Thanks to his long nights watching the barn and bookstore in his own village of Saxonby the previous summer, he was something of an expert on the calls of owls. This owl wasn't one he'd heard before, and he guessed it was Anne or Judith. He hoped the people they'd seen didn't know owl calls.

Almost at once, Bracken sat up growling softly. Bracken shushed him and they watched in silence as two figures approached, well bundled up against the cold night air.

Ramsay hoped the police constable had already radioed the arrival of the intruders to the waiting backup because he suddenly felt very visible to them. In his mind, the moonlight made him stand out boldly among the dark bushes. It seemed he wasn't so easily seen by the men for they began surveying the workings Ned had done and then down into the dip to where Ramsay had found the map and clues.

After whispered discussion, the two returned to the mill floor and circled the wall. They seemed not to have a plan at all, for they hadn't brought spades to continue Ned's work. They folded up the map and began making their way back to the Hall, while Ramsay waited for a safe distance to begin following them.

They stopped at the chapel and pulled aside the barrier that Ramsay and Isaac had placed across the entrance. With torches, they peered inside and conversed in voices so low, Ramsay couldn't make out what they were saying. Again, they had no equipment to enter the crypt, so they stood up and went on in the direction of the stable block.

A rustling in the bushes behind Ramsay made Bracken turn and growl. It was the police constable who came alongside Ramsay, patted Bracken, whispering, "Good boy," before saying, "Two of us and two of them, sir."

Ramsay nodded. He'd thought the same and he understood the constable's wish for action. After what had happened to Ned and Anne, he would like a few minutes alone with these two.

"When we hear police cars," Ramsay replied. "We go."

The man grinned and nodded.

They crept nearer, Ramsay holding Bracken's collar. He hoped Anne was doing the same with Rex, who may also feel there was a score to be settled.

The bigger of the two men swung open the first garage door and Ramsay smiled grimly to himself. The man had a way with locks. The two peered in, sweeping the now empty room with their flashlight beams. They even examined the roof trusses of the old stables, something Ramsay realized he'd neglected to do. He hoped they weren't going to find the last stash there.

Finally, in the distance, they heard car engines. "Go," Ramsay said, and set off. He realized his age when he saw the young officer halfway over the courtyard, Bracken at his heels, before Ramsay had even cleared the bushes.

Bracken's ferocious attack on the smaller man sent him reeling back into the garage while the constable hit the other so hard he tumbled over, only to scramble to his feet beside the smaller man. Arriving late, all that was left for Ramsay to do was shove the garage door shut, as Bracken and the constable stepped aside.

"That was disappointing," the constable said, watching Ramsay wedge the lock back inside the hook as the two inside attempted to push the door open.

"Very," Ramsay agreed. "But neither of them is up to your weight, constable. It wouldn't be a fair fight."

Police cars pulled into the courtyard as Anne, holding back Rex, and Judith rounded the corner and hurried to join the clamor of bells and shouting men.

When sufficient policemen were out of the cars, Ramsay removed the lock from the door and pulled it open, exposing Nigel and Terry blinded by the car's headlights. They were quickly grabbed by officers and marched out, where Anne stepped in front of Nigel, waved her arm and sling and shouted, "Why?"

Nigel stepped back, frightened by her anger, stammering, "I-I panicked."

Anne was taken aside by an officer, screaming, "Panicked? You panicked?" She was securely held as the two men were led to a black police van.

"And what about Ned?" Anne shouted after them.

Terry swung around so hard, the officer holding him couldn't prevent it. "He betrayed us," Terry snarled, his whole body shaking, and face contorted with rage.

Terry's fury was such that Anne took a step back in surprise and she was relieved when the two were bundled into the van and the doors closed. The van set off down the drive.

With the van gone, silence fell over the group as the excitement drained away. In the silence, a sergeant told Ramsay, he'd be wanted to give a statement. He turned to Anne and Judith and told them the same.

"We'll be at the station first thing in the morning," Ramsay replied, and he saw the two women nod their agreement.

"See you do," the sergeant replied, "Whitby Police Station, nine o'clock. Don't be late or we might feel obliged to come and find you." His face relaxed into a faint grin as he spoke. He signaled the others back to the cars and in minutes they were gone, leaving Ramsay, Anne, Judith, Bracken and Rex standing in the shadowy courtyard.

After a moment, Anne said, "I'm sorry this house clearance is over. I've grown attached to this wonderful old place."

Ramsay chuckled. "It's too soon for nostalgia."

"I know what Anne means," Judith commented, as they began walking to their cars. "The Hall has stood in this village for hundreds of years and its part of us. Even newcomers like me."

At the entranceway, they parted company. "Don't forget, we have a date at the police station tomorrow morning," Ramsay told them.

"Dates used to be more fun," Judith grumbled in reply.

28

ICEHOUSE TUNNEL

RAMSAY WAS SURPRISED to find Inspector Baldock in the Interview Room at Whitby, when he was ushered in.

"You were right," Baldock said, as the constable who'd brought Ramsay in closed the door. "Nigel did work for the safe company, and he was the one who opened the safe for the Fewsters."

Ramsay nodded. "To him, those jewels weren't just a 'quest' as they were for poor Ned. They were the 'pay' he never received for his work."

"What made you suspect him? He doesn't look a likely safecracker?"

Ramsay pulled the copies of photos from his pocket and selected the one with the group. "I think this 'treasure hunter' is a young Nigel." He pointed to a skinny, pale looking young man, ill-at-ease among the others.

Baldock nodded. "It could be anyone, but I think you're right. He does have something of the look of him."

"Has he told you what happened to Morris Saunders and Oscar Geary?" Ramsay asked.

"He doesn't know what happened to Saunders," Baldock says, "but he knows Geary was killed. Not by him and he doesn't know who. Nor does he know where the body is."

"It's early days," Ramsay said. "What about Ned?"

"He was alive when they left him," Baldock replied. "They didn't mean him harm. They put a hood on him while he slept and never spoke so he wouldn't know who they were."

Ramsay frowned. "Then how did they hope to get information from him?"

"Brent saw you hand papers over to Ned," Baldock replied. "That's what they were after. They thought Ned had thrown his lot in with you to get a share of whatever reward was going."

Ramsay's heart sank. "Ned handed the papers back to me but maybe they didn't see that. You know, I wouldn't have involved Ned if I'd imagined they'd see it as treachery. It explains Terry's comment about betrayal."

Baldock nodded. "It doesn't excuse what they did, not to a man of Ned's age."

Ramsay said, "They should have known old Ned wasn't the sort of man to take that kind of treatment."

"Exactly, he began lashing out and they tied him up. He was raging, shouting, so they wrapped a gag across the hood to quiet him," Baldock said. "The cigarette burn happened when Ned buffeted Terry so hard, Terry's cigarette fell from his mouth and onto Ned's hand."

"I don't entirely buy that," Ramsay replied.

"Nor do I but it's early days, as you said," Baldock responded. "The important thing in the eyes of the law is they didn't murder Ned. He was just too old for the things they *did* do."

Ramsay grimaced. "It can't have helped that he spent most of the day digging trenches in solid packed, root riddled, soil."

"Probably not, but you aren't to blame for that," Baldock agreed. "Anyway, we need your statement. I'll go, and let the constable here write it down." Nodding to Ramsay, he turned away. At the door, he stopped, looked back and added, "the York police say the Watson House Clearing company can have the car back. Let them know when you want to pick it up."

Ramsay's spirits rose. "That is good news. Did they find anything in the car?"

"Why? Should they have?" Baldock asked, puzzled. "The car was evidence of theft, and they took photos, fingerprints and samples, which is all they needed. They did search it for other evidence, but it had been well searched by someone before them."

Ramsay grimaced. "I searched inside too and, as you say, someone had been there before us. I just wondered if they had more luck."

"You want us to do your job for you?" Baldock mocked him. "You're the treasure hunters, not us." With this, he left the room and Ramsay gave his statement.

With their statements made, the three people and two dogs went in search of a café. As their mid-morning snack was being prepared, Anne said, chuckling, "The head man gave me a long lecture about my behavior last night and how he had a good mind to press charges."

"Well, Anne," Judith said, "you did rather lose your temper and say horrible things."

"Silly of me," Anne agreed. "I blame it on the pain in my shoulder from being brutally assaulted. If it should happen again, I'll be the very model of feminine sweetness. They'll give me a medal for it, I'm sure."

Ramsay laughed. "Baldock did give me some good news." He explained about the car.

"I'll phone York police the moment I get home," Anne said. "Ben and Isaac can keep that truck for one more day and collect the car from York."

"Tell Isaac he has to strip that car down into its smallest pieces," Ramsay whispered, looking around the room to see who might be listening. "I think we'll find Jeremy's share in there somewhere."

Anne also looked around and, seeing how many people could hear, whispered, "What about the two missing men? Did he say anything about them?"

"He said it was too early in the interrogation to have answers about those," Ramsay replied. "I'd like to have one more look for the tunnel entrance in the icehouse. I think that's where they'll find Saunders' bones."

Judith shuddered. "Then why look?"

"Like Ned, finding things is my quest," Ramsay replied. "Sometimes it's the truth I look for, and sometimes it's closure for some poor individual who has been lost. He may have family who would like to know what happened to him."

"You still think an accident?" Anne asked.

Ramsay nodded. "Somehow, he got into something and couldn't get out. The only place that fits that description is the tunnel that should go to the icehouse, but we can't find where. I suspect he found the entrance at the icehouse end but became trapped between the door and the dirt pile that blocks the tunnel."

"Someone could have closed the door behind him," Anne objected.

Ramsay shook his head. "If they'd done that, they'd have packed up his things and pretended he'd left, like they did with Oscar."

Anne responded. "Maybe it was their mistake over Saunders that gave them the hint over Geary."

Ramsay laughed. "Maybe. I'm still going to find that entrance, if you want to join me. I'd like a guard on the door. Bracken doesn't have opposable thumbs, you see. He can't open it again if it slams shut."

"I'll join you," Judith said. "Anne needs to be with Ben and Isaac as they finish the work. They need to be sure the developers can't claim the contract wasn't done properly." She smiled at Anne who nodded her agreement.

When they arrived at the Hall, Ben and Isaac had the truck almost loaded. When Isaac heard they were to pick up the car on the following day, he said he'd go today, right after they finished here. It took considerable persuasion to make him accept the arrangements Anne had made with York police during the phone call she'd had with them.

Ramsay had advised Anne to say nothing to Isaac or Ben about Jeremy's share of the loot until after the car was in Isaac's shop and securely locked up. Anne thought that good advice and she held her tongue.

"We're off to the icehouse," Ramsay said, when the others had sobered enough to continue loading the truck. "If we aren't back by quitting time, you come looking? Alright?"

They laughed and agreed they might.

With Bracken once again guarding the icehouse door, Ramsay and Judith descended into the slimy, damp darkness for what they hoped would be the final time.

They reached where Ramsay had searched last and paused. "This is where you'd expect the tunnel to join,"

Ramsay told Judith. "I searched most of the floor last time for a joint that might be the door and found nothing. This last bit of floor is our next best hope." He pointed to the area that was still covered in debris.

Judith said, "Maybe it doesn't join where you'd expect."

Ramsay considered this before saying, "You know, you may be right. Maybe the icehouse was built before the tunnel and the tunneling couldn't join up where you'd expect. Hard rock blocked them or something like that. After all, these probably weren't built by actual mining engineers."

"It's a big place to examine with what's left of today," Judith suggested.

"We'll go back outside and look at the front again," Ramsay said. "I've had an idea."

Bracken greeted them excitedly when they emerged. A thin rain had begun falling and he was happy to think they were going home.

"No alarms today," Ramsay greeted his friend. "You must have been bored. But I think you'd already shown us the way, if only we'd looked harder that day." He stepped away from the entrance and looked back. Pointing to the small cavern beside the entrance, he said to Judith, "That cave is where Bracken found the first box. Water was pouring out through the earth, creating the cave and exposing the box."

Judith nodded. "You think that's where the tunnel ends?"

"I do," Ramsay said. "I think originally, there was a covered walkway from there around to the icehouse entrance. It was probably made of wood, and it was demolished and used to block off the tunnel."

Judith looked unconvinced. "Wouldn't Saunders have been able to push wood aside?"

"I would expect so," Ramsay replied, "but maybe it was so unstable, it collapsed behind, or on him and he wasn't able to. He was the most interested of the treasure hunters in the icehouse and maybe the others, even when they came looking, didn't recognize the collapse for what it was."

Judith still unconvinced, said, "There's a lot of maybes in there."

Ramsay laughed. "I'm usually the one people call 'Doubting Thomas'." He grabbed a broken branch and began digging. After a moment, Ramsay said, "I'm going to ask Isaac for a shovel." Throwing the branch aside, he hurried off with Bracken trotting after him. Judith watched them for a moment, and then set off in pursuit.

"You didn't need to come," Ramsay told her when she caught up with him in the courtyard.

"I'm not staying anywhere alone in this creepy place," Judith retorted, out of breath.

Although he'd been confident Isaac would have a shovel on the truck, Ramsay was still impressed to find that he did.

"Never know when you might need to dig yourself out of somewhere," Isaac told him when Ramsay commented on him always having tools on hand. Ramsay decided not to say that didn't reflect well on Isaac or Ben's driving. He just thanked Isaac and hurried back to the icehouse.

It didn't take long for him to uncover a concrete slab, broken at the roof of what he knew would be the tunnel's exit point, and fallen at a forty-five-degree angle to the ground. Ramsay looked at it in silence for a moment before saying, "I suspect this is what Saunders destabilised when he found it. When it fell, all the earth on top of it and any loose on the icehouse roof that it was supporting, slid down and covered the collapse."

Judith said, in an awed whisper, "He's behind there."

"I imagine we'll find him at the dirt pile," Ramsay said. "If he wasn't crushed by the falling concrete slab. The dirt pile would seem easier to move than this." He hammered the shovel tip on the concrete.

"What are you going to do?"

"Phone the police," Ramsay replied. "We can't move that any more than Saunders could. Anyway, it's their case not mine."

"That only leaves the other one," Judith said, as they were walking back to the stable block.

"Nigel or Conn Fewster will have a good idea where he's buried," Ramsay replied. "Failing them, the two Fewsters in prison will. They may as well say now. It can't get worse for any of them."

"They may still have hopes of recovering the jewels," Judith suggested.

Ramsay shook his head. "Much as I'd like to leave the jewels in the hands of you, Anne and Isaac, where they might do some good, I can't. The law may be an ass, but it's all we have to keep society on an even keel. And once knowledge of the jewels seeps out, there'll be many people claiming them. Our villains will know soon enough the jewels are found and there's nothing to be gained by silence."

When they arrived back with the others, the truck was still in the yard and looked precariously loaded to Ramsay.

"Did you find it?" Anne demanded, as they approached.

Judith explained, while Ramsay and the two men discussed the load. They showed Ramsay the many straps holding the piled high junk and he, reluctantly, agreed it was probably safe. It wasn't his area of expertise, after all.

"I want to be here when they lift that slab," Anne said, as Ramsay turned back to her and Judith.

"I could get a digger, and we do it ourselves," Isaac offered.

Ramsay laughed. "It's best the police find the body, not us."

"We can phone from my house," Anne said, throwing her leather gloves in Ramsay's car. "Come on."

It was evening and growing dark when the police team lifted the slab and found the remains of Morris Saunders. He'd clearly seen the danger and tried desperately to stop the slab falling, only to be crushed under it.

Baldock had arrived before the slab was lifted and told Ramsay that the police had been given directions to an area on the moor where they should find the remains of Oscar Geary.

"Who killed him?" Ramsay asked.

Baldock laughed. "Now that we will never learn, unless one of them chooses suicide as a means to reduce his sentence."

"Then why was he killed?" Ramsay persisted.

"As you'd guessed, he came hunting for ghosts," Baldock said. "Unfortunately, he became involved with the treasure hunt and somehow came to realize it wasn't ancient treasure they were hunting, but the proceeds of the famous jewel robbery only weeks before."

"And being the man he was," Ramsay said, "he couldn't hide what he knew from them."

Baldock nodded, grimacing. "The usual fate of simpletons who get caught up with violent criminals, I'm afraid."

"Did Saunders or Geary have any family, do you know?" Anne asked.

Baldock grinned, glancing at Ramsay. "I doubt it. In their

own different ways, they were both private investigators and they're a sad, lonely bunch in my experience."

"Fortunately," Ramsay retorted, "I'm an amateur sleuth with private means, like Hercule Poirot or Lord Peter Wimsey, and not a lowly private investigator."

The others laughed. A little uncertainly, Ramsay thought.

29

TWO DAYS LATER

RAMSAY WAS RELAXING with a lunch time mug of tea, when he received an excited phone call from Anne. "Jeremy's portion was there. Like you said," she crowed.

"Isaac must have worked all night to have the car in pieces already," Ramsay replied. "You only got it back to his garage yesterday."

Judith laughed. "Not quite, but he worked late and started early, and the jewels weren't so deeply hidden. Oh, and I did the site completion inspection with the developer this morning and they've signed off on my contract. I can pay you now, well, when they pay me, anyway."

"I'm going to drive over and see these last few jewels," Ramsay told her. "It makes a fitting end to the whole affair."

Isaac was beaming with pleasure when he saw them arrive and excitedly waved them into his workshop.

"Didn't I tell you this car was worth a fortune," he exclaimed as they entered. He opened a cabinet mounted on the wall and pulled the dark, felt pouch they'd come to recognize as the bag used for the jewels, from among the tools hanging there.

He handed it to Anne. "Open it. It's like Aladdin's Cave inside."

Ramsay and Anne were more used to seeing the cascade of sparkling stones and glowing gold that Anne poured into her palm than Isaac was, but had to agree 'Aladdin's Cave' was a fair description.

"Can we keep them?" Isaac asked. "They were in the house we cleared."

"Mr. Ramsay thinks not," Anne replied, glancing at Ramsay. "I've asked my lawyer to look into the rights of it before we do anything with them."

"I went to Leeds again this morning," Ramsay said. "Something I read when I was investigating the robbery has been niggling me these past days."

Anne looked at Isaac. "This will be even worse news," she said, shaking her head.

"I don't think so," Ramsay replied, smiling. "I can give my information to your lawyer, Anne, and he can do further enquiries, but you all may be able to recover something from these jewels."

Anne regarded him suspiciously. "Why?"

"When we spoke earlier, I assumed the insurance company would have paid the owner for the loss and therefore, they belonged to the insurance company."

Anne gritted her teeth. "So, you said. What's changed?"

"The insurance company didn't pay up because they claimed the owner was to blame for the theft," Ramsay replied, "and it went to court. The court case ended when the businessman who owned them had a heart attack and died. He had no family and had made no will."

"You mean they're ours?" Isaac cried, once again excited.

Ramsay held up his hands to calm them. "You need your lawyer to confirm what I read in the newspaper's back numbers and then work out what that means. Normally, the Crown gets anything that is left behind when someone dies without making a will. You may get your 'Treasure Trove' after all."

"If he died ten years ago, or thereabouts, I don't see why the Crown should get any of it," Isaac growled.

"I agree with you, Isaac," Ramsay said, "but the law may not. Put the jewels in the bank, Anne, and we'll explain this to your lawyer tomorrow. He can take it from there."

Isaac still looked mutinous, but recovered enough to say, "The car is good. Come and look at this." He led them to the engine, where the cylinder head was removed, exposing the pistons and cylinders. "Still shiny," he said, running an oily cloth around one cylinder. "Smooth as a baby's bottom. They'll polish up a treat."

Anne reminded Isaac to keep track of his hours and his spending on the car, which didn't improve his expression. He still regarded the Jaguar as 'his'.

As they drove back, Anne said, "Nigel has gifted me the book he found."

"Kind of him," Ramsay said, smiling.

"Not really. He just doesn't want me suing him for my injuries," Anne retorted. "The important thing is we will get the value of that book, the value of the car, less Isaac's work, and now maybe something from the jewels. This just might be the job that makes me comfortable."

Ramsay laughed. "You haven't seen my bill yet."

"Nor Judith's either," Anne added, then continued, "Or my lawyer's bill. Oh well, if you don't dream, you don't live."

Ramsay pulled the third bag of jewels from his pocket. "We'll put these with the others before meeting with your lawyer."

"I'd forgotten you had them," Anne cried. "We should do that now."

When the jewels were all together at last in her bank safety deposit box, and they'd made an appointment with Anne's lawyer for the following day, Ramsay and Anne returned to Grassmount in relieved silence, until Ramsay asked, "What's your 'dream' for after we've set the lawyer to work tomorrow?"

"What?" Anne responded, momentarily puzzled by the word 'dream'. She grinned, "Oh, I see. Back to the grind for me, I'm afraid. Even a Treasure Trove won't let me retire. What about you?"

"Bracken and I will find another hill to climb," Ramsay replied. "It's what we do, when we're not solving mysteries."

Anne was puzzled. "You mean my letter was the only case you had?"

Ramsay shook his head. "It was the only case I liked the sound of. There may be another just like it waiting in the post box, and we'll be sleuthing again tomorrow. Winter is coming on and hiking up to peaks in the snow and ice isn't as enjoyable as it once might have been."

"You should advertise abroad in the winter months," Anne told him. "There are lots of English people in the South of France and the Caribbean. Some of them must have a mystery they want solving."

Ramsay murmured, "The Puzzle of the Planter's Punch. The Tom Collins Conundrum," he paused, and then said, "You know, I just might do that, if they'll let Bracken come too."

He dropped Anne off at her house, declined her offer of tea, and drove home.

"What do you say, Bracken?" he asked his friend who'd

taken over the passenger seat now Anne was gone. "Would a mystery on the French Riviera appeal to you?"

Bracken was too busy watching the hedgerows flying past to care where they might be tomorrow.

"I wonder if they have a newspaper for English people down there?" Ramsay continued. "I've never been abroad and never wanted to, but maybe we could consider it. After all, as Anne just said, 'if you don't dream, you don't live'."

Bracken suddenly flopped back down into the passenger seat and turned his attention to Ramsay. His expression was hard for Ramsay to read, but it didn't look like approval.

Ramsay sighed and nodded. "Maybe you're right. They wouldn't let you come with me anyway." He paused, and then added, "The Isle of Man might be suitably 'abroad' and we could both go there — only not in the winter. It's no warmer than here." Ramsay lapsed into silence as he negotiated a busy crossroad.

When he was once again motoring along a quiet lane, Ramsay continued, "I'll advertise in an Isle of Man newspaper over the winter and with luck we'll have a mystery-solving trip there next summer. We'll be like that television series, *Have Gun, Will Travel*. We're knights errant saving people from dastardly crimes all through the realm. What do you say, Bracken?"

Bracken said nothing and returned to the window. From his friend's tone of voice, he understood the 'dreams' had returned to reality and that was enough for the present.

* * *

READ the next Ramsay mystery here.

* * *

OR MY OTHER BOOKS HERE.

MORE BOOKS BY THE AUTHOR

On Amazon, my books can be found at the
One Man and His Dog Cozy Mysteries page

And

Miss Riddell Cozy Mysteries series page.

And for someone who likes listening to books, *In the Beginning, There Was a Murder* is now available as an audiobook on Amazon and here on Audible and many others, including:

Kobo, Chirp, Audiobooks, Scribd, Bingebooks, Apple, StoryTel

You can find even more books here:

P.C. James Author Page: https://www.amazon.com/P.-C.-James/e/B08VTN7Z8Y

P.C. James & Kathryn Mykel: Duchess Series

P.C. James & Kathryn Mykel: Sassy Senior Sleuths Series.

Paul James Author Page: https://www.amazon.com/-/e/B01DFGG2U2

GoodReads: https://www.amazon.com/P.-C.-James/e/B08VTN7Z8Y

And for something completely different, my books by Paul James at: https://www.amazon.com/-/e/B01DFGG2U2

ABOUT THE AUTHOR

P.C. James is the author of the quietly humorous Miss Riddell Cozy Mysteries, the One Man and His Dog Cozy Mysteries, and co-author of the Royal Duchess and Sassy Senior Sleuths cozy mysteries.

He lives in Canada near Toronto with his wife.

He loves photographing wildlife in the outdoors yet chooses to spend hours every day indoors writing stories, which he also loves. One day, he'll find a way to do them both together.

Printed in Great Britain
by Amazon